REBEL SPIES

— AND —

YANKEE AGENTS

St. Paul Street, St. Catharines, in the mid-1800s.

REBEL SPIES

— AND —

YANKEE AGENTS

LINDA BRAMBLE

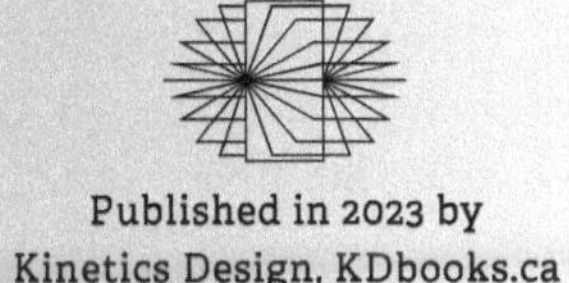

Published in 2023 by
Kinetics Design, KDbooks.ca

Published in 2023 by
Kinetics Design, KDbooks.ca

ISBN 978-1-988360-93-5 (paperback)

ISBN 978-1-988360-94-2 (ebook)

Edited by Michael Carroll

Cover and interior design, typesetting,
online publishing, and printing by Daniel Crack,
Kinetics Design, KDbooks.ca   www.linkedin.com/in/kdbooks

Image Credits:

Front Cover: Stock photo ID 489085076.

Page 2: Brock University's Digital Repository, John Burtniak Postcard Collection — RG 313.

Page 6: Brock University's Digital Repository, St. Catharines, Ontario, Canada, drawn by Charles H. Brosius, Shoberg & Co., proprietors, Chicago Lith. Co., 1875 (bird's-eye view), StCatharines-1875_col.tif.

Page 202: Richard Montgomery, 1864, image supplied by Linda Bramble, source unknown.

Contact the author at
lindabramble1@gmail.com

To my steadfast soulmate

Bird's-eye view of St. Catharines by Herman Brosius (1851–1917).

Contents

Prologue

Princeton, New Jersey

January 21, 1915

What matters most in the end is character. At least that's how
I had convinced myself to take an assignment nearly forty years ago
that compelled me to lie about who I was. In telling this story, I'll try
not to embellish it to fit what I had once vowed my life would be. God
only knows I needed embellishment. I'm still trying to unravel those
few months spent in Canada that were to change my life. My reputation
was the least of my worries. Good soldiers, men I knew who were acting
undercover, were being hanged for treason. It didn't strike me as
convenient to be one of them. I was twenty-six with enough experience
as an intelligence officer with Brigadier General Irvin McDowell, the
commander of the Army of Northeastern Virginia at the outbreak of
the Civil War, to make me unreasonably brash. I intended to prove my
worth to my country, or so I thought.

My name is Richard Montgomery. My assignment was to infiltrate
a newly organized Confederate spy mission in Canada that had been
established to stir the growing discontent of farmers in the "Northwest"
Union territory. The Northwest in those days was composed mostly
of farmers who were fomenting rebellion from the Union for very
different reasons from the Confederate states in the South. It could be
argued that both parts of the country had economic motives for wanting
to leave. For the farmers of the Northwest, it was because Abraham
Lincoln had closed off the Mississippi to their trade. Without the river
to ship their crops, they were quickly becoming financially ravaged.

The Confederate government saw the farmers' move as an opportunity to weaken the Union.

If the Confederates supported their bid to break away from the Union, the former United States would splinter into three pieces, thus better assuring the survival of the Confederacy. It was a conceivable scenario. To more directly wage war against the Union, the Confederates also conceived of several invasions into Union territory from Canada, which I might add was a neutral nation at the time.

To co-lead these clandestine activities, they sent two of the most unlikely men: Jacob Thompson, the former secretary of the interior when James Buchanan was president, and Clement C. Clay, a senator from Alabama in office until secession. It would soon become clear that sending two politicians to lead a spy mission was naive. Their considerable political skills would be of little use as spies. I wish I had known that at the time.

Richard Montgomery

1

A New Town, a New Identity

I arrived in Canada in the town of St. Catharines on the morning train from Washington City, sleeping most of the way, unharrassed by inquisitive travellers. I hadn't yet grown accustomed to this new version of myself to feel comfortable enough that I wouldn't arouse suspicion due to some inconsistency in my comments or demeanour. I was relieved to be left alone. Nor had I thought through under what circumstances it was right to pretend to be someone I wasn't in order to learn information that could benefit one side in that terrible war. No matter how morally unassailable my goals, I was still about to behave unethically to achieve them.

St. Catharines was close enough to the U.S. border to sabotage Northern states from the relative safety of neutral Canadian territory and far enough away from any swift Union retaliation. My intelligence work behind enemy lines for General McDowell had involved gathering information on Confederate troop encampments, estimates of size, and approximations of the duration of their stay. Doing that depended on my agility and a bit of foolish intrepidness to think I could enter enemy territory unnoticed. Yet I succeeded doing so for a year.

When I was called upon by Assistant Secretary of War Charles A. Dana himself to serve in a different type of intelligence work — espionage — I accepted out of immodest pride, I guess, plus a sense of duty. My new identity contained a blend of true elements from my own background that I hoped would lend plausibility and coherence to my cover. However, for McDowell I had to hide from the enemy. In Canada I would operate in its presence. In civilian life I had practised law. It was natural that in Canada I would be a clerk and secretary. I was born, raised, and schooled in Virginia, so I had an understanding of the Southern mind and politics; I just had no sympathies for its cause.

Even though my papers were in order as James Thomson, including a letter of introduction from Jefferson Davis, the president of the Confederacy, prepared by impeccable Union forgers, I was still edgy at the border crossing. Detectives from Canada and the United States had proliferated making any clandestine activity extremely hazardous, but I got through.

After I arrived in St. Catharines, I decided to do a bit of reconnaissance around the town before registering at the hotel where I was to perform secretarial work for the owner and his guests. When I reached the market square, it was like a Breughel canvas of shoppers and vendors, kaleidescoping into colourful arrangements of activities. Among them was a community of blacks. I counted thirty-seven of them, all vendors selling commodities from the backs of their wagons — ducks, chickens, eggs, butter, cheeses, hams, bacon, vegetables, and fruits of all kinds. A henna-skinned woman peeling a peach caught my eye. She sat beside her wagon of peaches, plums, and early pears she had displayed neatly in cascading, orderly rows. Jars of jams and jellies edged one side, and along the other under a small glass case were cakes, cookies, and breakfast muffins sitting on fancy hand-embroidered doilies. When she saw me, she sliced a piece of peach, skewered it on the end of her knife, and held it out.

"How dee do. You new in town or just visiting, son?" She was buxom, assured, and as lavish as the fruit she sold.

"Just a guest for now, ma'am." There was something so familiar about her — like my own mammy from my growing-up days on my father's plantation in Virginia. I loved her as much as I loved my own mother. "How much are your peaches?"

"Well, sir, these big 'uns is quarter dollar a half peck."

I raised my eyebrows in mock outrage. "Isn't that rather steep?"

"These peaches not just peaches, my friend, they's a stairway to heav'n. Rich as cream, they is. Here, you jes' try another."

She cut off an even larger piece this time, offered it to me, and watched as I tasted with an air of certainty in the merit of her product. It was the most flavourful peach I had ever eaten. "I'll take six. You and your peaches have weakened my ability to resist."

She laughed as she carefully selected six of her finest and laid them

  LINDA BRAMBLE

on top of a newspaper and started to wrap. "You a sweet talker, mister. You too young to git so smooth."

"You're the one with honeyed words. Sounds like they were learned at the foot of a mammy from Virginia. Am I correct?"

"Ooo-eee, lordy. How'd ya know'd dat? Is ya from dere, too?"

"I did spend some time in Virginia, but I'm most recently from New York City. How did it come to pass that you came to Canada?"

She stopped wrapping and peered directly into my eyes, her mood visibly changed. "Ain't no foolin' matter, so I's get serious 'nuf to tell ya that me and my man wanted a place of our own to raise our young'uns ourselves and hold their li'l dark-skinned faces to the light and be counted like the rest of you white folk. We come with that saucy li'l Harriet Tubman that's brought us here with her kin. We forever grateful to that caution of a woman — mean as a snake, but righteous as a saint." She tied string around the parcel of fruit and handed it to me as she accepted my money.

I indicated for her to keep the change. "How have you found it here?"

"Been here now five years, and, no mistakin' this is the Promised Land, but many of the white folk up here sees the colour of our skin long before the countenance of our souls. They's no diff'rent in that regard than other folk south of the border. If they could own us, I 'spect they would. But the law up here says they c'aint. That's the diff'rence. So we obstinate and we stays and makes a merciful life."

"But there are Southern guests in town, many of whom have large plantations of their own. Doesn't that threaten your people?"

"Is you one of 'em?" She checked over her shoulder as if ready to call any one of the other black vendors to her aid.

"I'm originally from Virginia, but I'm just a humble New York lawyer and clerk."

"Then I is proud to admit that dems rich Southrens here aren't dat hard to outsmart, honey." She bellowed a deep, pleasing chuckle as she handed a muffin to me as if sealing our confidence. I accepted the muffin and reached for my bag. She raised her hand; "You pay me by saying your prayers tonight, young man. I gets the feeling you gonna need the wisdom of the good Lord. And, lordy, lordy, unless you's lookin' for work by the docks, better git your sweet face a shave before you do any more prancing around dis town. Dere's a good brother who's a barber at the Stephenson House Hotel."

"As it happens, that's where I'll be newly employed."

"Mighty fine employment for a newcomer," she said, then wished me well.

The Stephenson House Hotel was elegant and large with four storeys of accommodations for four hundred guests, a bowling alley, a croquet court, and formal gardens, as well as walking trails that coiled through woodlands. It reclined languorously at the top of the Salina Street hill like a trusted courtesan privy to the secrets of the men and women who stayed in her rooms. I found the barbershop on the first floor with access doors to both the street and the lobby and was shown to a barber's chair where an assistant prepared me for a shave by swathing me in steaming towels. The towels made me so relaxed from their warmth that I didn't bother to acknowledge the assistant standing behind me stropping his razor. *Swish … swish … swish* it went against the leather strap.

"Don't move, Montgomery," the assistant whispered, his hot breath suddenly erupting in my ear like a trapped wasp. How did the man know my real name? Had the black woman in the market square lured me into a trap? But I hadn't told her my name. In the split second it took me to register what was happening, it was too late. The barber's assistant pulled the cape tightly around my arms, immobilizing me.

"What's that all about?" demanded the customer in the next chair.

"Nothing," I said. "Nothing at all, but this shave will have to wait." I unravelled myself from the cape and towels and raced out of the shop without catching sight of the man who seemed to be threatening to defeat my mission before it had even begun.

2

Colonel Stephenson

Many of the early risers at the Stephenson House Hotel were having breakfast on the veranda, busy reading American papers that had been delivered on the morning coach from Buffalo. The veranda encircled the first floor of the hotel's four storeys, splitting into two levels, one to a more secluded addition that tiered down the hillside from the main sections, the other at street level. I had located a barber on the other side of town and had arrived at the hotel smelling of pomade and tonic. Feeling more presentable to meet my new employer, I took a seat near the rear of the veranda to wait. From this vantage point I watched the activity on the canal. A three-masted barquentine was being loaded at the dock as the ship's chandlers supervised supplies of produce, meats, and fowl being transported to the galley doors. Cranes hoisted what looked like bales of cotton, barrels of beer, and other bound crates onto the decks as sailors manoeuvred ropes and wires to make way.

I smelled the nutty aroma of hops being boiled into malt. The brewery couldn't be far away, and then I spotted it and its wagon yard at the bottom of the hill. My stomach knotted a bit. What had that barber's assistant wanted? I was fit enough to defend myself, but I couldn't afford to have my mission aborted before it even began. From what I could see, getting to the wagon yard at night would present no problems. If I was capable of securing intelligence as a Union scout within Confederate territory, I could certainly take on a barber's assistant if I had to.

Evasion wasn't the worst of my fears. Nor was bullet or bayonet, or even the chance of capture. I was more concerned about a chance blunder, a mispronounced word, an unwarranted phrase, a blind spot that would inadvertently disclose who I was and the mission I was on. I didn't need an extorting barber's assistant who could arouse suspicion or betray me. How did that damn man know my name?

My interview with the hotel's proprietor, Colonel Eleazer Stephenson, was scheduled for eleven o'clock. I had dressed appropriately in a black one-button coat with grey-line trousers. My derby had an immaculate white satin lining that I knew bore the marks of a professional man. I draped a gold watch and fob from my vest pocket to my trousers. To round out my new identity that, as I said, wasn't far from my own before the war, I carried an oil-silk bag with compartments that organized documents, paper, nibs, seal, wax, and spoon. The oil-silk bag was a gift from my father when I was studying for the bar, just before he ended our relationship for good. The bag was my only remaining connection to him.

I checked my watch: nearly eleven. It was time to meet Colonel Eleazer Stephenson, the man for whom I would work undercover as a secretary and clerk. Two massive carved front doors opened into an expansive room with ornate two-storey columns and arches that opened into a centre atrium. An elaborately ornamented skylight filtered sunlight into the interior. In the centre of the room was a circular table of considerable size holding an imposing arrangement of fresh flowers and greenery artfully arranged in all directions. Flowered chintz settees and damask armchairs set in twos and threes were positioned casually around the room. I walked to the reception desk, which was beside a set of stairs that split at the top landing to the right and left leading to the north or south wings of the hotel.

"I'm here to see Colonel Stephenson, please. He's expecting me. My name is James Thomson." I took a breath to settle my nerves, then set my writing case on the counter. A clammy imprint persisted on the case where my hand had been. I casually wiped it away with my elbow, hoping it would go unnoticed.

"One moment, sir. I'll see if he's free to see you."

I picked up a leaflet on the desk that explained the services of the hotel and the background of its entrepreneurial owner. Colonel Stephenson was a native of Springfield, Massachusetts, and had immigrated to St. Catharines in 1826 to open a livery stable and stagecoach company. When the railroad came, his business slackened off, so he turned his eye to a local saltworks that had gone out of business. There was no particular enterprise in salt with the competition from the United States, but salt wasn't Stephenson's interest. The water that filtered through the salt was.

Stephenson had sent a sample of the brackish water to a chemistry professor at the University of Toronto. When the professor reported that the water sample contained chlorides, iodides, and bromides of calcium, magnesium, and sulfates approaching the composition of some of the most important and fashionable European spas, Stephenson began building a stylish spa of his own. The promise of good health gained through the extraordinary medicinal qualities of the waters and baths that lay in store for the invalid or traveller was convincing. A patient could expect "a speedy cure for a range of digestive and urinary disorders, lassitude, seasickness, and eruptions of the skin."

The ample Stephenson burst into the lobby, sliding one hand along the top of the entry table to check for dust. He extended his other hand to greet me. "Good morning, my good man. Mr. Thomson, I presume? Thank you for responding to my query. Pray your trip from the City was without event." He was impeccably tailored in a single collar linen shirt with starched cuffs and jewelled links, a buff vest, and a blue satin cravat.

"Yes, Colonel Stephenson. It was most scenic. I spent the better part of the early hours walking through your most commodious town. It lacks for nothing."

"You're too kind, Mr. Thomson. Our guests do find St. Catharines a peaceable place to sojourn." Stephenson smoothed stray strands of hair that had slipped away from a low-slung part. "But we natives also find life here most pleasant. Come, come, sit down." Stephenson ushered me to a settee in the corner, arranging himself so he could monitor the activity in the lobby. "I hope you don't mind meeting out here. My office is covered with painter's cloths and ladders. My rooms are the last, of course, in the hotel's renovations."

"I see business is prosperous in spite of the war."

"Our rooms are fully occupied because of it, Mr. Thomson. But I should hope not at the expense of the poor souls who have suffered irretrievable losses in kith and kin, home and spirit. My heart goes out to them." He placed a reverent hand in the centre of his abundant chest. "Thank goodness the battlefield hasn't gotten any farther north than Pennsylvania. I still have relatives in New England. You'll find our clientele composed of mostly Southern refugees. I understand that although you presently hail from New York City, your political disposition is sympathetic to their cause."

"Yes, Colonel. Will that be an impediment to my work here?" My back stiffened. *Did Stephenson notice? The lies had begun.*

"No, of course not. I don't expect you to be fraternizing with the guests, anyway, but should your sympathies become obvious on occasion, I should think our Southern guests would feel consoled. Most Union sympathizers take rooms at one of the other hotels. I, for one, am indifferent. Blue or grey, Reb or Fed, their money's all the same to me. I'm a British subject now. I think you'll find many Canadians, on the other hand, are on the side of the Southern cause."

At that moment Stephenson recognized someone entering the front door, and with a sense of urgency, raised his elbows like a large bird attempting the first flaps of flight. With hands firmly braced on the settee's cushions, he hoisted himself to a standing position. "You'll excuse me, Mr. Thomson. I must attend to a guest. Please comfort yourself with a glass of juice made from our fresh local peaches. I will return."

Stephenson fluttered to greet a frail man wearing a heavy black gabardine cloak despite the summer morning's warmth. I could hear the man wheeze a request for Stephenson to order him a stage and driver to take him to Hamilton. "Certainly, Senator Clay." Stephenson clapped his hands toward an orderly who then escorted the patrician senator to the hotel's steam room.

When Stephenson returned, his chest had visibly expanded. "That was Senator Clement C. Clay from Alabama. I'm sure you're acquainted with him. We're most pleased to have such a distinguished guest at our baths."

"It hasn't been my good fortune to meet a man of such distinction, but I'm aware of his accomplishments in the U.S. Senate as an eloquent advocate of states' rights and now as a current supporter of the Confederate cause."

"Yes, yes, of course. I would have been so pleased if he could have honoured us at this evening's Salon. He would have been quite a draw, but he seems under the weather. Pity." Stephenson frowned momentarily as if he had just heard painful news, then he brightened.

"Say, Thomson, why don't you attend? You must observe the effects of our waters on the dispositions of our guests, many who are men of merit with whom you might be familiar. It's a most invigorating evening of conversation hosted by my own lovely niece, my sister's child from Louisiana, Miss Sarah Stephenson. This will be a fine opportunity to introduce you and inform our guests of the services you can provide." Stephenson looked pleased with himself for coming up with such a good idea.

"I should be honoured to attend."

"Good. That's settled. Now, may I be so abrupt as to bring us back to the business at hand, Thomson? When might you be able to start?" he said quickly as if pre-empting any other interruption from the lobby.

"I'm prepared to begin immediately," I replied, relieved I had apparently passed my first test.

Stephenson slapped his knees, then clasped his large hands over mine. "Well, then, do so!" he bellowed with pleasure and rose to leave. I reminded him that he hadn't yet given me my duties. "Oh, yes, yes, of course," he said, scratching his forehead, slightly embarrassed.

He then proceeded to tell me that he expected me to prepare all of his correspondence and also to act as secretary and/or courier to any guest who requested such service. Sunday nights would be my own, and I could use the baths only between seven and eight o'clock at night. The staff would acclimatize me to the hotel's routines, my meals would be in the kitchen, and a bellman would show me to my quarters. The floor clock in the lobby chimed eleven-thirty, which seemed to startle Stephenson.

"Must go now, Thomson. Workmen idle around this time of the morning." With those words, the good innkeeper excused himself, signalled the bellman, ducked behind the desk, and vanished into the sanctum of his private office.

Would I meet tonight the men of the Confederacy's "secret mission" or at least their minions? Either would suit "James Thomson."

3

Fomentation

By the time I settled in my room, I could smell the preparations for the first luncheon sitting. I followed the aromas to the kitchen where the staff members were already seated at a long table. I introduced myself to the head chef, who pointed to a table of salads, cold meats, ice tea, fruits, cheese, and cakes. Sitting nearby was the front-desk clerk, who nodded in the direction of an available seat at the end of the table. My "place," I discovered, was next to the tender of the baths, Superintendent Cyril Spears, a congenial Englishman who proceeded to regale me for the course of the meal on the merits of hydropathy.

"It has curative powers, you realize," Spears told me. "We maintain the finest sanitary conditions and possess a splendid range of practices available should you want to enjoy the service at those times staff are permitted to partake. The colonel likes his staff clean and to be familiar with the health benefits of our offerings."

"Most interesting, Mr. Spears. Tell me more."

"Well, we equal the best treatments as those found in Europe or Saratoga Springs in New York, such as wet packs, body bondage, spinal slapping, and head baths. We have a bath for every cranny in the human anatomy — sitz baths, douche baths, Turkish baths with either vapour or steam, followed by towel rubbing, fomentation, limb packing —"

"Excuse me, Mr. Spears," I interrupted. "I'd like to learn more about … fomentation?"

The superintendent put down his fork, dabbed each corner of his mouth with care, and prepared for a full discourse, supremely pleased at the opportunity to explain it. "Fomentation," he began, clearing his throat, "is a very beneficial application of warmth we've adopted here at the hotel to relieve pain. First, we spread a mackintosh sheet on the bed, then two blankets, on which the person, with only the trunk of his body undressed, or wholly undressed, is placed. One of the fomenting flannels, previously steamed, is wrung of hot water, then positioned under the back of the neck and another over the chest and bowels."

The desk clerk shouted good-naturedly to me as he was leaving the kitchen, interrupting the superintendent in mid-sentence. "Hey, Thomson, you'll learn soon enough not to get the old man started — pity. *Courage, mon brave.* He does take the odd breath every now and then, but don't get him on his theory of nether garments unless you're less a gentleman than you appear." The desk clerk swatted the doorframe for emphasis and ducked away, but not before feigning injury as Spears tossed his linen napkin, just missing the clerk's head.

"Do finish your description, Mr. Spears. I find it most interesting. I've never used a facility like this before."

"Of course. I should be happy to oblige. Where was I … oh, yes, the fomenting flannels. The guest is wrapped where he lies for about an hour, after which we place a cold dripping sheet over his body, followed by a spray of tepid water." Spears picked up his fork to resume eating and concluded, "It's a very pleasant encounter."

"I can see that it would be," I said, finishing the last bit of cold meat on my plate. "You must tell me about your nether theory someday." We laughed. "This evening's salon ... can you tell me when and where I should expect to attend?"

Spears sniffed as if slighted. "The colonel invited you, did he?"

"Only to introduce me to the guests and let them know in an informal manner of the secretarial services the colonel is now able to provide them, through me, that is, should they so require. My debut, so to speak."

"Well, although I've never been invited to attend, I've heard that between the posturing and airs you'll find some interesting conversation. It's a most worthwhile evening. Seven-thirty in the Crystal Room."

4

"Military Necessity"

The Crystal Room was on the top floor of the hotel with the potential to offer a generous view of the Canadian countryside below. However, since the drapes were drawn to keep the room cool, the outdoors couldn't be seen. The space was softly lit by a crystal chandelier, the room's eponymous centrepiece, which had been newly adapted to modern gas lighting.

The colonel's niece, whose name, if I remember the colonel correctly, I learned was Sarah Stephenson, stood by the arches at the entrance to the Crystal Room, looking poised as she greeted the arriving guests. With one hand she held a decorated folding fan and with the other she gracefully touched each guest's arm or gestured toward the cellarets around the room on which stemware encircled bottles of sherry. "Do feel free to help yourself or perhaps I may offer you some ice tea or lemonade instead, both cooled by ice harvested from fresh Canadian waters just last winter?" Then she whispered something confidential or amusing, and the guest laughed easily with charmed familiarity.

She made quick note of me the moment I entered the anteroom. I must have seemed unsure because she left her place by the archway and walked over to me. As hostess of the Salon, etiquette permitted this overture by an unmarried woman to a man. "Mr. Thomson, is it not?"

I quickly extended my palm. She offered her hand, which I lifted to my lips close enough for her to feel my breath but not touching her skin. I held it a second longer than might have been considered proper.

"Why, Mr. Thomson, we've only just met. Do you have plans to sweep me off my very feet?"

"James Thomson at your service, Miss Stephenson. It's a pleasure to make your acquaintance." I was aware of my own heartbeat as she spoke and became light-headed at the sight of her flawless skin.

"The pleasure's all mine, I'm sure. My uncle told me you'd be joining our friendly circle this evening. I hope you'll find it to your liking." Her voice was resonant and slow with the cadence of the Mississippi Southerner, so distinctive in the midst of the other prevailing British-sounding accents I'd encountered. "Have you an interest you'd like to pursue? I should be glad to introduce you to those who might entertain the topic you'd be most inclined to enjoy."

"Thank you, Miss Stephenson, for your kind consideration of my ability to remain in harmony with the evening's agenda, but I should feel most comfortable merely to observe and listen, and when appropriate, meet those guests who might need my services. The colonel would like his guests to feel at ease with me and to become aware of the clerical services I might offer should they so require."

I knew I didn't have to explain my presence to her. The colonel would have briefed her, but somehow it helped me to gather my thoughts.

"I'm here to make your evening as comfortable yet as thought-provoking as time will allow," she said. "May I offer you some sherry, Mr. Thomson? We've grown particularly fond of the style produced locally. Come." She offered her arm as she lithely glided her skirts around end tables and seated guests to the sherry. "Now there's a group of gentlemen you must meet," she whispered, discreetly placing her fan across her mouth as her eyes gave the direction in which she wanted me to look. "Do you recognize anyone?"

She poured my sherry as I scanned the corner. I recognized two of the four men from photographs I'd been shown during my Washington briefing. The third man seemed familiar, but I couldn't be sure. The fourth man I was certain I'd never seen.

"No, ma'am," I murmured, bending close enough to breathe her in. "I don't think so. However, the tall gentleman with the side whiskers —" Sarah nodded "— looks very much like the Honourable Beverly Tucker, the former U.S. consul to Liverpool." Tucker might have been fifty yet he had the bearing of a younger man, tailored, slim with a slightly protruding lower lip that gave him a constant appearance of circumspection, which seemed to be the steadfast features necessary for an international trade negotiator.

Sarah tapped my arm with her fan. "You're absolutely correct, Mr. Thomson. You *are* a clever man."

Tucker had been originally against the Southern states leaving the Union, but when his home state of Virginia seceded from the Union he felt it was his duty to resign his post in Liverpool as a Union representative and return to defend his Confederate comrades. Confederate President Jefferson Davis used Tucker's experience and trade contacts to arrange deals to sell Southern products on behalf of the Confederate government. It made sense to me now. The bales of hay I'd seen being loaded near the Welland Canal that morning were part of Tucker's trade mission in Canada. In St. Catharines, Tucker could monitor the arrival and departure of Southern commodities through the canal such as cotton, which provided him access to both European, and Yankee markets. His interests, for the time being, were solely commercial.

You are a clever man echoed in my brain. It was one thing to worry about pretending to be someone else, but I hadn't anticipated how difficult it would be to separate the United States Secret Service agent from the *clever man.*

"Thank you, Miss Stephenson. You're most kind."

"Allow me to introduce you to them," she said. "I'm certain they'll be as charmed as I am with your most promising acquaintance." Again, she gathered her layers of skirts, then measured her passage with grace, gliding around bobbin-turned chairs and chintz sofas, between French flowered damask chesterfields, and around occasional tables dotted with delicate porcelain figurines.

Four men stood in the corner where the second man I recognized was holding court. As we approached, he was placing his sherry on a bookshelf behind him to free his hands so he could more forcefully underscore a point he was making. I immediately recognized him from the U.S. Senate confirmation hearings a few years back. It was George N. Sanders, a distinctively short and stocky man with untamed curly hair. He was known in government circles as "the wirepuller," a master puppeteer manipulating the strings of political marionettes, invisibly moving events behind the scenes.

In the 1850s, President Franklin Pierce had wanted to recognize the contribution Sanders had made during the campaign to annex Texas in 1845, so he had appointed Sanders consul to London. Sanders's reactions soon caused quite a scandal. Without waiting for confirmation, he left to take up consular duties but became embroiled with refugee European revolutionaries, including the two Giuseppes Mazzini and Garibaldi in Italy, and became an outspoken supporter of the former and his theory of the dagger that justified tyrannicide as a reasonable act in the face of oppression. In France, Sanders joined forces with other radical freedom fighters who called for the assassination of Napoleon III. Because he had been too impulsive a man for a diplomatic post, the Senate refused to confirm him. Consequently, Sanders was without portfolio and stayed in Europe to hobnob with Europe's most passionate defenders of freedom, but only for the select few who were white male landowners. As a staunch Confederate, Sanders endorsed slavery with unflinching conviction. His views were so antithetical to my own that it would test my ability for restraint to remain indifferent, or worse, seemingly supportive of his cause.

When the Civil War started, it was well known that Sanders had become a self-appointed emissary of the Confederacy as a negotiator of financial and trading agreements with European officials and bankers. He was never without money or beautiful women. Many people were repelled by his appearance and questionable politics, but most had no doubt that this ill-kempt man was willing to take any initiative to influence events.

Sanders was complaining about the recent aborted peace initiative between the Union and the Confederacy that he had helped to arrange in Niagara Falls, New York, through Horace Greeley, the editor of the *New-York Daily Tribune*. Sarah and I waited by a corner screen until a moment presented itself to step in. Sanders hardly noticed.

"It was that sanguinary philanthropist and paltry abolitionist Greeley," railed Sanders in nasal tones caused by an apparent deviated septum, "who thinks himself astute and sagacious." He slapped the back of one hand into the palm of the other as if hammering his point in place. "He's nothing but a contriving bungler who placed both parties at cross-purposes." His contempt for the unwitting Greeley was unequivocal.

Sanders was rehashing how he and other Confederates had consented to meet with an emissary from Washington on the neutral Canadian

                                                  LINDA BRAMBLE

side of Niagara Falls and how they had been under the naive impression that President Lincoln was willing to negotiate peace. "That idiot Greeley," Sanders continued, "made us such fools. He has the wits of a field mouse. Lincoln no more wanted to meet with us to consider peace than drive a mule team to France." He took another sip of sherry.

This tirade was for the benefit of his audience. Sanders knew full well that Lincoln would be stubborn and he was also aware of Lincoln's preconditions for peace ---which were nothing short of the reunification of the country and the end of slavery. Sanders was clever, though. He reckoned if the North could witness Lincoln's intransigence in the face of the loss of so many lives, Lincoln's perceived bloodthirsty insensitivity would surely cost him his bid for a second term in office at the upcoming November election.

Sanders left his listeners without rejoinder. Sarah saw this as her cue.

"Please excuse my intrusion, gentlemen. I see you're deeply engaged in airing a most irksome issue, but may I take this opportunity to introduce you to Mr. James Thomson, originally from Virginia, the hotel's new amanuensis and a law clerk by trade. He'll be at your secretarial and courier services on call."

The four men opened their circle to accommodate us.

"You're never an intrusion, milady," Sanders said with an overstating sweep of his hand. "Mr. Thomson, welcome. What brings you to these northern parts?"

Sarah interceded. "It's my good uncle's intention to bring to his guests a needed service. You'll find Mr. Thomson a trusted clerk highly recommended for confidential service by our very president, Mr. Jefferson Davis himself."

"How did you know President Davis, Thomson?" Tucker asked.

"I worked in the Richmond legislature as an administrative assistant. When President Davis relocated there at the outbreak of the war, I served his cabinet. Subsequently, I was redeployed to Baltimore on special assignment. My mother currently stays in Niagara Falls visiting her sister and is in poor health. I've been furloughed for a few months to be near her as she convalesces. When this position arose to clerk at the hotel, I took advantage of the opportunity."

Tucker seemed satisfied. The real James Thomson had just such a scenario, working in the Richmond legislature until recently when he was moved to the intelligence section of the Confederate legislature.

Since no one in the government would verify his location, only his good standing for the time being, my alias could be safely confirmed.

I shook hands all around as the conversationalists introduced themselves. However, the third fellow, an Englishman named Godfrey Hyams, made me feel uneasy. There was something not as forthcoming in his manner. He had allowed his long, coarse beard to reach the second button of his coat. I shouldn't have judged the man for an unsightly beard, but it hid a fuller comprehension of his expressions. He was a hard man to read because of it. Sanders introduced the fourth man as Dr. Louis Contri, a physician from Italy who was also Sanders's new son-in-law. The doctor was unusually tall for an Italian and had straight blond hair. He was probably from the Veneto or perhaps Trentino, closer to the Austro-Hungarian border.

"Mi scusie," Contri volunteered. "English no so good. I listen. *Grazie.*"

"It is indeed a pleasure to meet you all," I said. Seeing that I was introduced, Sarah politely excused herself and joined another group to stimulate conversation.

"Mr. Sanders," said Hyams, who seemed to be almost as new to the conversation as I, "am I correct in recalling your connections in Europe to the great Mazzini?"

Sanders seemed pleased to have the chance to leave the aborted Peace Conference initiative behind and talk about his European escapades. "Ah, yes ..." He sighed as if dreaming about happier days. "My reputation precedes me even to Canada West." He picked up his sherry and recounted the days of Italian freedom fighting against the oppressive rule of King Victor Emmanuel II, then said, "And I think the Italians have an extraordinary legacy in Machiavelli's political philosophy that's bred in the bone, upon which they so sensibly draw from time to time." As Sanders baited his listeners, his dutiful Italian son-in law, Louis Contri, nodded in agreement.

Hyams took the bait. "Tell us more, Sanders."

"It's quite obvious," Sanders said dismissively. "Their eminently sensible theory of tyrannicide, of course. 'He who oppresses earns the dagger.'"

Hyams nodded slightly as if to acknowledge his understanding of the theory. In retrospect I remember a slight asymmetrical purse to what could be seen of his lips, which I ignored then but may have suggested he felt more contempt with the notion than approval.

Tucker shifted his weight and tugged slowly at his side whiskers. "What are you implying, Sanders?"

"I'm not implying anything, Tucker. I'm outright stating that the oppressive Lincoln deserves to be dead." Sanders had lowered his voice and gravelled his last three words, looking Tucker straight in the eye. A gentleman sitting in a chair a few feet away stood up, folded his newspaper, and slowly approached us.

"Good God, Sanders, you don't mean that," Hyams said as if his proper British notions of the canons of war had been violated.

Sanders smiled enigmatically. "Oh, but I do. This very day I received word that the Confederate Command in Richmond found orders on the person of Colonel Dahlgren in his failed attempt to capture Richmond, our beloved capital — orders that explicitly required him to capture President Davis and, may I add, to assassinate him. Only the tyrant Lincoln is responsible for this planned atrocity." He stood back and folded his arms as if to say 'Now, what do you think of that?'

"Yes, that boorish backwoods buffoon who eats with his fingers and blows his nose with his thumb has ordered our president murdered," Sanders continued. "Only Lincoln would have had the imperial gall to send in an army against his own people. I ask you, do we stand idly by and let these whoresons destroy us more? The time for retribution has come. If it's considered murder in the time of war, so be it. Get to the oppressor, I say. Without that head of state the Union will fall."

Sanders's face was flushed as he spoke, amplifying the coiled blue veins at his temples. Tucker was about to ask Sanders more about the Dahlgren raid when the man who had been observing the conversation approached the group with hesitation, mindful of the seriousness of the topic and the power of Sanders's words.

"Excuse me, gentlemen, but I couldn't help but overhear your most passionate debate and should like to inform you that I know of others who share your view." In the spirit of the salon, the newcomer was welcomed, so again the men opened their circle to add another.

"Go on," urged Tucker to the newcomer, slipping his hand into his waistcoat as if withholding judgment until hearing more. "Do you know of such men?" The men tightened their circle, drawing in like filings to a magnet.

"I do," said the newcomer, his eyes still averted as if the information he was about to deliver was too heavy to bear. Had he been talking about the weather, his listeners would have responded with the same attention, for he had the commanding presence of a statesman — tall, slim, with slow, observant eyes, and with the exception of a slight aquiline nose, the kind of well-proportioned features that might have inspired the artist Titian. His face was clean-shaven all for but a well-groomed moustache with waxed ends. He wore a double-breasted frock coat in black with fawn twills and a white shirt, its collar edged by a saffron cravat with a pearl stud. He impressed me as a man of pleasing gentility and carriage. "Let me introduce myself. My name is James Watson Wallace of Maryland."

The Maryland Wallaces were well known in the South as having made their fortune in manufacturing. Wallace nodded, tilting his head to the group. They, in turn, returned the ritual with polite acknowledgement.

Beverly Tucker spoke first. "Tucker here, pleased to meet you. And this is Mr. Godfrey Hyams, Mr. George Sanders, Dr. Louis Contri, and Mr. James Thomson. Now, do continue. You've piqued our interest."

"My pleasure, as dubious as it might be, given the topic I shall relate. Let me explain. The man at the heart of the plan is a Colonel George Margrave of South Carolina, but I have it on good authority that this is merely a *nom de guerre*. His real name is Rhett. He was at one time a member of General Beauregard's staff and at the battle of Shiloh was shot through the body and carried off the field for dead."

Wallace spoke to each man in the circle, aware of the rapt interest his news of the front was garnering. "Fortunately, his life wasn't extinct, and he was discovered again working to preserve the rights of the South, but this time his efforts have gone underground. Some call him a cool and reckless villain, one who can smile and murder while he does it. For such an enterprise as assassination, no better leader could be found. They say he's now somewhere in the Canadas, heading a group of men loyal to the Confederacy."

I had been warned of Margrave's activities but hadn't heard that he might be in the Canadas. "Where in the Canadas do you think he is?" I asked.

"Should he be in our midst, we might further his initiative," Sanders interjected with enthusiasm.

"How did you meet him?" Hyams asked.

                                          LINDA BRAMBLE

Wallace turned to accept a glass of sherry being passed by a black servant. *"Prosit!"* he said, sipping slowly, not to be rushed. "I should be pleased to respond to each one of you. Mr. Hyams," he began, peering into Hyams's eyes with a disturbing directness, "my acquaintance with Colonel Margrave began last year in Baltimore when my firm was approached to participate in a project initiated by a group of *effective* citizens of Richmond to raise money to manage a military operation by individual enterprise rather than by the government."

Wallace took his eyes off Hyams momentarily to gauge the attention of the rest of his listeners. Satisfied, he continued. "In spite of the Union occupation of Baltimore, Margrave was secretly asking others at that time to volunteer their services in order to play a more conspicuous part in what he referred to as the destruction of that great hydra-headed monster of civil discord." Wallace paused. "I admit to having considered the idea at the time." The others, not yet part of the dialogue, stood silently as if weighing what Wallace had said.

Hyams broke the silence. "You're very forthright, Mr. Wallace. A less congenial group might find your knowledge of the possible murder of a head of state an abetting act of treason, only reconciled by the noose. I can't help but wonder if thou dost protest too much."

"You're correct in challenging me, Mr. Hyams, but I need not remind you of the justness of our cause, for it rests on the sacred principles of '76, '89, and '98 and the American experiment of limited government." Wallace had reverted to an aggressive tone more common in a courtroom than a salon. "Nor do I need to remind you of the doctrine of military necessity. It's a measure that's indispensable for securing the ends of this godawful war. History attests to its justifiable use and the future will no doubt do the same. I, too, regard the removal of Lincoln as a military necessity. The war has loosed much anger in the world, which someone must have the integrity to stem." Feeling vindicated by the alacrity with which he had deflected Hyams's parry, Wallace took another sip of sherry.

Sanders stepped in. "Precisely. Couldn't have argued better myself. Now, where can we find this Colonel Margrave?"

Wallace turned cordially in Sanders's direction to respond to his ally. "He spoke of meeting with Southern gentlemen in Toronto at the Queen's Hotel. Whether he's there now, I don't know. I'm on my way there as soon as I finish some business I have in town here. I can scout around and let you know."

It was no secret that Lincoln had been plagued by assassination plots from the day he was inaugurated, yet he took none of them seriously, much to the dismay of his cabinet and military officers. Nevertheless, I knew I needed to follow Wallace's actions closely.

"I'm going for a cigar on the veranda," Tucker said.

His abruptness didn't surprise Sanders, who waved him on and said within earshot of Tucker as he was leaving, "This talk of military necessity quickens his nerves and agitates his stomach. Lincoln was an old friend of his. But sometimes he acts as if the ambiguities of loyalty and betrayal that war forces on a man troubles only him."

Tucker ignored Sanders's reproach and continued walking. Sanders shrugged and returned his attention to Wallace and Hyams. Contri had left the conversation a few moments earlier. In the meantime I noticed Sarah motioning to me from the anteroom, so I excused myself.

She handed me a folded and sealed piece of paper. "Forgive me, Mr. Thomson, but this just arrived for you. The courier said it was urgent. I do hope everything's all right." She watched with concern as I broke the seal.

"Thank you, Miss Stephenson. I hope so, as well." I glanced at the message: "Man can never escape from himself … at your peril forget our appointment."

I checked my watch. It was 9:45 p.m. "As I expected," I reassured her, "nothing of concern, but it does require my immediate attention."

I thanked her again and strode away, trying to appear unhurried — a gentleman never rushed. I passed Louis Contri in the hallway, who asked if I had seen Sarah. As I motioned toward the anteroom, I wondered if he needed a refill of sherry. Italians, I knew, loved their wine. When I reached the veranda, I first made certain Tucker was on the other side. Then I started to run down the Salina Street hill behind the hotel toward the canal. My adversary had shown his hand.

5

The Meeting

Parked in the brewery yard was a large, hitched, but empty dead-axle dray, sturdy enough to deliver at least twenty barrels of beer.

"You be the man from Virginia?" asked the muscular black driver perched high on the wagon's platform.

"Yes."

"I got orders to tell you you'd best be takin' a seat or else I needs to take serious steps to prompt you aboard."

"No need," I said as I got on. "I'm complying." The wagon bounced along the towpath that skirted the canal, barely clearing the steep embankment to the water's edge. One misplaced boulder could have unhinged the wheel of a lesser vehicle and we would have gone toppling into the water below. We rode silently, indifferent to the other's company — apparent enemies without cause other than the colour of my skin. He drove with half-lidded eyes, his arm resting confidently along the back of the seat. The man knew the team needed little prompting along the path, but I also got the sense he was enjoying what he imagined to be the trouble that lay ahead for me.

The driver let me off at the base of the hill, pointing to a trapdoor built into the side of the embankment beside the creek that fed into the canal. "Lift dat door and go through. He's a waitin'."

I opened the door cautiously. All I could see was a series of steps that spiralled just below the waterline to what looked like a tunnel under the creek. As I proceeded, I found along either side of the narrow passage barrels of beer kept from spoiling in the summer heat by the cooling effect of the surrounding water. I had to crouch as I made my way toward the man sitting on a crate with a beer in his hand, waiting for me.

"Man can never escape from himself," I said, "nor from you. That gave you away."

"My intention. I was afraid the yellow streak down your back might have stopped you from coming." He feigned a jab at my arm.

"I have to admit your assistant in the barbershop rattled me when he mentioned my real name. I can see now that he's one of your men."

"Sorry about that. Yes, he is. So, you asslick, who said the words in my note?"

I grinned. "Give me something tougher than that."

"You don't know, do you?"

"I'll embarrass you, Aaron. This is fair warning."

"Go on."

"Goethe, *Torquato Tasso*, 1790."

The black man rolled his eyes, cuffed the side of his leg, and handed me a beer. "Damn, I'll catch you yet, Richard."

Of that I had no doubt. Aaron Young was a bright and fearless black man, sturdy, well over six feet tall, with broad shoulders and serious eyes that could move anyone from his path. His parents had escaped bondage in Virginia in the late 1850s and had travelled to Canada West with the intrepid Harriet Tubman. The plantation from which they escaped was my own family's estate where we boys had grown up together. As far as I was concerned, we were brothers. I couldn't have loved Aaron more. When I was in university, I would buy two sets of books for every course I took so that Aaron could study along with me.

When Aaron's family ran away, I wished them Godspeed and never warned my father they were planning their escape. After the overseer noticed they weren't in their quarters, he pounded on my father's door to awaken him. The two of them rounded up men and hounds to chase down the fugitives, but I refused to go. When my father realized I had not only betrayed him but was an accomplice to the loss of his property, he disinherited me and refused to ever lay eyes on me again. Without slaves he couldn't run the farm and would eventually be forced to sell it. I detested slavery and believed change had to begin somewhere. My father had resources; his slaves didn't.

Eventually, my father moved to New York City where he opened a small import/export company. I finished my schooling by cashing in a small trust in my name that my mother had provided and never saw my parents again.

Aaron Young and I had lost touch with each other for a few years until 1863 when the Emancipation Proclamation prompted him to volunteer as a scout for the Corps of the Army of the Potomac led by Brigadier General McDowell where, by chance, I had also volunteered as a scout. So we met up again in the familiar mountains of Virginia. On quiet evenings while waiting for Confederate armies to advance or their campfires to dim, I'd listen while Aaron recited flawless passages from the *Aeneid* or related profiles from *Plutarch's Lives* to keep his mind agile when he resumed his studies after the war. When the fighting changed theatres, we were both reassigned to separate campaigns and lost track of each other until now.

"I got a thirty-day furlough, so I came home to be closer to my family for a while," Aaron told me. "Jobs are always easy to get in summer at any one of the hotels in town. My intention was not to get drawn into the war again for the duration of my rest, but before I could blink I'm cutting the hair of Confederates I'd only read about in Union newspapers. It's the curious presence of these distinguished Rebels that brings you here."

"How would you know that?"

"When I informed the War Department about the Rebel activity in St. Catharines, Assistant Secretary of War Dana had me commissioned here. So much for a furlough. I was the one who requested you to join me! I needed someone I could trust." Aaron took a pry bar and opened a crate of four-quart bottles of beer, unlatched the stoppers on two, and handed me one.

"So it's you I have to thank for this mission?"

Aaron nodded. "It is. I need your help, and you can use mine. You can get into places I can't and vice versa."

"Let's not waste any time then. Tell me what you know. Let's start with Clement Clay."

Aaron took a swig of beer. "You've probably been briefed, but let me review the facts so far. My information is that Clay and Jacob Thompson — the former congressman from Mississippi and secretary of the interior under President Buchanan — were both sent by President Davis to advance the cause of the South any way they could by establishing a secret mission in Canada to plan operations from here. They call it 'fire from the north.'"

Aaron wiped some beer foam from his lips with his hand. Although he had made a conscious effort to speak impeccable English and lose the vestiges of the language of an uneducated slave, his words were slow and rhythmic like those of a Southern storyteller. He paused often at the end of a description to check if I was following him.

Taking another swallow of beer, he continued. "Jacob Thompson became one of the richest and meanest planters in the South, owning hundreds of slaves, then lost it all in a Union raid. He now seethes with the desire for retribution. He's operating out of Toronto and can usually be found at the Queen's Hotel, bossing everyone around him, even the Canadians who come to do business with him. From what I can see, he's a scheming and uncouth man despite his so-called blue blood."

"Why is Clay in St. Catharines?" I asked.

Aaron sat up, scratched his head, and laughed. "Because it's a fact that these two former upstanding Southern gentlemen who supposedly wouldn't say shit if they had a mouthful absolutely hate each other. By the time they ran the blockade from Bermuda to Halifax on a rather unaggressive sidewheel steamer, they were so vexed with each other that Clay refused to join Thompson, and Thompson's secretary, William Cleary, for the next thousand-mile overland leg of the trip from Halifax to Toronto. The other reason Clay is here is because of the water treatments at our local hotels. Seems he has chronic asthma that needs taming when he's under stress."

"How did you scout all this out?"

"The baths, my friend, the baths. It's just the same here as on the plantation. Either the Southerners don't see us, or they think we're too dumb to understand anything we hear. I've got neighbours who serve the very masters from whom they ran away. These Rebels don't notice a dark man's face. They see only the white uniform he wears."

I sighed. "I know, I know … However, I imagine with that unseen presence comes a certain covert satisfaction to be able to outwit them."

"Sometimes, yes, that's a fact. But it's risky. The authorities can report you to hungry bounty hunters or track you down at night, pull you from your bed, and murder you even here in Canada. So it's risky. Freedom's given my brothers and sisters a new boldness, though. They're like gamblers, I swear, who've been forbidden to return to the cards because they beat the house too often. Then, with the boldness of a fox after a lion, they come back in disguise and present themselves right in front of the dealers who once banished them. They're audacious, I agree, yet they hear and see, then report back to me in the barbershop."

"You've got quite a nest of informers working for you," I marvelled.

                                                          LINDA BRAMBLE

"That's right."

"Tell me more about Clay."

"Frankly, he's pitiable. The mission is supposed to be clandestine, so Clay makes these feeble attempts at secrecy by doing such things as using an anagram of his name — L-A-C-Y — in secret dispatches to Richmond. Thompson is as vulgar and greedy as Clay is feeble and trusting, but they're still both committed to their cause, even if they're unwilling to submit to the judgment of the other and are equally inept at pulling their mission off."

"This should make my job that much easier, but fools are unpredictable. You said you needed my help. What can I do for you?"

"You can begin," Aaron said, "by simply gaining Clay's trust. We'll then devise our plans as events dictate. I know it's early, but do you see any place where I might help assist you?"

"Yes. There's a way you can help me. Clay's going to Hamilton tomorrow. I would have found a reason to join him, but I need to stick around here to keep my eye on another fellow, James Watson Wallace, before he leaves town. Do you know anything about him?"

"No, he's new, but I'll ask around."

"Good. Clay has ordered a stagecoach for nine o'clock. He's not the type to travel just to see the sights. Could you follow him and tell me where he goes and with whom he meets?"

Aaron grinned. "Consider it done."

The next morning a coach-and-four picked up the wheezing Clement Clay in front of the Stephenson House Hotel. A jovial Irish driver punched Clay's ticket while an indifferent but very tall black footman with a coachman's hat and cape lifted Clay's valise to the roof carrier and seated him for the thirty-five-mile journey to Hamilton. By eight o'clock that evening, an envelope was slipped under my door with a note that read: "He met Hyams and Dr. Luke Blackburn."

Blackburn was a physician renowned for his work fighting yellow fever. I had to find a way to get word to the U.S. War Department very fast.

6

First Dispatch to Washington City

I should have waited until morning to find Aaron when a shave could have easily covered the nature of our meeting. I wasn't even sure where to begin looking for him, but I found myself reaching for my coat nonetheless. Being seen with a black man at night would look suspicious, but something had to be done. I placed my room key in my pocket, grabbed my kit, and headed for the veranda.

It was one of those tranquil summer nights. Guests dotted the grounds, lingering in the cool twilight and listening to the nostalgic music of a military band playing on the lawn in front of the hotel. Late-blooming linden trees honeyed the evening air. For a moment I wondered what it would be like to sit on the veranda next to Sarah — so closely I would feel the sweep of her fan. The thought vanished when I noticed two sailors strolling down the Salina Street hill. I took the veranda steps two at a time to catch up with them.

"Excuse me, mates!" I called out.

The sailors stopped abruptly, their hands braced at their sides, taut for a fight — a way of life on the canal. "What would you be wantin'?" demanded the taller of the two.

"Just the location of the nearest telegraph office."

"Would ya be lookin' to send a wire at this hour of night?" inquired the second sailor.

"Yes, it's rather urgent that I do."

"Would you be knowin' the way to the St. Paul Street Bridge?" said the less suspicious second sailor.

"Yes," I replied, wondering if these Irish sailors could answer a question without asking one.

"Stay straight. It'll be on your right," said sailor number one, now willing to be helpful.

I thanked them and headed off before they could ask me anything else. I would look for Aaron after sunset. Right now I needed the last remaining light to trace the route of the telegraph lines.

"Head right toward the train depot and hold tight your pockets!" sailor number two cried out. "Damn fool dandies goin' down the road alone at night."

The low-level swing bridge across the canal was available for me to cross. Once I was past the shipyards on the other side, the city quickly surrendered to the country. Classic Italianate and Georgian townhouses were replaced by gingerbread-and-gabled farms, then barns and orchards beginning to give way to carriage houses and industry. The lines of the Montreal Telegraph Company edged the right-hand side of the corduroy road that led to the train station. I speculated that the road probably paralleled the Niagara Escarpment, an eight-hundred-foot ledge that linked an upper plateau, extending east toward Toronto and west to Buffalo, New York, where the next relay stations were located.

I walked the telegraph line until I was well out of the curious eyes of the nearest farmhouse. The sun was low in the sky, casting long, slim shadows along the road. When I found a telegraph pole with enough surrounding spies bush for camouflage, I removed my jacket, placed it beside the base, sat down, and opened my kit bag, the one I used as a military scout. Aaron had one, too. From it I removed a pair of spurs we used to climb trees in order to gain a broader perspective of encamped enemy troops. I buckled them over my boots, adjusting the long metal spikes to fit under the arch of each foot. Then I waited until darkness completely enveloped the landscape.

With my kit bag criss-crossed over my chest and shoulder, I started climbing, testing each crevice of the pole for safe footing. I jabbed the spur into one side, then the other, hoisting myself up, one secured foot at a time, until I reached the top. The orchard below looked like an entire regiment on parade, standing tall in meticulously aligned columns and rows.

In order to create a one-way line to the Buffalo relay station, I had to break the telegraph wire so that my outgoing message wouldn't go back to the St. Catharines telegraph office. I removed a pair of gloves, wire cutters, and a spool of copper wire, which I tucked under my arm, then snipped the open line, careful to hold the end going to Buffalo and let the other end fall to the ground. Taking the end of the copper spool, I spliced it onto the telegraph wire, forming a rattail with the malleable wire. I cut enough wire from the spool to what I guessed to be the length of the pole plus a few feet. Then I dropped the wire to the ground and climbed down.

The moon provided enough light to install a makeshift field station at the base of the pole by connecting a coil to the wire and a receiver magnet, which had a small rotating armature and battery. I was now ready to send. With every touch of the wire, in varying lengths of contact, I tapped my coded message to the War Department in Washington City: "Hyams and Clay met Luke Blackburn in Hamilton, Ont. Stop. Advise tonight. Stop."

Only a reply would confirm whether or not my message got through. The Buffalo relay station was a twenty-four-hour operation. Messages from all points would be relayed there first and then redirected. My Washington contact also had a twenty-four-hour direct line receiving, which meant I could expect a reply within the hour. I prepared to wait, making myself comfortable at the base of the pole.

I liked this part of the work, pitting myself against a problem, challenging the night to give up its secrets. A mockingbird performed his entire melancholy repertoire, never repeating another bird's song, yet never singing a song of his own. I remember thinking, *Would this be my fate, too? Telling someone else's story. Never telling one of my own?*

The armature began to move as if operated by a phantom, clicking out a message in Morse — I had made a connection! The message, however, was addressed to a guest at the hotel: "It's a boy. Stop. All fine. Stop. Love, Theodore. Stop." Three more messages came through the wire before I heard my call letters. No sooner had I placed my ear close to the apparatus to better pick up the incoming clicks, than an approaching depot baggage wagon came rattling down the road. I wouldn't be able to hear the armature's faint clicks spelling out the message if it arrived before the wagon passed, and I couldn't afford to miss the reply. I had to do something and do it quickly.

The driver's dog began to bark, aroused by my downwind scent. I had seconds before the canine would be beside me, alerting the driver to my operation. First, I placed my fingertips gently on the armature to feel the message, hoping each pulsation would feather my fingers with meaning, but my fingers weren't sensitive enough. I dug one spurred foot into the pole, grabbed my receiving unit, and stabbed my other foot onto the pole for better grounding. Then the armature started to move in ghostly taps.

My only recourse was to place the ends of the one hundred and thirty volts of wire in my mouth. Every pulse of meaning sent a charge through my body that felt like an explosion.

"H — OK. Stop. LB — NO. Stop. More LB. Stop." That was followed by the sign-off letters. It was over. I had received the message, plus the lingering bitter aftertaste of wire and acid and a disturbing tingling in my head.

I let go of the unit and wire, jumped down, and crouched low out of sight but not out of scent. The dog barked louder and became more anxious.

"Hush up, hound!" ordered the driver, but the dog persisted. I threw a large rock across the road. The dog jumped out of the wagon and ran to the rock, determined to be the victor of the chase. The driver, unwilling to be part of a fray between a field skunk and a depot dog, muttered something about "varmints," then snapped the whip and reins, hollering "Hee-yaw" and picking up enough speed to worry the hound, which flew between the fruit trees to catch up with his master.

When the driver was out of sight, I disconnected the apparatus, placed it in my kit, and left the wire on the pole dangling. Linemen would find the break in the morning and reconnect the wires. I brushed off my coat, repacked the spurs, and slung the kit across my chest. Now I needed to make contact with Aaron before morning. It was ten o'clock on a Sunday night. I had a hunch where I might find my friend, or at least someone who might know him, and headed for the north side of town to the black settlement. The heart of any community of blacks was its church. Surely, this community would be no different. Sunday night was for gospel singing and prayer meetings. There had to be someone who knew where to find Aaron.

After a brisk walk, I reached the black settlement where moonlight reflected off the clapboards of the single-peaked British Methodist Episcopal church, giving it a holy glow. Men and women were gathered in small circles, talking quietly before heading back to their homes in the surrounding neighbourhood. The church was indeed the heart of this community. I approached, trying to look inconspicuous. However, the more I tried the more obvious and out of place I felt. A tap on my shoulder made me almost jump.

"Lan' sakes, child, why you in this neck of the woods this time o' night? You realize the stir you's a causin'?" The woman from the market square when I first arrived in St. Catharines stood there, wagging her finger at me.

"Begging pardon, ma'am, but I was out walking and heard such heart-rending music that I thought I'd find the source. I certainly didn't mean to affront your congregation's spiritual privacy." I could see this wasn't washing with the market vendor.

"A white man in our part of town is usually up to no good. Our brethren seem to just *disappears* whenever white folk comes this way after dark." She flicked her hand high in the air to indicate the ethereal mystery of their disappearances. "A face so pretty as yours with such a look a'yearning is bothersome to our womenfolk, too, if you knows what I mean. And I's not sure to trust you, neither. One minute honest as the day is long and the next —" she paused and squinted "— you eyes all a dartin' like a fox out for a coop. What you *really* doin' out here, young man?"

There are some people I knew I could charm, but the old woman wasn't one of them, and I needed her. "You're right, ma'am. I'm looking for someone. That barber you recommended to me at the Stephenson House Hotel — Aaron Young."

The old woman put her hands on her hips in defiance. "What you want wif him?"

I tried to lower the barrier she was erecting between us. Years of survival had taught her to trust few. "Just to give him a message. My concern is to find a courier I can trust to get it to him tonight."

She raised her arms in exasperation, shaking her head. "You talkin' trust to me now, child? You sure is a cheeky one. I'll tells you I knows him and I might deliver somthin' to 'im, if'n I had a mind." She glanced away, pushing a disdaining chin into the night.

I knew this feigned slight was part of the negotiation, so I played my part as the ameliorator. "I mean no harm, ma'am. I'm not a bounty hunter or a crimper aiming to enlist such a sturdy lad. Mr. Young can act upon my message or let it be."

She studied me up and down, then drew closer to my face and spoke slowly. "Now you listen and listen good. This once, just this once, but not again unless you comes clean with me, ya hear? Now what you want him to know?"

She had the comforting home smells of celery, garlic, biscuits, and bay that I remembered so well from my own mammy. "Tell him, 'Every physician almost hath his favourite disease.' He'll know what I mean."

"That it?" She repeated the cryptic message.

"Yes, ma'am, and I'd thank you to see that he gets it as soon as possible."

"Aaron's a smart boy and not taken in by no pretty white-boy trap," she said, trying to convince herself her co-operation wouldn't be seen as an act of treachery.

"Yes, ma'am, he's smart and this is no trap. I guarantee Aaron will know."

The streets of town were Sabbath quiet, deserted except for a few arguing sailors. I went the shortest route I knew along the canal to the beer storage tunnel where Aaron and I had met the day before. I would wait for him there. Before I set out I sat beside the canal for a few minutes to be sure no one followed me to the service road east to the brewery wagon yard. When I arrived, I raised the doors to the tunnel and entered cautiously. Lanterns lit the narrow passageway that stretched under the canal from one bank to the other. Halfway down, I spotted Aaron with his feet up on a crate, having a beer.

"That didn't take you long," I said. "I see the old woman was true to her word."

"Careful what you say, old man. That 'old woman' is my auntie. She was sold to another Virginia plantation. That's why she didn't know you. When we left your daddy's plantation, she and my uncle were waiting for us at a safehouse so we could all come up north together. Wasn't easy. She might be old, but she's got grit like no other."

"No wonder she seemed a bit cranky. She was protecting her kin. Of all the people I could have met in town, I meet your auntie."

"Wouldn't have mattered. We look out for each other. Now what's this message all about?"

"I got word from headquarters tonight."

"How?"

"More on that later, but they indicated that this Hyams fellow is okay. He must be a federal agent. I was uncomfortable when I met him last night. Maybe that's why. But they want to know more about Blackburn and what Hyams, Clay, and Blackburn were up to in Hamilton. My guess is so they can cross-check Hyams's story. He could be playing both sides. What else did you get in Hamilton?"

"This Dr. Blackburn is being financed by a Canadian from Toronto named William L. McDonald, a munitions manufacturer who backed a trip that Hyams recently made to Halifax where he met some trunks Blackburn sent from Bermuda. Hyams was to have them shipped to some key Northern cities. Their meeting seemed to go well with one exception. Hyams refused to ship a special valise to someone in Washington. They argued about that for a while, but Hyams was adamant. Who's this Blackburn, anyway?"

"All I know," I said, "is his reputation for putting down a yellow fever epidemic in Bermuda. Are you thinking what I am?"

"Oh, good Lord!" Aaron cried. "If he's filled those trunks with infected clothes or blankets in this weather, the next person who uses them could be infected."

"Yes, innocent people, children, women — it could start an epidemic that would wipe out more people in the North than any amount of gunfire. If we're right, it's damn diabolical. Have you ever witnessed an outbreak of smallpox?"

Aaron nodded. "Yes, once. It advances with a vengeance. Victims suffer internal bleeding and a rotting of their organs. They vomit black putrid spit, and in a week they're dead. Those trunks must be traced."

7

Orchids

The next morning I arrived in Colonel Stephenson's outer office just before seven. The desk clerk announced my arrival.

"Send him in!" bellowed the innkeeper, holding each word like a tenor in a *recitatif*. The desk clerk rolled his eyes affectionately at his employer's exuberance and motioned toward the door for me to enter.

Stephenson was bending over some plants by the window, tenderly moving leaves to make room for the watering can's long spout. His attention was divided between me and his plants. "Good morning, Thomson. I trust you slept well."

I stood by the door, taking a moment to measure the proximity to Stephenson I could reasonably stand without betraying the inevitable smell of last night's beer on my breath. "Yes, sir, and I hope you did, as well." I entered the room and stood behind one of two chairs positioned in front of Stephenson's rolltop desk.

"Mmmm-hmmm," murmured Stephenson, concentrating on his plants. The sun reflected off the petals of an exquisite white orchid with brilliant yellow stamens. Dust particles in the sunlight flecked around it like sparkling gold.

"Isn't it magnificent?" asked the Colonel, beguiled by its beauty. "Did you know, Thomson, that there are twenty-six different varieties of orchids that grow wild right here in Niagara?"

"No, sir."

"Who would have thought a region so north could produce flora in such delicate variety?" mused the colonel as he gestured, one arm spanning the entire length of his flower collection.

It was a different side to the entrepreneur from the one I had first encountered. *We contain so many different people.*

"Ah," said Stephenson, brought back to the moment. "It's vital that we see, really see with eyes wide open, the beauty in the world around us, especially in such dreadful times as these. Gives the soul a lift, don't you think, Thomson?" He placed the watering can on a nearby shelf.

"Wasn't it Edgar Allan Poe who said 'Beauty of whatever kind in its supreme development excites the sensitive soul to tears'?"

"Yes, how apt," said the colonel. "Poe, you say? From a man so disposed to horror? But then again, we all have inconsistencies and contradictions, wouldn't you say?"

Not too close, I thought. *Not too close.*

Stephenson puttered around his desk as if postponing the time he had to begin the work of the day — tidying papers, straightening the inkwell, sweeping dust from far corners, and pushing to one side two large ledgers. With nothing left to put in order, he sat down in a great puff, settling into an oversized spindle chair.

"Well, then, I've good news. Your first customer has engaged your services this morning at 9:30. He's scheduled for therapy at 8:15, so he should be spruce and fit to dictate. I took the liberty of offering him samples of your penmanship and he approved. He has a letter he must complete and get through the lines to Richmond. I understand a courier is to arrive by noon. Any questions?"

"His name, sir, and where should I meet him?"

"Ah, right, yes, yes, right here in my office. There's good light and privacy and the senator should be quite comfortable."

"The senator?"

"Why, yes, didn't I say? The esteemed Senator Clay." Stephenson enjoyed drawing out the last bit of his good news. "Yes, do well with him and we'll indeed have something to boast about to our other guests."

When I returned to the colonel's office at 9:30, Clement Clay, the lawyer, statesman, and slave owner, was sitting in one of Stephenson's wing-backed chairs, his tall, thin frame barely indenting the cushion. He seemed to be studying a space just outside the windows as though there might be a source of inspiration or at least a consolation for how he came to be sitting in the colonel's office in Canada on a mission for which he had little preparation, desire, or confidence to lead. I could see that this frail man was inadequate for the job. His face was sallow and sunken and his clothes drooped off his shoulders, dragging over his wrists and nearly topping his knuckles.

"Excuse me, Senator, you requested a clerk? The name's Thomson. I'm honoured to meet you."

I took a seat at a table that had been prepared with paper, ink, nibs, wax, and envelopes. Preferring to use my own pen and nibs, I put my oil-silk bag on the desk and removed them, setting each side by side for quick access. Nibs especially were personal. Clay barely acknowledged my presence in the room, making me feel as Aaron must have felt most of the time — invisible. I was merely a disembodied hand sent to put Clay's words to paper. Uncapping the inkwell, I positioned my paper at a comfortable angle. All the while Clay continued to stare somewhere beyond the window, his eyes transfixed, his hand shaping and smoothing his sparse black beard.

"Are you related to Jacob Thompson?" the senator finally asked, his eyes narrowing as he waited for my reply.

"No, sir. Mine's Thomson without a *p*. The Virginia Thomsons, sir. Not Mississippi."

Clay nodded slowly as if calibrating my social status and lineage, unknotting the furrow in his forehead, apparently more satisfied that

I wasn't related to Jacob Thompson than any serious concern over my family lines. "Fair enough. Are you ready?" He pushed the words through his chest with effort.

"Yes, sir," I replied, aware of a sour sulphuric odour on Clay's breath. I shifted slightly to avoid its foul effect.

"Then let's begin. My hand's been unsteady of late and I appreciate your assistance. I trust what follows is in the strictest of confidence. Have I your word on that?"

"You do, sir. My honour defines me as a man to be loyal to the cause and committed to your confidence. Colonel Stephenson has a letter of reference from our noble leader, President Davis, should you have any question." *I am loyal to the cause, just not the same one you are*, I thought. But more bothersome was the knowledge that this internal moral volley was going to emerge every time I enacted my charade.

Clay coughed as he spoke. "Yes, I understand you came with high recommendations. I trust you."

Satisfied, he opened a brown leather journal of what appeared to be drafts of confidential letters — undoubtedly his personal record of private correspondence. Selecting one, he began to dictate. His Southern speech was articulate and slow. As he spoke, he watched my every dip of pen, every word I formed, indicating punctuation as we went along, courteously pausing to allow enough time for me to write and blot. There was an art to dictation.

As Clay dictated a letter to Jefferson Davis, I saw how much the man was a product of the South — he *was* the dignified South, the orator whose honour rested on portraying his ideas with pedigree and eloquence in equal proportion to their significance. The preliminaries of the letter dealt with, he looked away from my hand to review his thoughts, then continued. "Mr. George N. Sanders had directly or indirectly invited many gentlemen to visit the Falls and interchange opinions with us upon various subjects and among others that of the possibility of making peace ..."

Clay was giving Davis his side of the aborted Peace Conference in Niagara Falls, explaining to Davis that Lincoln was uncompromising in his refusal to redefine the terms of peace. The senator's composure and breathing was getting increasingly agitated as he spoke. He was becoming shorter of breath, straining and tugging at his chest as he wheezed. Beads of sweat collected on his pallid forehead, yet he gathered a shawl from the back of the chair and swept it across his shoulders.

"Read me the last line, Thomson, if you will."

"Of course. 'We did not deem it inexpedient to chaffer about the terms of peace at this time and shall regret to see anything to prescribe those terms in the Southern papers, especially at Richmond, until our mission is concluded.'"

Clay stiffened in the chair, then leaned forward and placed his hands on his knees, arching his back while taking quick, shallow breaths to expand the area in his lungs to bring him sufficient air.

"Are you all right, Senator? Can I get you something?"

"No, no, I'll be fine," Clay said, dismissing my offer, his voice now weaker and more laboured. He bent over, clinging to his knees and gasping for breath as he spoke.

I was getting very worried. His fingernails were turning blue. I put down my pen and moved toward the senator, who now seemed to be suffocating from the unyielding spasms of asphyxia.

He held up his hand to ward off my overtures. "Don't panic, man. Continue. I can finish this correspondence." He then asked in his letter if Davis would inform the wives of Beverly Tucker and Jacob Thompson, as well as his own, that they were well and signed off as "Your most obedient servant, C.C. Clay, Jr."

I gave the letter a final blot and handed it to Clay to review and sign. He took the paper, his breathing greatly accelerated and raspy. Too weak to hold the letter, it slipped through his fingers to the floor.

"You'll excuse me, sir," I said. "May I help you to the veranda for fresh air, then I should like to find the hotel's doctor."

I had no doubt he was having a reaction to the orchids, an hour ago considered so lovely and now so potentially deadly. This time he consented to my assistance. I placed my arm around his waist to lift him and offered my other arm to steady him as he stood still, struggling for air. When a breath did come, it was wheezing and high-pitched. Once in the fresh air, he was able to brace himself against the veranda railing and stand upright. When his coughing started to lessen, I raced to the desk clerk. "The doctor? Where's the doctor?"

"Dr. Mack?" the clerk said. "His office is down the hall to your left, but he's with a patient right now."

The doctor was setting the broken arm of a young boy when I burst in. "Excuse me, Dr. Mack?"

He glanced up through half-rimmed glasses, annoyed with my abrupt entry. "I say, young man. Don't you see I'm busy? Get back in the foyer and wait your proper turn."

"But, sir, this is an emergency. I'm with Senator Clay who's having severe problems breathing. What should I do? Is there something I can give him? His lungs seem to be collapsing." I was trying not to give in to the panic I was beginning to feel. *Stay calm. Think clearly.*

"I can't leave this boy," said the doctor. "And my nurse is away. Who are you, anyway?"

"Thomson, sir, James Thomson, the new secretarial clerk for the hotel."

"I'm familiar with Clay's condition. All right. Pay attention to me. You must not pick the wrong compound. In my cabinet, get the bottle labelled potassium iodide and mix one tablespoon of the salts in a glass of water."

I found the compound, showed it to Dr. Mack to confirm I had the correct bottle, then complied with his directions to put a tablespoon in solution.

The doctor continued wrapping papier mâché around the boy's arm and splint as he spoke. "It will enter Clay's bloodstream quickly to help liquefy the secretions plugging the tubes in his lungs."

As fast as I could without spilling the medicine, I walked back to where Clay was slumped on the veranda. "Take this, Senator. It's a potassium iodide solution from Dr. Mack, the hotel physician." I tried to remain matter-of-fact to spare the proud Clay the indignity of being seen by a clerk to be vulnerable and in need.

The senator lifted his arm slowly without looking up, sniffed the solution, and sipped it between breaths. The pace of his breathing started to slow to the extent he was able to speak to me. As if nothing had happened over the past life-threatening fifteen minutes, he reached for a packet of papers from his breast pocket and requested that I retrieve the letter to sign that I had helped him prepare. "Will you add these papers and address an envelope to Mr. C.C. Nelson? Can I trust you to meet him in the front lobby at noon?"

"Yes, sir. I should be glad to oblige." I was starting to view Clay as a man with no want of personal courage and readiness to commit himself to his country in spite of the debility of his health. Given different politics and circumstances, he might have earned my loyalty and regard, but I quickly reminded myself of the treason this kindly gentleman was committing.

At noon a dishevelled farmhand who I thought vaguely resembled one of the Rebel soldiers I'd seen in the pub when I first arrived answered to the name C.C. Nelson. After handing over the letter and getting a receipt, I returned immediately to the veranda to check on Clay, who was waiting for my confirmation that the courier had arrived and his papers were on their way.

"Thank you, Thomson," he said. "I appreciate your service and kind attention. I'll see you again, I presume?"

I realized then that I had his trust, but I questioned whether I deserved it.

8

A Near Miss

It was lunchtime and I was hungry. Smells from the kitchen did little to lessen my appetite. By the time I reached the lunch table, the chef was ordering the staff to clear the buffet.

"Wait, if you please!" I exclaimed. "May I avail myself to some bread and cheese before you clear?"

The chef glanced at his watch with military scorn. "This time, all right. Next time you eat in town."

Spears, the superintendent of the baths, was still eating, so I joined him. "Mr. Spears, how are you today?"

"Not badly, Thomson. You?"

"First day on the job and all's well."

I tore off a chunk of bread with my teeth, then topped it with a rather large wedge of cheese and some of the chef's peach chutney. Spears looked the other way. I realized that this fastidious man of tidy habits found my table manners crude.

"Please forgive me, Mr. Spears. I'm hungrier than I thought. No excuse for bad manners, though, is it?"

Spears shrugged. "Make no never mind, Mr. Thomson. It's me mum's to blame. Years of table nagging that's created an unnecessary reflex I try to ignore. We're not dining with the queen now, are we?" He glanced at his watch.

"You needn't stay, Mr. Spears. I'm away shortly." I could see that the kitchen maids were anxious to tidy up.

"I should be getting back, but tell me, how did your 'debut' at the Salon go last night?" Spears asked.

"Very well, thank you. Not the least of which was meeting the fair Miss Stephenson."

"That she is, Thomson. A lovely one, to be sure, and very well connected." Spears cleared his throat for emphasis. "She knows 'em all. Who else did you meet?"

"An interesting collection of gentlemen from the South — Messieurs Tucker, Sanders, Contri, and Hyams, plus another chap from Maryland named James Watson Wallace."

"James Watson Wallace, eh?" intoned Spears, repeating the name as if he were speaking in capital letters. "Puzzle, that."

"How so, Mr. Spears?"

"Well, as the desk clerk disparaged the other day, I do confess to an interest in the nether garments people choose to wear. It goes with my trade, I guess. Sort of a hobby. But more important, I regard these times as ones of great change, you see, and no place are the times and a man's character better reflected than in his nether garments."

Spears pulled his chair closer to me to speak more confidentially. "The discarding of men's corsets for reasons of ease rather than convention has been fashion's desideratum, except for women, of course. This relaxing of a man's appearance, if you ask me, reflects a dissipation of national strength and military prowess." He cleared his throat again and tightened his lips to suggest his complete objectivity. "In this I take a purely academic interest, of course."

"I have no doubt."

"I'm glad you see the validity of my study. What I find most intriguing is the correlation between what one wears beneath the surface with one's, shall we say, trustworthiness?" The kitchen maids were now

acting more like a soldier complying with an order than a spy feeling relieved that his worst fears hadn't materialized.

Clay led me to a large parcel on the desk. "Your employer has guaranteed your bond. His trust in you confirms my own. By the way, your concern for me and display of cool-headed thinking the other day at the hotel was most appreciated."

"Thank you, sir. I'll do my best not to let you or Colonel Stephenson down."

Used to giving instructions, Clay spoke slowly and sequentially. "This is what I need you to do. Take this box to Toronto where you'll be met at the station by Mr. John C. Walker. You'll hand over this parcel to him only if he gives you this handshake." Clay grabbed my right hand and shook it with his forefinger touching the inside of my palm, a Freemason's acknowledgement of trust and brotherhood. "He'll squeeze your elbow three times with his other hand." He demonstrated again, his squeeze noticeably weak. "He'll then say to you the following phrase — 'The sun can liberate the spirit on a fair day.'"

I repeated the phrase.

"You'll reply 'When the spirit is willing and the day is fair.' Do you understand?"

I indicated that I did.

"Walker's a man of about forty years, shorter than most and distinguished by very large hands. Don't give the parcel to anyone unless everything fits. It will be very costly if you do. Many lives depend on it, including your own, I may add. Now, then, do you have any questions?" Affording me little time for a thoughtful response, he handed the parcel over and concluded, "Well, then, be on your way. The stage will be at the hotel to take you to the depot in fifteen minutes. Hurry. Guard the parcel safely. As you can tell by its heft, it's gold. Godspeed." I was about to leave when Clay stopped me. "By the way, Thomson, may I ask a personal favour?"

"Of course, sir."

"Would you pick up a few things for me?" He took from his waistcoat pocket a piece of paper with several items listed. "My dearest wife, Ginnie, would be ever so uplifted given the privations of war she's suffered at home to receive these staples. Our land has been so depleted of the simplest of goods. I haven't the opportunity to shop, so if I may prevail upon you, I'll give you expenses and notify your employer not

　　　　　　　　　　　　　　　　　　　　　　　　LINDA BRAMBLE

to expect you until tomorrow's late train. Would that meet with your approval?"

"Yes, of course, sir," I replied.

Clay handed me the list, along with some British pounds sterling for which he requested receipts on all goods purchased. Then he gave me some expense money and bid me safe journey. I left wondering about the irony of my mission. I was about to advance the Confederate war effort, then shop for lace and taffeta.

10

Abetting a Conspiracy

My legs were stiff by the time the train arrived in Toronto. I travelled with the gold between my feet throughout the two-and-a-half-hour journey. As the trained pulled into Union Station on Front Street opposite the Queen's Hotel, I spotted a man I guessed was Walker — stocky, straining to see into each car. Walker was a Copperhead, one of those Democrats seeking to reunite the Northwest wing of the party in a coup against the Lincoln Republicans in power. I knew that the secret mission in Canada would play a central part in their plans, but I didn't know what, when, or how. I did know that the gold I was about to hand over to Walker would be used to support a conspiracy of some sort in collaboration with the Southern Democrats.

I had barely stepped onto the bottom step of the train when a little man rushed over to me. "Thomson, I believe?"

I nodded. "And you are?"

"Walker's the name." He shook my hand in the manner of a Freemason, then squeezed my elbow three times. "Well, hello, my good man, and welcome to Toronto. The sun can liberate the spirit on a fair day."

Walker was built like a bulldog — close to the ground with power I reckoned that at the slightest provocation would be unleashed in short, stunning stabs and with a furious strength capable of killing a man twice his size. His hands were disproportionately large and meaty with thick fingers — tenacious, unbreakable, informing fingers that told me not to be misled by this man's lack of height.

"When the spirit is willing and the day is fair," I replied, sealing the code required for the exchange.

"I trust you had a pleasant trip." Walker peered behind me with the awkwardness of a man trying to be discreet but more inclined to Midwestern directness than subterfuge. I hadn't yet handed the gold over to him.

"Yes, Mr. Walker," I said, keeping him at bay, "but I could use some lunch." I heaved the parcel to my shoulder and balanced it with one hand as we moved off.

"A good lunch can be had at the Queen's Hotel across the street," suggested Walker, obviously not wanting to postpone the exchange by taking the time to search for a place to eat.

The Queen's Hotel was the largest and finest, the newspapers had assured, in the entire British Empire. It was a place known for its slow-paced dinners, its international wine cellar, and its gracious service. It was also a notorious sanctuary for the Confederates in Canada.

"I recommend their steak-and-kidney pie," Walker said, "and the honey porter. English victuals, don't you know, and darn good, if'n I do say so myself. Bit pricey, but what the heck." Walker then gave me a convincing slap on the back. "Perhaps you'd like to wash up a bit first and allow me to take that heavy parcel off your hands. Are you staying here? Mighty fine hotel, the Queen is, if'n I do say so myself."

"Not sure yet." *The least said the better*.

"Be glad to offer my room and basin for a quick wash-up if you'd like." Walker was still eyeing the gold.

"Be obliged."

"May I help you?" asked Walker, eager to touch his prize.

"Soon enough, Mr. Walker, soon enough."

Once inside Walker's hotel room, I handed him the long-awaited gold. He proceeded to ignore me the moment he received it, too busy unwrapping the inauspicious parcel in order to examine its contents. After splashing water on my face, I was downstairs in the taproom within minutes.

When I gave the barkeep my order, I avoided the steak-and-kidney for some cheddar, pork, and bread, but did order a draft of the porter Walker had recommended. Then I took a table by the front window. Among the

Rebel soldiers in the crowded taproom were merchants and traders who kept to themselves.

The driver of a double brougham carriage had just tied up in front when I spotted Walker meeting the men getting out. Among them I recognized the brown spade beard and feverish eyes of Jacob Thompson, Clay's fellow commissioner, along with William Cleary, Thompson's secretary, and Godfrey Hyams, the same Hyams of the infected-trunks Blackburn affair, who was presumably a Union agent, if Washington's return wire to me was accurate. The fourth man I recognized but couldn't place. The men entered the taproom, with Walker doing most of the talking. Thompson scanned the room before taking a corner table. Within minutes, Cleary approached me.

"The Honourable Jacob Thompson requests that you join him at his table," Cleary said with the dubious charm of a dueller's second. Thin lips gave him a pursed expression, as if he had for so long kept his true thoughts contained that his mouth was now permanently clamped and could only utter short phrases each time he spoke. His red whiskers were an eerie contrast to his tallow complexion. "My name's Cleary and I understand you're Thomson."

"Glad to meet you, Mr. Cleary."

"I'm sure." He sniffed and led the way to Thompson's table where the politician was already conducting affairs. As I approached, I noticed the fourth man scrutinizing me. Then with what seemed to be a jolt of recognition he leaned over to Thompson and whispered in his ear. I should have left then but, like a fool, I stayed on to meet the notorious Jacob Thompson.

"May I present James Thomson, Clay's courier from St. Catharines?" Cleary spoke my name as if he were a bailiff announcing the next witness.

"Thomson?" said Jacob Thompson. "Curious coincidence, our names." Clouds of cigar smoke hovered above the Confederate agent's head. "Sit down, Thomson, if indeed that's your name."

I tried to stay calm. Now that I was up close I recognized the fourth man as Benjamin Wood, the publisher of the *New York Daily News*, a pro-Confederate tabloid.

"My friend here, Mr. Wood, seems to think that Thomson's not your real name."

It was hard to explain what went through me at that moment. I felt as though I had been struck by a bolt of lightning that penetrated my core.

I had to remain calm. All I could think of was not betraying my terror at being discovered. A twitch at the wrong time, an averted glance, a lip lifted, a crossing of my arm could communicate to my adversaries the lie standing before them. I became resolute, keeping my eyes on Thompson, and breathed naturally, allowing no emotion to be expressed on my face. Thompson drew slowly on his cigar and exhaled in my direction, squinting through its haze as he studied my reaction. I made no move.

"He says your last name's something like Moore or Monty and that you're a weevil in the cotton field. We don't like weevils in the cotton field."

He drew on his cigar again, tapping the ash near my shoes. I couldn't allow this slight to faze me. As he addressed his colleagues at the table, his tone turned to one of derision.

Thompson paused, narrowed his eyes, took another drag of his cigar, and glared accusingly at me while talking to the others around the table. "Have you noticed, gentlemen, the bane and curse of carrying out anything in this country is the surveillance under which we act? Detectives, or those ready to give information, stand at every street corner. Two or three can't interchange ideas without a reporter. I must admit to having a powerful aversion to this most annoying of situations. What say you to that, Mr. Weevil?"

I wasn't about to give this oaf satisfaction. "I, too, have noticed the proliferation of men with ears stretched like a coyote's in all directions. And on the matter of my likeness to another, if I have a resemblance to this poor Mr. Moore or Mr. Monty, I offer him my condolences. I'm a law clerk and secretary currently from St. Catharines, Canada West, and formerly with the firm of Case, Pepperidge, and McAllister of Virginia. Please feel free to check my credentials. You'll find my references most reliable." I looked boldly at Thompson, then at Wood, so they could get a better appraisal of my face. "Begging your pardon, but you're mistaken, Mr. Wood."

At this point Hyams got up, whispered something to Jacob Thompson, and left the room. I made little concern of it at the time.

"Keep your letters and your nose out of our affairs, Mr. Weevil," retorted Thompson. "We don't need the questionable help of men like you. I don't care who you are." He leaned toward the others again to confide his mocking disgust with Clay. "That damn fool puts his trust in any itinerant who merely says 'Trust me, trust me.'" Trying to catch me off guard, he turned with a maniacal abruptness, raising his hand to emphasize his point. "This is a warning to you. I have friends all over the Northern states ready and willing to go to any lengths to serve the cause of the South."

Thompson rocked back on his chair, smiling at first, then lunged at me, slapping his fists on the table. "That goes for the tyrant Lincoln or any of his advisers, who I could at any time that I chose put out of my way. I would have but to point out the man that I consider in my way, and my friends would put him out of it and not let me know anything about it if necessary. Nor would they consider it a crime when done for the cause of the Confederacy. Do I make myself clear?"

The venom in Thompson's eyes took me aback, but I remained calm. Thompson's Southern treachery was all the more sinister, since Lincoln was a man Thompson had once called a friend. The war had done that. The bonds of friendship that were once capable of transcending a conflict of loyalties were lost. The tacit moorings of trust were vanquished. No matter who won this scurrilous war, it was clear neither side would ever recover any trust it once might have possessed in the other. If trust returned, it would take generations to do so.

Thompson emptied his glass, slammed it on the table, and stood. Then Cleary leaped to his feet and gathered their papers as Thompson made his exit. I collected my satchel, and ostensibly unmoved, left Wood and Walker at the table, and not a moment too soon. Wood kept repeating, "Moore, Mat, Mon ..." As I neared the door, I heard Wood's chair grate against the wooden floor as he slid it away from the table. I walked a little faster, then heard Wood shout, "Hey, wait!" I continued out the front door, with the newspaper publisher following closely this time and shouting, "It's Montague, isn't it?"

11

Better Lucky Than Rich

A town coach was slowing down in front of the hotel, its passenger-side door opening just as I slipped through the front entrance of the Queen's

Hotel. Hyams was inside, slightly hidden from view, signalling to me to hurry and get in. He had tucked his long beard into his collar and wore a slouch hat that made recognizing him all the more difficult. I wasn't sure it was him, nor was I confident about what I was getting myself into. But with Wood trailing closely behind me, however, I grabbed the door's frame, hoisted myself into the moving carriage, and slammed the door, thus narrowly escaping Wood's loud insinuations that I was attached to the U.S. Marshals' Office in New York City with Robert Murray.

"The man's fairly accurate, isn't he, Montgomery?" asked Hyams.

"Hell, no," I replied, thinking what a step down that would be from a sergeant major to a U.S. marshal, even though I had, in fact, worked with Murray. "And to what do I owe this lift, Mr. Hyams?"

Godfrey Hyams, the Brit from the South whom I'd encountered the evening I attended the Salon at Stephenson House, the same Hyams who had met Dr. Blackburn with Clay in Hamilton, leaned forward to give the driver directions to an address on King Street. The same man my Washington contact had said was okay, yet I remained cautious until I had further proof.

"You live right, Montgomery," said Hyams. "Better lucky than rich, I always say. Hyams reminded me of a university tutor: thin lips, high collar under that long beard he sported, wire-rim spectacles with straight temple pieces and oval rims. "Headquarters in Washington wired me yesterday regarding your arrival in Toronto. You surely sliced things close to the bone in there," he said, indicating my near collision with Jacob Thompson and Benjamin Wood.

"What do you mean?" I asked. "The way I see it, it seems to me that any person even seen communicating with the Confederates, let alone doing business with them, is being shadowed by detectives from both sides of the border. You could have been arrested as a spy, you know."

Hyams shrugged.

"Either way Hyams, it's you who slices things close to the bone, not I. Besides, why would you take a chance with me? If I were working for the federal government, the Confederates would have your neck if they saw you here with me."

"Fair enough, Montgomery," said Hyams. "There's not much time to debate the matter. We'll be at our destination on King Street in a few minutes and I have to brief you on some of the schemes these men have concocted. They're capable of the most plausible but odious deeds, clinging to prejudice as if it were principle. I'll be leaving Canada soon, and each plot necessitates constant vigilance."

"What makes you think I can be trusted?" I demanded, speaking in a louder voice than I was comfortable with to overcome the clatter of the carriage. Even carriage drivers could be in the service of the Confederates.

"My Washington contact says you are," Hyams said. "He trusts you, as misplaced as that trust might or might not be, given your perhaps limited usefulness as an agent now. I heard Wood calling out very close approximations of your real name. If he convinces Thompson of your identity, your career as a special agent will be extremely short-lived."

The driver took a corner sharply, forcing me to slide a little too close to Hyams for comfort. "Tell me what you have to say," I said, resuming my side of the carriage.

"Don't be cavalier. They might seem naive and ill-equipped to wage a covert campaign, but make no mistake, they're serious when it comes to eliminating those they think betray them. I've seen them in action."

"I'm listening," I said. "What's the publisher of the *Daily News* doing in Toronto with Jacob Thompson, anyway?"

"Ever since the war started, President Davis has been paying Wood off to print stories favourable to the South to arouse antagonism against the North. Now Wood has guaranteed to help Thompson orchestrate an insurrection in New York City."

"An insurrection?"

"Yes, it sounds mad, but they believe it can work. At an outbreak of violence a small force will be responsible for setting off a series of fires while some other Copperheads from the Northwest take control of the major federal and municipal buildings in the city, including the police department and the army. They figure by sunset the Confederate flag will fly over New York City."

"When is this insurrection supposed to take place?"

"Don't know."

"What does Wood have to do with it?"

Hyams stroked his beard. "Thompson's giving him a cheque for $25,000 to buy arms."

"He's trusting a newspaperman to do this?"

"Yes. Thompson's been given some pernicious power to finance this entire Confederate mission up here. Millions in gold."

Hyams might have been prone to hyperbole, yet having witnessed

Thompson's imperial countenance myself, he might not be far off the mark concerning the Confederate's overreaching menace.

"His judgment," Hyams continued, "is suspect when you consider his obstinacy and uncompromising opinions. He's in awe of anyone who claims influential connections with those in high places in Richmond. Wood knows Davis. And, as far as I'm concerned, although he complains of Clay's misplaced trust in you, Thompson's committing the most unpardonable of errors."

What's that?" I asked.

"He's underestimating the enemy and overestimating his allies. But this is just a diversionary tactic to mask the real activity of making the most out of the disloyalty in the Northwest."

Hyams's eyes bore into me as if the more intently he glared the more seriously I would take his story. "The Copperheads, with the help of Thompson's funds and a few soldiers, plan on capturing the Great Lakes steamer *Michigan*. It's guarding the access to the prisoner-of-war camps in Chicago and on Johnson's Island, near Sandusky, Ohio. With these Confederate soldiers freed, they plan on taking over the state capitals of Ohio, Illinois, and Indiana, which would give them, that is, the Copperheads, political leverage in the coming presidential election to get Lincoln defeated."

I nodded. "It's plausible."

"The scheme could succeed if we fail to do our work."

"What's Walker's role in all of this?"

"You just passed him $10,000 in gold so that he can arm his Copperhead farmers, who will then free the rebel POWs. Are you starting to get the picture?"

"What are their chances of pulling it off?"

"Who knows? But we have a man on it. Tomorrow Walker has to hand over the money to Judge Bullitt, the grand secretary of the Sons of Liberty, a branch of the Copperheads. If all goes well for the Union cause, Bullitt will be arrested en route to Montreal and placed in custody with the gold and an incriminating cheque for another $10,000."

The carriage was slowing onto King Street.

"I understand you had me watched in Hamilton when I met Blackburn with Clay," Hyams said.

"What were you doing with them?"

"That's another contemptible scheme, but if it works, half the people of the major cities in the Northeast will have yellow fever by September." We could hear the driver coaxing his team to a stop. "I'm doing my best to alert the authorities," added Hyams, his voice more hushed than before, "to be at the auction when the infected trunks Blackburn shipped from Bermuda are sold. Clay and Blackburn wanted me to hand-deliver an infected valise to Lincoln. I refused. I told them that it smelled too rank. It would never reach the president, anyway. But for as many men like me who refuse, they have others, Canadians included, willing to do their dirty work. A Canadian explosives manufacturer right here, for instance, is financing this whole escapade in Toronto, a William L. McDonald, Larry, to his friends. I'm on my way there now." He leaned across to my window side of the carriage. "But this whole thing isn't your concern." He separated the curtains slightly and said emphatically, "But that man is!"

Standing in front of a haberdashery was James Watson Wallace, the dandy from Maryland. "Keep your eye on him, Montgomery. I haven't felt right about that one from the beginning. He could be trouble."

"Did you know he'd be here?"

"Wallace wired Clay to make good an offer of his personal tailor because Clay mentioned his intent to get some bespoke jackets and trousers made while in the Canadas. Clay wired Wallace back telling him about your 'shopping assignment' for his wife and thought Wallace's sartorial sources could help you shop. The man at the telegraph office is one of ours and forwarded the information to me." Hyams slid into the corner of the carriage away from the door to avoid being spotted by Wallace. "Now, be off and be careful."

12

Shopping with Wallace

I was relieved that another agent was tracing the infected trunks. I now needed all of my focus to figure out who this Wallace character was and what he was up to. The south side of King Street East was Toronto's Regent Street. Lining the avenue were coordinated rows of shops in buildings graced with extravagant confections of cast iron and carved stone fronted by plate-glass windows glittering with jewellery, china, filigreed silver, gowns, and furs. When I opened the carriage door, the impeccably dressed Wallace greeted me with the felicitousness of an old friend, standing by as I stepped onto the footstone.

"Thomson, my good man, I've been expecting you. Clay forewarned me. I hope your trip was smooth and your engagement at the Queen's Hotel went well. It's nice to see you again."

Wallace held my elbow and eagerly guided me toward the embossed oak door of an impressive dry goods shop. I felt dishevelled next to the consummate Wallace, who was dressed in white linen and a wide-brimmed summer straw hat. He looked much the Southerner — prosperous and refined.

"Senator Clay informed me you'd be shopping for dry goods for his beloved Ginnie," Wallace said. "I volunteered my services to aid and abet your mission, so to speak. I do hope you find my assistance one of service and not an intrusion. I think you'll find the establishment before you to be one of outstanding quality and reputation."

"I welcome your assistance, Wallace," I replied gratefully. "Please do carry on." I didn't know the first thing about fabrics and lace.

The shop was an impressive four-storey building with heavy masonry that seemed to float above thirty-foot-high panes of glass. The shop-keeper, dressed in pinstriped tails, greeted us with detached deference.

"Good afternoon, Mr. Wallace. I gather this is the fine gentleman about whom you spoke."

"Yes, Mr. Simpson. May I introduce Mr. James Thomson, lately of New York City by way of Virginia, so to speak? Isn't that correct, Mr. Thomson?"

"Yes, but …" I wondered how he knew my background. How much more did he know?

Wallace leaned toward my ear in an aside. "I hope you don't mind, Thomson, but I interviewed your good employer last week regarding the provenance of some of the more interesting guests I met at the Salon and your name came up. I can appreciate that one might be disquieted to learn others have been snooping around, so to speak, but I assure you, it was with the noblest of intentions on my part."

"That's fine," I said. "It's what we do in times like these where trust is at a premium." *It's what we do, so to speak.*

                                        LINDA BRAMBLE

Wallace raised the volume of his voice to include the elderly shop-keeper in our conversation. "And, Mr. Thomson, I present Mr. Simpson, the proprietor of this most splendid emporium, The Golden Lion. He's the finest importer of dry goods in Canada West. The two fearsome lions whose life-sized presence peer above the shop door and again on the balustrade above lash their golden tails at all competitors, leaving the range and scope of his goods superior to all."

Simpson bowed his head modestly, accepting Wallace's praise with exaggerated humility.

"I think you'll find Mr. Simpson, and might I boldly include many of the other Toronto merchants and hoteliers I've met, to be altogether on the side of the Southern cause. They believe it's a battle for sovereignty or subjugation. The fact is demonstrated by the avidity with which they celebrate every communiqué of the North's military reverses. Isn't that so, Mr. Simpson?"

"Yes, completely, sir. If I may offer an opinion ..."

"By all means," Wallace said with princely permission.

"I assure you that I believe the current administration in the United States is mismanaged and corrupt and is finally getting its due." He turned away and dabbed his eyes, visibly upset.

It was unusual that a shopkeeper would reveal such a personal point of view to a prospective customer so soon in a service encounter, but I nevertheless tried to be sympathetic to what appeared to be his lingering grief. Wallace motioned that we should walk toward a display of hats so he could explain the shopkeeper's emotional reaction.

"You see, Thomson," he began in a rather secretive voice, even though he knew the shopkeeper could overhear him, "Mr. Simpson still grieves the loss of his beloved older brother who was felled while coura-geously defending Upper Canada against marauding Americans during the War of 1812. However, you do see what I mean in terms of Canadian regard for the Southern cause? Feel comfortable in this bantam bantling of Britain. Despite their proclaimed neutrality, you're among friends — feisty but friendly."

Wallace noticed that Simpson had finally composed himself and was waiting patiently to be summoned. "Ah, yes, Mr. Simpson, as I informed you, Mr. Thomson's errand is at once simple and complex. He must select something of quality for the taste of another. But I believe the delicacy of his task can be mitigated by your kind intercession." Looking at me, he added, "Does that meet with your approval, Thomson?"

Hundreds of bolts of fabrics lined the walls from ceiling to floor — paisleys and stripes, worsteds, tweeds, twills, gabardines, all quite overwhelming me. "Yes, yes, of course," I said. "I most gratefully yield to your superior knowledge, but forgive my impertinence. My errand, you see, is for a woman, and as impressive as this display of men's fine suiting is, she might be more inclined to fabrics of a more delicate nature."

Wallace laughed. "Of course, my good man."

The shopkeeper took his cue. "Right this way, gentlemen." He led us to the rear of the shop, which opened into a two-storey section with a light well in the centre encased in a dome of cast iron and plate glass. Women's fine fabrics and accessories covered the walls. On the table was *Godey's Lady's Book and Magazine*, referencing Simpson's display as one of the finest on the continent: organdies, satins, silks, chiffons, with taffetas in six different jewel colours and yards of laces from France, Italy, Belgium, and Greece.

Thankfully, Clay had indicated the fabric and the yardage his wife desired, which narrowed our decision-making quite nicely. I say "our" decision-making immodestly, because in actual fact, it was Wallace at this point who took over the list, working with Simpson, requesting this bolt and that to be flung onto the cutting counter to compare with other samples so distributed. Wallace studiously placed one fabric between his fingers to test its texture against another. Such theatre might have been for my benefit, but I didn't care. He was accomplishing my task for which I was ill equipped, and I was glad. His efforts were no doubt to get into Clay's good graces, assuming I would give him credit for the purchases.

Once Wallace indicated that the items on Clay's list had been selected, I paid the shopkeeper and got receipts as Clay had requested, feeling quite satisfied the goods would please both Clay and his wife. I was also indebted that this most dreaded part of my assignment was completed. Could I separate my indebtedness from an objective appraisal of Wallace's character? It would remain to be seen.

"How can I repay you for your kindness, Wallace?" I asked, thinking Hyams might have misjudged this man. Granted, earlier he had seemed of a different stripe, but when our shopping was done, I felt he was

　　　　　　　　　　　　　　　　　　　　　　　　LINDA BRAMBLE

downright collegial. If he was a Southern collaborator, I would have been more on my guard, or so I thought. Then again, like Hyams, Wallace might be a federal agent trying to infiltrate Confederate cells as was I. I had to learn more about the fellow.

"It would have taken me days to find this shop on my own, if I found it at all," I confessed. "Clay will have little choice but to look upon our efforts with favour. Might you consider being my guest at dinner tonight?"

Wallace smiled. "It would be my pleasure to have the opportunity to get to know you better. I accept, but would you mind awfully if Colonel Margrave joined us?"

13

Dinner with Wallace

On the way to the restaurant, I noticed how the planked city sidewalks gave Toronto a northern fragrance of pitch and pine. The roadways, on the other hand, were dangerously striated by carriage wheels that had created hazardous crevices in the summer-dried dirt, making travel treacherous. Back in New York City, I knew of carriages that tipped if caught for any distance in a deep rut.

"It will be miraculous if our carriage makes it to the restaurant without misadventure!" cried Wallace over the driver's loud admonition to his team as we sideswiped a pony cart.

"I've never seen a city as prosperous or as negligent of its streets" I said, supporting Wallace for the sake of likeability, even though I had actually seen worse.

"Almost there," said Wallace, checking the street for landmarks as the carriage made a precipitous turn onto Toronto Street. "This is one of my favourite haunts. A lovely street for window-gazing, with less bustle than on King, don't you think? Ah, there it is!" he called to the driver, beaming with anticipation. "Bacchus, my favourite bookseller and steakhouse. I expect Margrave will be in the back regaling newsmen with his politics. I hope you find him as entertaining as I, however radical his cause. I think he's a most gregarious and gifted conversationalist, with an overabundant flair for the grandiose perhaps, but nevertheless he has a zest for life. But I caution you, my friend, he can weave a magic spell around you if you submit. I've witnessed many strong men blinded by the clever way he can awaken dormant tendencies and trigger desires so bone-deep his victims surrender to his cause and have hardly known they've done so."

Wallace might have been describing himself, but at this point I was more eager to meet Margrave than to assess Wallace's motives more deeply. "Forewarned is forearmed," I said, ready to meet the mastermind behind the most current assassination plot against Lincoln.

"I warn you, indeed," Wallace said. "If you're not careful, he'll have you joined up in no time as part of his cadre of co-conspirators."

"How have you resisted his allure?" I asked.

Wallace laughed. "Me? I don't know that I have." The cab had scarcely come to a stop before Wallace paid the cabbie and unlatched the door. "I'll run in and see if I can locate Margrave to firm up our dinner plans. Meet you in the bookstore."

Once inside, I browsed for a few minutes, waiting for Wallace who, when he finally appeared, was slightly out of breath. "Margrave doesn't seem to be around, but I've left word for him to join us in the steak-house." He wiped a faint spray of perspiration from his forehead. "I'm ready to eat. How about you?"

I wondered what Margrave's absence meant but figured I'd soon know. As in The Golden Lion, I deferred to Wallace when it came time to order, which my companion assumed with great fervour.

"We'll have a joint of sirloin of a nice weight for three with horse-radish and Yorkshire pudding," Wallace told the waiter. He paused momentarily to appraise a row of at least twenty porcelain multico-loured draft beer pumps, then added, "And two Faversham best bitters while we wait."

Dinner was one of the most relaxed I'd had in months. Wallace told fascinating stories about his family in Baltimore, his businesses, and Baltimore society. He described the war and got particularly exercised by the unconscionable way in which it was being conducted, but even worse, how it was being reported. He held in particular contempt the newsmen who embroidered the slightest event of the war into "a wall-sized tapestry of misstatement and lies."

                                              LINDA BRAMBLE

We were finishing dinner over a glass of port when Wallace finally conceded, "I guess Margrave found more pressing obligations elsewhere, eh, what?"

"He missed a fine evening," I said, feeling relieved that I was able to enjoy a meal without constant vigilance, yet was still able to gain insight into the machinations of the Rebel mission in Canada. Wallace seemed to be an insider. He knew all about the Rebel plan to release prisoners on Johnson's Island. He praised the Confederates and Copperheads for their courage despite their flagrant violations of Canadian neutrality, referring to them as "neutral marauders." Perhaps I should have wondered more how he knew so much.

14

Close Calls

On the train going back to St. Catharines the following day, I read some of the newspapers I had purchased at the bookstore side of Bacchus. I was anxious to learn what was being said about this so-called "secret" northern flank of the war. The *Richmond Examiner*, a secessionist newspaper but critical of Jefferson Davis's administration, contained a piece about the ill-fated Peace Conference in Niagara Falls that surprised me with its caustic review of the events. It chastised Clay and Sanders as "officious individuals who go creeping round back doors asking for interviews with Lincoln." The article took issue with the Canadian complaint of violations of neutrality and suggested that the Confederates in Canada were "indifferent to the world clamours of this bantam bantling of Britain."

The train sped through the plain that separated Lake Ontario and the north-facing ridge of the Niagara Escarpment. Hawks circled a promontory that protruded close to the lake, providing thermals on which they sleepily glided. I put the paper down. It all seemed faintly familiar, not just the news of the plans to free prisoners of war but the words "bantam bantling of Britain." I followed four hawks effortlessly hitching rides on currents, their dihedral wings fully spanned and still, their bodies weightless and invulnerable. Either Wallace had read the same article and repeated the correspondent's view or he was a very smooth Union agent supplying information to the *Examiner*. If so, why hadn't Assistant Secretary Dana told me Wallace, like Hyams, was a Union agent?

When I arrived in St. Catharines, I went first to Stephenson House to check my mail and messages before reporting to Clay. Spears was working at the partner's desk we shared.

"Good day, Spears," I said. "Working hard, I see."

Spears appeared to be organizing his attendants' work schedules for the afternoon. "Yes, Thomson. How was your trip? I understand you were Toronto-bound."

"It went quite well, thank you. Met up with that Wallace chap and spent a most satisfying evening at Bacchus. Do you know the place?"

"Ah, Bacchus," said Spears, "a read and a feed, so to speak." His shoulders shook lightly up and down in soundless amusement at his own play on words. He placed a finger against his lips, feigning shame. Collecting himself, he glanced at his appointments before I could reply. "I see your friend Wallace beat you home. He's already scheduled for a douche bath this afternoon."

"Really, Mr. Spears. A douche bath?" I asked, ready to receive his second lesson in the wonders of hydrotherapy.

"It's one of our more invigorating applications."

"How's that?"

The superintendent pulled a watch from his pocket, no doubt noting he had only a few minutes to spare to accommodate me with a brief explanation. "Well, it's like this. The patient stands beneath a stream of cold water, from one or two inches in diameter, with a fall of twenty feet." He paused, knowing this would get a reaction from me.

I obliged. "Twenty feet? Good God, man, he'd faint from the blow."

"No, no, no. It's a most gradual encounter. We first wet his head. Then he receives the column of cold water upon the spine from the neck downward and next to the rest of his body for two to three minutes. An attendant follows with an invigorating rub with a starched Turkish towel to rid the body of morific matter."

"Did you say cold water?" I groaned. "My apologies to your profession, Spears, but from what unbearable condition must a man be suffering to subject himself to such a chamber of horrors?"

Spears chose to overlook my remark and answered haughtily,

                                                     LINDA BRAMBLE

"Congestion of the lungs, constipation, dyspepsia, nervous tremors, and indigestion. By the look of you, you could use one!" Spears slapped the desk with great satisfaction at having evened the score.

"I'll stick with fomentation. By the way, when is Wallace scheduled?"

"Let's see," said Spears, checking his list. "Two-thirty, bath unit number 4. Hmm … looks as if Senator Clay is scheduled around the same time. Fancy that." Spears closed his foolscap. "Must be off. Ta."

It was nearly 2:30. I was putting off delivering the parcels I'd purchased for Clay until I had a better sense of whether Benjamin Wood or Jacob Thompson had wired Clay with their suspicions regarding my true identity. In my mail, I found a note from Clay requesting me to see him as soon as I arrived back in St. Catharines. Clay's therapy, however, would give me some leeway to check out Spears's observations about Wallace's mismatching monogram. Who was Wallace working for? Maybe his monogram could shed some light.

I had helped myself to an appointment form from Spears's desk and assigned myself to a fifteen-minute steam bath. The reception attendant took my slip and scrutinized me momentarily, enough for me to feel compelled to allay his concerns. "Too much of the grain last night. Superintendant Spears allowed that it would benefit the hotel if I steamed it out."

The attendant shrugged. "S'okay with me if Spears says so. Just don't let the colonel see you, though."

"I'm so advised. Thank you, my friend." I received my robe, sandals, and towel. "Busy today?"

"Yes, just about full up. Better hurry if you want a steam box."

"Any change cubicle in particular?"

"No. Whichever's free."

Those in use had an opaque muslin privacy drape pulled across the front. I heard men in the far end of the room, so I had to work fast before anyone found me rifling through the guests' personals. Cubicles lined both sides of the aisle, doubling my mission.

I started down the first aisle, moving quickly from side to side, looking for the feet of a guest in mid-change. If no feet appeared, then I slipped inside, searching for something of Wallace's that might be familiar.

Nothing. Then I ranged up the second aisle where only three drapes were drawn. No luck. Just as I was turning to go down the third row, I recognized Clay's voice. I stopped to learn, without being seen, who the senator was speaking to. It took what seemed like an eternity to recognize the voice, distinguished by its low pitch and pleasing resonance. And then it dawned on me. It was the voice of another Confederate commissioner named Joseph Holcombe. *Damn!* I thought. *Of all the men to meet now.*

Holcombe was one of my former tutors at the University of Virginia. If he caught sight of me, he was sure to remember me not as James Thomson but as Richard Montgomery. Quickly, I slid into a nearby cubicle, tore off my clothes, wrapped myself in the robe, and stole into the steam room, or tepidarium, as the sign above the door indicated. Clay's and Holcombe's voices were closer to the door than before.

Lining three walls of the room were five large units four by four feet, large enough for a man to sit in. The front of each unit was open, revealing an adjustable seat inside and a lid with a hole large enough to allow a man to slip his head through. Steam entered the box through a pipe with an outside handle to enable the bather to alter its force.

As the two men outside twisted the knob to the tepidarium, I motioned to the black attendant, a man I recognized from the British Methodist Episcopal congregation, and put my fingers to my lips, asking him to be silent regarding my entrance into the steam box. The attendant complied, holding the door and lid until I was crouched into an uncomfortable knot of arms and knees. Then he sealed me safely in and out of sight.

Clay and Holcombe entered, choosing two cabinets near enough to me that I feared they would pick up the claps of thunder beating in my chest that seemed to vibrate my entire body against the sides of my box. I manoeuvred the towel over my head in case either man decided to approach my box and peer inside. This was a ridiculous and unbefitting ruse for a Union spy, but I had no other option.

I heard both men settle into their respective cabinets, patiently waiting as the attendant tucked towels around the neck holes while telling them he would stand by with glasses of cold water that he would serve them as requested. Once settled, they resumed the conversation they had started in the change room.

"I'm learning to place little reliance on not only the truth of that man's utterances but the sanity of his faculties," Holcombe said above the hiss of steam.

"Mark my words, Holcombe, that sallow lack-wit will attribute any failure in Chicago to the peace negotiations at the Falls. He's sure to blame us for his shortcomings." Clay breathed the moistened air deeply to loosen the congestion in his lungs, coughing on occasion but gradually clearing the rattle in his chest.

I slid my towel between my head and lap, allowing it to sponge away the perspiration beginning to sting my eyes. They were talking about Jacob Thompson. A deeper split in their ranks perhaps?

"His so-called revolution in the Northwest," continued Clay, "is doomed. When Judge Bullitt was arrested yesterday, they found the plans for the uprising, membership lists of the Sons of Liberty, plus the money I gave them, so I'm confident many more arrests will be made. I don't think the judge advocate general will look fondly on their treason."

"You're right, Clay. I fear for the South."

"At least the South has a leader."

I remembered Hyams's prediction that Bullitt would be arrested. He was right.

Clay summoned the attendant for water, then asked to be moved to the massage room for a rubdown. It had to be nearly three o'clock, and Wallace was sure to be finishing his douche therapy. I had to hurry and locate Wallace's cubicle before he returned.

When Clay and Holcombe left the tepidarium, the attendant focused his attention on me. "You alive in there?" He unlocked the steam box and extended a hand. "They's gone now, son. You can come out, but don't rise too quickly and go and faint on me. I ain't 'bout to aks no questions, but I figures any soul fearing to be seen by those noose-deserving Rebels cain't be all bad. Now stand, son, and let me helps you out."

I unfolded my legs carefully. "Hell, that's hot in there!" I cried, towelling my drenched face and chest. "I'm beholden to you, my good man. Thank you for your help. I'd appreciate your confidence," I whispered, tightening the robe around my waist.

As he wiped down the box, the attendant muttered, "Got no reason to tell a soul. Got no reason, no suh."

I had to work fast. Wallace would be coming out of unit number 4 within minutes, and I had an entire double row of cubicles to check. From side to side of the aisle I dashed, pulling apart the muslin drapes and checking the hanging contents for any sign of Wallace's belong-ings. Then I spotted the familiar linen chemise. On his under drawers in embroidered elided script read "CAD." The only person I knew with those initials was my boss, Charles A. Dana, the assistant secretary of war. Wallace wasn't Dana — that was for sure. But he wasn't Wallace, either. CAD? Were they his real initials, or did he secretly enjoy a most eccentric but harmless private indiscretion?

Returning Wallace's clothes to the hook, I poked my head out of the curtain to see if the aisle was clear. Standing in front of me was Wallace, about to simultaneously swing open the drape to catch his intruder while the crime was blazing.

"Thomson! What are you doing here among my things?"

"Wallace? These yours?" I asked, feeling clumsy being caught off guard.

"Yes, I'd say so," he said loudly, not about to lower his voice.

"I'm most embarrassed. This is the first time I've used the baths, against my employer's request, of course. I thought I heard Colonel Stephenson's voice and hurried into the wrong aisle and pew. You can see mine is the same, only the next aisle over, but once I was in here I didn't have the nerve to come out until I was sure the colonel was gone. Can you excuse me this most unfortunate incident? Thank goodness it was your cubicle and not an unfriendly guest's."

"I should say."

I peered out the curtain, tilting my ear as if to better hear. "I guess the coast is clear. I'll be going."

I knew I hadn't fooled Wallace for one minute. If he could be trusted, I fully expected we'd have a good laugh about this one day. Wallace would nevertheless now be suspicious of me but that would work both ways. Most spies weren't revealed by investigations but by their own mistakes or by other spies.

15

Through Enemy Lines

The next day Clay greeted me more cordially at his Park Street residence than he had at our previous meetings — almost too cordially. He escorted me into the study where Beverly Tucker, one of the men I'd met at the Salon my first night in St. Catharines, sat. Tucker was the former U.S. consul in Liverpool, and now he was ensconced at a desk dropping a dab of warm wax onto an envelope, then pressing it with Clay's signet ring to seal the letter. *I felt as if I were the sacrificial lamb being led to slaughter.*

"I understand your trip to Toronto went without event," Clay said.

"Quite so, sir," I replied, waiting to learn whether Jacob Thompson or Benjamin Wood had wired regarding their suspicions about my identity. If they hadn't, perhaps they were colluding in Clay's inevitable and humiliating downfall for trusting a Union spy. Their bad blood could well be my lifeline, for the time being at least.

As I handed Clay the parcel of fabric and lace, along with his receipts, I debated whether or not to mention the Benjamin Wood incident. Then I decided I better and said nonchalantly, "There was one unfortunate encounter with Benjamin Wood, the New York newspaper publisher. He thought I was a person of his acquaintance who favoured the Union cause. Other than that nothing untoward happened on my journey. I assured Wood he was sorely mistaken. I guess I have a common face, but surely not a Union one!"

Clay nodded, somewhat distracted as he separated the personal receipts from those he would classify as part of the war effort. Once that was done, he reviewed the contents of the parcel, apparently dismissing the Wood accusation entirely. "You've done exceedingly well, Thomson. My compliments and gratitude. I'm sure the assignment wasn't easy, particularly the shopping for my dear Ginnie, but Wallace tells me you met and performed the task together."

"Yes, he was most helpful," I said. At that point my eyes met Beverly Tucker's. "Good afternoon, Mr. Tucker. It's a pleasure to see you again."

"Mutual, Thomson, I'm sure."

"Mr. Tucker here has served as my secretary in your absence, Thomson. His hand is nearly as fast as yours, but I must say, not as clear." Smiling at Tucker, Clay added, "No offence, Beverly."

"None taken, Clement," replied Tucker, now a bit preoccupied with tidying the papers at the desk. "Will you excuse us, Mr. Thomson?" he asked. "I need one last word with the senator before I leave."

"Certainly, sir." I returned to the foyer outside the study, but not quite out of sight and earshot. Tucker moved closer to Clay, putting his arm around his shoulder for greater intimacy and making it more difficult but not impossible for me to hear.

"I don't mean to doubt your judgment, Clement," Tucker said, "but are you sure you can trust this man? Maybe Wood was right."

"Yes, Bev. President Davis himself has endorsed Thomson's integrity and trustworthiness. I saw the letter with my own eyes, and it was in Jefferson's own hand. I recognized it immediately. "

Pulling away from Tucker, Clay tugged his shirtsleeve through the edge of the cuff of his long coat to assert the resoluteness of his assessment. "I had another trusted Confederate keep an eye on him the entire time, and he conducted himself with perfect decorum. If I'd sent him to Richmond with my last dispatch instead of that Canadian rotter Nelson, I could have spoken more freely about the events at Niagara Falls instead of the couched phrases I was forced to use. I might have nipped Richmond's mistaken assumptions in the bud and avoided this whole embarrassing debacle. Secretary of War Seddon in the War Department must understand how Dame Rumour ruled this affair, causing such intemperate declarations by reactionary newspaper editors. Our role is difficult enough. We must be judged with charity until we can be heard in our own defence. Trust me on this."

Clay had pulled rank. He then summoned me to return.

"I have another assignment for you, Thomson, more arduous than the last, but if you're willing, I'll pay you well."

Tucker scowled, registering his displeasure.

"Yes, sir, how may I be of service?" I glanced at Tucker, who was now reaching for his hat and cane.

"I need you to get through the enemy lines to deliver this dispatch to

Secretary of War James Seddon in Richmond, telling him our version of the so-called peace talks fiasco. I'll finance you and provide a letter for your safe passage once past Union lines, but getting to that point will be up to your own wit. Are you willing?"

"For my country I offer my humble services and my life. I can accept no pay, but thank you just the same." As much as I dearly needed the cash, I had to establish myself as a trustworthy man. To an aristocrat, money exchanged made the purity of one's motives dubious.

"You are loyal, indeed," said Clay, who then excused himself to see Tucker out. Returning, he gave me expense money to buy a horse once I was in Pennsylvania and wished me Godspeed.

I returned to the hotel and informed Colonel Stephenson that the senator had asked me to perform another courier service, which pleased the innkeeper to think his employee would be so trusted. "Well, then," said the colonel, "what are you waiting for? Pack your satchel and wangle some pickles and cheese from the chef for the trip."

The journey was uncomplicated but nevertheless tense. From St. Catharines I took the train to Niagara Falls, New York, where authorities checked and rechecked my documents, which were in order. I used my certificate of employment issued by Colonel Stephenson, showing me to be a resident of Canada. Then it was on to New York City where I wired my Union contact, Assistant Secretary of War Dana, telling him I was on my way to Richmond. I informed Dana that the dispatch I was carrying involved Clay's rebuttal to the criticisms of the Niagara Falls Peace Conference and wasn't even in cipher, so the assistant secretary surmised it was probably inconsequential and suggested I bypass his office in Washington and head straight to Richmond. I could always wire him if I discovered my information was of any significance.

From New York City I boarded a train to Washington where I bought a horse to get to Richmond farther south, arriving two days later. Soldiers stopped me on the outskirts of the city but let me pass once they received confirmation that my letter from Clay was valid.

Delivering the dispatch to Confederate Secretary of State Judah Benjamin tested my patience. I waited and waited. When the secretary finally came out of his meeting, he greeted me, scanned my countenance, accepted the letter, thanked me, and returned to his meeting. *That was it?* No "How was your journey? Did you find it arduous? Dangerous? How are the commissioners in Canada?"

I returned to St. Catharines the same way I travelled to Richmond, this time sharing a compartment as far as Syracuse with two card-playing, port-drinking salesmen from Schenectady who, once they tired of their game and finished their bottle, fell asleep and snored loudly. At Niagara Falls, New York, I went through customs and boarded a Canadian train for St. Catharines. Once on the Canadian side, I somehow felt safe to admit to myself that this first trip through enemy lines was without event, as Clay had put it. At that point I recognized someone passing my compartment door among the passengers who had just boarded. I rushed to the door before another compartment swallowed her out of sight and had to shout above the blare of the whistle and steam. "Miss Stephenson, it's Thomson here! Hello!"

Sarah Stephenson peered around her travelling companion and servant, a young mulatto woman with sea-green eyes. "Yes, so it is. Fancy meeting you here." She bowed slightly, offering an encouraging flirtatious smile.

"Won't you both please join me? My compartment's empty and I'm longing for company."

"Why, Mr. Thomson, we'd be delighted. Isn't that right, Lizzie?"

"Yes'm."

"Your company would most enliven my journey," I said, standing aside as they took their seats, then shifting awkwardly to allow the porter to stack their parcels in the overhead rack. I took the seat opposite Sarah. When she looked up to speak, I realized I had never really seen her face well before — full face, complete, with no fan or evening shadow to hide her features. She was lovelier than I remembered. Her skin was so iridescent it was as if I were gazing into a bubble, reflecting prisms of pink and gold. Her small foot touched mine inadvertently as she tucked her skirts between her and Lizzie. She held her foot very still next to mine, and I fought the current of energy that surged through me at so intimate an encounter.

"You've been sightseeing at the Falls?" I asked, feebly acknowledging the obvious.

"Yes, Mr. Thomson. Lizzie and I also bought some linens for my uncle at a sweet little Scottish shop on the Canadian side. I wouldn't venture the trip alone through the line to the American side. I find those Yankees too troublesome in their inquiries of anyone Southern, as innocent as any trip of mine may be destined."

"They can be troublesome in their vigilance. There's no doubt about that."

"Yes, they can," Sarah said as she adjusted her hat, tucking safely behind a ribbon some errant netting that had slipped around her forehead. "On such a busy train, we're most fortunate indeed to find you so accommodating as to share your compartment. It allows us to travel unmolested by the hordes of soldiers and detectives on this line. We're truly grateful for your kindness, Mr. Thomson. Aren't we, Lizzie?"

"Yes,m."

Sarah leaned forward, so close that I smelled the rose she'd pinned to her lapel. As she whispered, every soft word seemed to enter me, filling me, supersaturating me with her confidential tone. "I know where you've been, Mr. Thomson. My uncle told me, and I'm mighty proud to have an association with a loyal man of such courage and gallantry."

An association? What did she mean? Don't read more than she intends, I told myself. Her foot remained next to mine. "Is that right?" I said, affectionately mimicking her whisper. "I shouldn't think my whereabouts would be cause for your inquiry."

"Well, yes, your presence was noticeably missing, Mr. Thomson. Noticeably missing." She smiled at me directly rather than averting her eyes.

This was my opening. "I've been gone nearly a week and should look forward to an appointment in Mr. Spears's tepidarium when I return, but only to make me a more fitting escort, if you would honour me with a promenade to town after dinner tonight. I know a small confectionery recommended by Dr. Mack that sells a fine vanilla iced cream. That is, of course, if you have a mind to stop for some." I found myself studying the buttons on my jacket, preparing to hear the reasons why she wouldn't be able to accept my invitation on such short notice.

"We should be charmed, Mr. Thomson. Absolutely charmed."

"I'm so pleased," I said, trying to assume a composure more confident than that of the nervous adolescent I currently felt and no doubt appeared.

"Now tell me all about your adventure to Richmond," she prompted. "I want to know everything."

"There should be things only a courier knows, for your protection, ma'am, but I should be glad to offer what I can," I said, sensing that if I wasn't careful I could, in my desire to have her like me, be easily teased into revealing something I shouldn't. She seemed to thirst for knowledge of Richmond. Were the Union troops as close to the capital as the newspapers had led her to believe? What was the weather like? How did I make connections undisturbed? How did I find Secretary of War Seddon — worried? In good health? I answered her questions briefly without equivocation or elaboration. She knew I'd made the trip, so denials would have been futile. Besides, her pleasure seemed to grow with every bit of information I offered, or was that my imagination?

"You have the courage of a soldier, Mr. Thomson. Are you?"

"Am I what, ma'am?"

"Why, a soldier, of course?"

"No, ma'am, I'm just a lawyer struggling to serve my country in a civilian capacity wherever my skills are needed."

"Were you sent here, Mr. Thomson?"

"Why do you ask, Miss Stephenson?"

"Because as I was attending to my uncle's bookkeeping, I found a letter from President Jeff Davis in the files. It spoke on your behalf."

Her questions were making me nervous. "I came with letters of reference, yes," I replied, hoping to avoid answering directly. "If there was an additional letter, perhaps it was Senator Clay inquiring after the reliability of my credentials, as I suggested he should." Thankfully, the Union's War Department operatives had infiltrated Richmond's Government House and had access to Davis's penmanship.

"Yes, no doubt, he did." Sarah glanced out the window as the Canadian countryside sped past, then returned her attention to me. "Well, I guess what's good enough for the president is good enough for me. You seem like such a gentleman, but one can't be too careful these days. Yes, we should be charmed to join you for a promenade and for a vanilla iced cream. Isn't that right, Lizzie?"

"Yes'm."

The evening was a cooling relief from the mugginess that had thickened the afternoon. Soulful cicadas reverberated in the trees like a cautioning

Greek chorus. But I paid little attention. We passed hotel guests fanning themselves, heading for the cooler banks of the canal, municipal leaders emptying the town hall in clouds of cigar smoke and continuing rhetoric, but I still couldn't settle my excitement at the fact that I was actually walking beside Sarah. Lizzie ambled behind us, stopping to gaze longingly inside the shops lining St. Paul Street, or to stroke the mane of a chestnut Arabian, or flirt with its groom, and then she'd run wildly to catch up. In the time we were left alone, Sarah and I strolled a little closer to each other.

"Mr. Thomson, what do you think will happen to us all when this war's over? Can we ever live in peace with the Yankees? Land sakes — with ourselves?"

Sarah was so earnest that I wanted to reach down and embrace her. "I guess it depends on who's seen as the victor. Humiliation is a bitter pill that some never swallow without recrimination and the desire for retribution."

"Who has ever borne humiliation with indifference?" she asked.

"I guess you're right. We're all fragile beings when the things we believe matter are seen as having no consequence. Perhaps it boils down to whether or not the victor is noble and the defeated are strong."

"The North is going to win, Mr. Thomson, isn't it?" she asked, half yearning for me to deny the inevitability of the events that were sure to transpire within the next few months. "We haven't the strength to go on, do we? I'm so afraid for what the future holds. When it happens, will you stay in Canada or will you return to Virginia?"

As much as I could, I would tell her no lies. "I don't know, Sarah." Too late I realized I'd called her by her first name. I stopped walking. "I beg your pardon, Miss Stephenson. I didn't mean to be so familiar. My rudeness is exceeded only by my desire that you find it in your heart to overlook my indiscretion."

"I'm flattered, James," she said, putting her arm through mine and bringing me closer. "May I call you James?"

I covered her hand with mine. "I've longed to say your name aloud since we first met."

"I know," she said, and we walked quietly for a while, now hearing the cicadas' warning song. We had crossed a threshold and knew what followed from this point could determine our future together. "Tell me about your trip to Toronto?" she asked, breaking our nearly unbearable silence.

I told her about The Golden Lion, Mr. Simpson, and the bolts and bolts of fine fabrics, which she thoroughly enjoyed hearing about. Then I recounted my dinner with Wallace at Bacchus and the pun Spears had made, which made her laugh, as much at the pun as at the fact that the usual dour superintendent of the baths had made it. Next, I mentioned my curiosity about Sanders's son-in-law, Louis Contri, and my suspicions that Wallace could be masquerading as a journalist or perhaps even a spy for the Union or the Confederacy.

"I, too, have misgivings about Signore Contri," Sarah said. "He's a skittish, flirtatious man who doesn't inspire trust. I think he understands much more than he professes, but what are you suggesting about Wallace?"

"I'm saying that he might not be who he says he is." I knew I was walking a dangerous line in my own imposture, but perhaps Sarah could help me uncover the identity of the man. "Given the nature of the times, it's a mystery worth unravelling. If it turns out to be innocuous, so be it. On the other hand, people we know might be placing unwarranted trust in him."

Sarah stiffened with resolution. "If your superiors are confused and he really is a Yankee posing as a Southerner, he's got to be up to no good, else why would he lie? To expose him would be serving our country, wouldn't it, James?" She was asking for my reassurance. "No service too small," she concluded. "We must do something, but what?"

16

Wallace's *Noms de Plume*

Sarah Stephenson was a few years younger than I, perhaps twenty or twenty-one. Most women her age would have been driven by the prospect of finding a suitable husband but that didn't seem to be Sarah's preoccupation. She was filled with an independence of mind and spirit that gave her an air of resourcefulness and stability, qualities most men found unnerving. But not me, or so I thought. She wasn't easily disturbed and much too self-sufficient for what I now recognize was my need to protect her when she was quite capable of doing so herself.

On the veranda the next morning, I saw Sarah saying goodbye to Wallace. I caught her eye, walked toward the south wing, and waited. When she arrived, she was holding the carved wooden handle of a room key.

"He's taken the Tally Ho to connect with the train to Windsor to meet someone. I saw him get on. It's a day's journey, so he should be away a few days, but let's waste no time. He's staying in room 203 here at the hotel. I'll meet you there in five minutes."

I hadn't anticipated that the fair Sarah would be quite so adventurous. From the end of the corridor, I saw her unlock the door to room 203 and enter. I waited until I was sure no guest would see me do the same. When I slipped into the room, I found her standing in the middle of it, looking quite bewildered.

"He's not as fastidious as he seems, is he?" she whispered, commenting on the layers of clothes draped over chairs and bedposts.

I whispered back, "No, he's not. We had best move quickly. Shall I check the armoire and you the desk?"

"Oh, dear," she said with a worried expression on her face. "I don't mind saying that I do feel odd to be in the presence of a gentleman's intimates, but then again, perhaps he's not a gentleman at all, so we might as well begin."

We worked rapidly, trying not to disturb what was already an inordinate amount of clutter. Mounds of clothes, books, papers …

"The man can't be said to travel lightly," I said quietly, aware how easy it was for passersby to overhear from the hallway voices inside a hotel room.

"Nor without the accoutrements of his trade," added Sarah from the other side of the room. "Come, look at this." Inside the desk drawer Sarah had found a number of stories in draft form. Some were addressed to the editor of the liberal *New-York Tribune* and signed by Sanford Conover. Others were addressed to the conservative *New York Herald* and signed by Harvey Birch. However, the same hand had written both of them.

"What do you make of it?" she asked.

"I'd be less disposed to think him a Yankee infiltrator in disguise

My motivation in accepting the assignment to infiltrate the Confederate mission in Canada was solely idealistic. I was often torn between my patriotism and my instincts to tell the truth. It was always a relief to be with Aaron so that I could relax my deceits. I enjoyed the complexities of the man. When Emancipation came, he was as patriotic as I and unruffled in spite of the indignities we suffered at the hands of my father: Aaron as a slave and myself as the son of a dissolute man. That was the bond we shared. Not that we suffered, but that we survived. Somehow that made us both resilient and willing to take responsibility for our own lives.

"It's safe to talk," he said. "There's no one here now. We can be seen through the shop window, but we can't be overheard."

"I'm seeking," I said. "So what will I find?"

Aaron winked. "It's not what you'll find but what my good auntie has found." He walked to a desk in the back of his shop while I stayed at the front in plain view.

"Your auntie?" I asked when he returned.

"Yes, I told you she was good. But you won't know how good until you see this." Aaron handed me a newspaper with a letter tucked inside, then busied himself with a broom while I read the letter as if scanning the news. It was addressed to Clay from a Lieutenant Bennett Young.

"How did she get this?" I asked.

"Seems Senator Clay shops frequently at the market square in town and has taken a liking to my auntie's biscuits, so she delivered some to him for breakfast one morning, right out of the oven. While Clay was searching for money to pay her, a postman delivered a letter to Clay and handed it to her, thinking she was the housemaid. She tucked it under her turban, assuming I might be interested, since it was from a man named Bennett Young. She's always concerned about family."

I grimaced at Aaron's facetious comment. "Presence of mind, that woman. If it's the same Bennett Young I know, he going to be trouble."

Aaron placed the barber's cape around my chest and tipped the chair back to prepare me for a shave, then stropped the blade and stirred the soap until it frothed into a creamy lather as he had done the first day I was in town.

"Bennett Young is about twenty-one years old," I continued, "but a very busy Rebel as the son of a wealthy slave owner from Kentucky and a theology student who got kicked out of Kentucky a few years ago for preaching the gospel according to Jefferson Davis."

Aaron put steamed towels across my chin. I didn't really need a shave, but all this was a necessary subterfuge. Although he stood with his back to me as he arranged his shaving tools, we could see each other's reflection in the mirror. "What have you heard about this Young, Aaron?"

He glanced at me. "Bennett Young sought refuge in Canada in 1862 after being labelled a traitor in neutral Kentucky. When I arrived in St. Catharines on leave a few months ago, I was told to watch for him."

Aaron circled the bristles of the shaving brush in the cup until the foam became a rich cream. Once he was satisfied with its consistency, he applied it to my face with deft swirls. "He was supposed to be in Canada West until he could sign up in the Confederate army, riding with Morgan's Raiders. Unfortunately, the entire band was captured in 1863 and sent to Camp Douglas, the prisoner-of-war camp near Chicago. Shortly after that, I heard he escaped and ended up in Canada again, but this time he enrolled in the University of Toronto for studies in theology."

Once I felt the straight razor skimming my skin, I could only listen.

"We know he met Clay in Halifax when Clay first arrived three months ago," Aaron continued. "Presumably, he was there to brief Clay on what might be accomplished for the Rebel cause from a Canadian position, the so-called 'fire from the north.' I don't know any specifics, only that Richmond gave Bennett Young the go-ahead to invade Vermont entering the state from a covert point in Canada." He finished my shave in silence, wiped the remaining cream from my face, then applied a brisk spray of cool water and towelled me off.

"That go-ahead," I said, "seems to have been with Clay's blessing. This letter confirms Clay is financing a new and quite dangerous mission."

"Yes," said Aaron, "and the target's a land raid into Vermont, but when and exactly where, it doesn't say."

"I'll get a wire to Dana in the War Department as soon as I can," I said. "In the meantime we've got to get this letter back into Clay's hands as soon as possible."

"My auntie could always make some more biscuits."

"No, Clay might get suspicious. Leave it with me."

I took the newspaper and its purloined contents and returned to my desk where I scrawled a copy of the letter and placed it in a false bottom I'd constructed in the centre drawer. The colonel had signed the letters I'd prepared earlier, which were now ready for mailing. I folded them into their respective envelopes, addressed them, and informed my employer that I was going downtown to post them.

"Is there anything else you need from town, Colonel?" I waited patiently at his office door as he placed an invoicing pencil to his temple to consider the possibilities.

"Yes," he said. "Pick up the *New York Herald* at the smoke shop on James. I had a guest requesting one this morning."

"Yes, sir. Be glad to."

On my way to the post office, I stopped at the Montreal Telegraph Office and sent a wire to a trusted Union contact in Rebel-occupied Virginia that Assistant Secretary of War Dana had given me. The contact would forward my message directly to the assistant secretary in Washington City. At the post office I got three letters stamped, plus a third, which was carefully resealed, and requested they be remailed, explaining that somehow they had gotten delivered to the hotel by mistake. On the way back, I stopped at the smoke shop for the paper and a cigar, both of which I enjoyed under a tree by the canal for a fifteen-minute interlude, careful not to wrinkle the newspaper before presenting it to the colonel for his guest.

On page 1, column 4, there it was. The headlines read: "The Rebel Raid from Canada — How It Was Plotted — Its Inside Story — More Plots — What the Canadians Say." The byline was Sanford Conover, James Watson Wallace's *nom de plume*. Given his inside sources in Toronto, Wallace had obviously gone to Windsor to cover the aborted Rebel operation to liberate the prisoners at Johnson's Island, and this was the story he'd filed.

The article explained how the plan hinged on seizing the warship USS *Michigan* that guarded the prison on the island. The surprise attack was to be made easier by a Confederate on board who was to host an all-night drinking party where he would see to it that the Union captain and crew drank themselves blind. The *Michigan*'s guns were then to be used to liberate the Confederate prisoners on the island.

An informer told the *Michigan*'s captain about the plan, and the Confederate on board was arrested a few hours before the scheduled drinking party. But the Rebel in charge of seizing the warship, Captain

John Beall, was unaware of the arrest and was still carrying out his part of the scheme. Beall boarded the lake steamer *Philo Parsons* with sixteen scruffy other men carrying a large trunk. As the vessel steamed toward Sandusky, Beall seized the *Philo Parsons* and herded the passengers and crew into the hold.

Conover's, or I should say, Wallace's coverage of the escapade was compelling. He described how everything had gone smoothly until the Confederate pirates approached Johnson's Island and saw the *Michigan*'s decks cleared and guns pointed directly at the *Philo Parsons*. Beall and his faint-hearted crew turned tail and headed back to Canadian waters loaded with booty they had pilfered from the steamer and its passengers.

The failure of the mission was laughable. What was interesting was that Wallace/Conover stated it was Jacob Thompson, a Confederate commissioner in Canada, who had financed the plot, underscoring the fact that it was planned on Canadian soil and in direct violation of neutrality laws. Wallace/Conover's plea for action by the Canadian government to step in and condemn potential international treaty violations was articulate and adamant. It was the last sentence that suggested that Wallace/Conover was probably working for the North: "We should have great cause for remonstrance if Canada became the castle from which our enemies could assail us while we could not reach them in return."

Even if this were true, at this stage I felt I still needed to be cautious. Imposture was Wallace's currency, so he could still be capable of betrayal if it was expedient to do so.

18

The Eye of a Spy

I refolded the large single sheet over once and propped it against the tree, placing a rock in the centre to prevent a breeze from carrying it away. Tilting my hat forward, I rested my head against the trunk to savour my smoke.

"*Gah-rrrrr-ate* blend, that," came a voice with *r*'s tumbling against one another in a melodic Scottish burr. "Must have been *rrrr*-rolled on the hip of a maiden."

Tipping the brim of my hat, I spied a man in his fifties dressed in stripes and a long coat, anchoring his foot onto the side of the hill as he steadied his balance with an ebony cane.

"I'm like a wee bairn in Hamlin drawn to the lilt o' the pipe," he said, "but in this case, it's the fine aroma of your cigar. It's braw, it is."

I made a move to stand up out of respect.

"Stay seated, man. My object wasn't to bestow a disturbance on your private reverie on so fine a day."

"Not at all, sir," I said. "I'd best be going now, anyway."

"It's no business o' mine, but where, may I ask, is your destination?"

"Stephenson House at the top of Salina Street and Yates."

"If you could spare this old man the company, I'd welcome the chance to breathe in the aroma until its last wee ash falls to the ground."

"I'd gladly offer you one, sir, but I bought only one."

"No hardship, lad. I don't smoke. Never have. Never will. Too costly a pleasure for me. That, however, has never lessened my enjoyment of a good leaf. Yours smells robust and has a darker leaf, so it must be sun-grown. Because of its aroma, I'd say it's a Cavendish."

"You're very knowledgeable for a man who doesn't smoke."

"The lads back home have enlisted the practice of smoking, much to my wife's grief, so she makes them go to our wee yard whenever they decide to indulge. But I find pleasure in it."

We stepped onto the towpath beside the canal and took in the traffic of brigs, schooners, and cutters crowding the waterway, waiting their turn to enter the locks.

The Scot noted an American sidewheeler being loaded and pointed to it with his cane. "I take by your accent you're an American."

"Yes, sir, I am. Not hard to note that you're a Glaswegian."

The man laughed.

"But how did you know I was American? I've said so few words."

"We cannae hear the distinctions in our own speech, can we? What I heard in yours was the way ye said *anyway* a few moments ago. A dead giveaway. It's a good thing you're nae a spy, because a good ear would catch ye right off. You say *eh-nee-weigh*." The man exaggerated the last syllable, stretching it into two.

"And what would a Canadian say?"

"A Canadian, nae from Glasgow, mind ye, would say *enny-weh*. Do ye hear the difference? It's a subtle one, for sure, but it's there. My guess is you're from downstate New York. Am I right?"

I wasn't sure how to play this. Imposture was the art of telling the truth in the details and letting your target think he was discovering something about you. "My mother was a New Yorker, and my father a Virginian," I said cautiously, hoping this would satisfy my new acquaintance, who could be a spy himself. There were so many detectives about one could never know for certain. "I'd say you're from Canada East. Perhaps Montreal. Am I right?"

The older man stopped walking and peered at me in amazement. "Glasga' isn't hard to figure, but Montreal? How'd ye deduce that?"

"Your trousers, sir. They betray you. You see, I have it on good authority that the stripe is available only at Morgan's in Montreal and in Toronto by special order. You could be from Toronto, but the ring you wear bears the Masonic crest of a Montreal chapter."

The man placed both hands on the knob of his cane to hold his weight as he bent over in laughter, thoroughly enjoying my detective work. "Very good, laddie. I judged ye too soon. You might not have the ear of a spy, but ye have the eye of one. Better yet, with your eye for detail, ye should be a photographer like me. My name's Notman. William Notman. A pleasure it is to meet ye."

I was visibly impressed. "Am I walking with *the* William Notman, the noted photographer of figures both distinguished and common? Why, I have a *carte de visite* with your very imprint displayed."

"Aye, your humble servant," Notman replied with a bow.

"I'm much obliged to make your acquaintance, Mr. Notman. What brings you to St. Catharines?"

His attention was diverted to some activity he spotted in the canal. "Be with ye momentarily, lad. Right now, set your wee lamps on that." A large clipper was starting to rise in a lock as the floodgates opened, spilling channels of water into its berth. "Amazin' feat of engineering, that. I wish I had my camera."

"Without your camera? Do I assume you're here on holiday then, Mr. Notman."

"I'm nae here on my own free will. 'Twas my guid wife. She thought I was gettin' too cranky for my britches and needed a rest."

"You've been working too hard?"

"Aye, ye might say. I had the pleasure of takin' the photos of the politicians from Ottawa and Montreal headin' to Halifax to wyse and coax the Maritimers to unite with them and form a new union. You've heard of their plan, no doubt?"

"Yes, I'm aware. It's strange, isn't it? We Americans are trying to break apart and you Canadians are trying to come together."

"Aye, out of self-preservation, it is. By the way, what's your name?"

I extended my hand. "Thomson. James Thomson."

"A'm glad tae meet ye," the photographer said, gripping my hand with both of his.

"Your work must be a fascinating line — meeting with all those interesting people."

"Well, I dinnae really *meet* them to talk to, like this, Mr. Thomson. I'm at their service. But, yes, my work has some fair moments. And your line of work?"

I puffed the last of my cigar until its ash glowed and fell to the ground. Notman inhaled deeply, savouring the last of the aroma that lingered.

"I'm just a law clerk, sir," I said as I tamped the ash in the grass, "with a great admiration for your craft. Perhaps you'll allow me the honour of your business card."

He reached into his waistcoat and handed me an embossed calling card with the words "Photography, William Notman, Artist, 11 Bleury Street, Montreal." "When ye go to Montreal, please let me know if I can be of service."

"I shall, Mr. Notman."

19

Clay Resigns

I spent the next couple of months carrying dispatches back and forth to Richmond for Senator Clay, stopping off in Washington City prior to their delivery. Then, in October, Lieutenant Bennett Young made his move, which infuriated Clay. Originally, Young's idea for the raid into Vermont had seemed feasible to Clay. Jacob Thompson thought it was worthless, so he washed his hands of the entire affair. But the government in Richmond overruled Thompson and gave Young full authority to do whatever he thought necessary. Clay had originally funded the mission, which made him the authority in charge, but when fourteen of the twenty Rebel invaders escaped over the border into Canada East and were quickly captured and jailed in Montreal, Clay denied involvement.

The raiders foolishly thought by invading the border town of St. Albans, Vermont, they could claim it for the Confederacy. While they were at it, they also robbed its banks of over $200,000 and ended up killing a man. This kind of conduct wasn't what Clay had agreed to, yet it was quickly becoming a focus of international concern between the Union and Great Britain. Clay expected that only the Union would retaliate against the Confederacy. That retaliation would deflect troops fighting in the South to a campaign in the North. But when it appeared that Great Britain was primed to execute reprisals for violations of neutrality, Clay drew the line and wanted no part of it.

Young and his men felt betrayed and demoralized by Clay. They remained in jail, awaiting trial without money for their defence. But what they needed even more was a confirmation from Richmond that they were legitimate soldiers of war commissioned by the Confederate government to invade Vermont. If their commissions weren't forthcoming, they could be extradited and hanged from Yankee gallows.

I had received a message that Clay wanted me to deliver another dispatch to Richmond. Now I stood at his front door, watching leaves swirl around my feet as they were chased by the November wind. A tall black servant let me in, took my derby and coat, and conducted me to a seat in the foyer where he instructed me to wait. I overheard Beverly Tucker's voice in the adjoining room.

"Clement," said Tucker, "I confess I really don't know much about your business here. As you're aware, I usually leave the room when you have callers."

"Yes, yes, my friend," replied Clay as if impatient at what he could anticipate was advice he didn't want to hear.

"But on one occasion I couldn't help overhearing that you made it clear to Lieutenant Young that the object of his enterprise was to destroy property of the enemy by burning and that robbery wasn't contemplated in your instructions to him."

"Yes, Bev, I felt strongly about that. Now we'll soon be mired in an embarrassing international case of extradition. I'm disgusted with the greedy lot of them." Clay was uncharacteristically critical of another Confederate. Then I heard the servant knock on the anteroom door. "Have him wait," Clay almost growled. "I'll see him shortly."

The servant returned, gave me the message, and stood at the end of the corridor, waiting to be summoned. Clay's conversation with Tucker was audible to us both.

Clay continued his tirade. "They're nothing but a gang of thieves, and I wish all of them, except Young, in hell."

The senator's intransigence came as no surprise to me. In Clay's world the canons of war were shaped by the principles of probity and honour, and the men who invaded St. Albans had violated both.

"A civilian died unnecessarily in their childish melee," Clay told Tucker. "Raid, indeed. It was pure and simple robbery! What was Young thinking? And *I've* abandoned *them*? I'll be going to Montreal myself to see to it that Sanders will have control of $6,000 for their defence. That will be the extent of my support. They refuse to hand over the money they took from the Vermont bank. If they need more than I can allot, let them use that money for their defence."

I had never heard Clay so adamant. Then I heard Tucker take steps closer to Clay, perhaps to reason with him.

"You realize that Governor General Monck is anxious to placate Washington?" Tucker asked. "I understand he's appointing a clerk of the Crown to work on the prosecution of our soldiers. If convicted, they could be extradited and hanged from Yankee gallows." Tucker's voice had risen in his attempt to try every angle to get Clay to change his mind.

"I'm not sure I understand your tone," Clay said. "What do you expect of me?"

"Support them," pleaded Tucker. "Help them demonstrate they were acting on orders from our government. You could avoid an international court battle if you requested the papers from Richmond to prove they were soldiers of the Confederacy and not marauders."

Tucker seemed exasperated with Clay. Five months had gone by since the senator's arrival in Canada, and he had little to show for it. From my perspective that was a good thing, but for such an honourable Southern patriot, it must have felt humiliating.

"I've summoned a courier here today to carry a dispatch to Secretary of War Seddon," Clay said. "I'm requesting reassignment. I'm weary of the whole thing."

"Reassignment?" Tucker now sounded dismayed.

"I'm of no use up here now," admitted Clay. "As soon as testimony starts at the raiders' trial, the Canadians will arrest me for neutrality violations, for which, I fear, I'm guilty. Plus, with the approach of winter, I also fear for my health."

Tucker raised his voice another notch, now with an unmistakable tone of incredulity. "You fear for *your* health when the lives of fourteen men are at stake?"

"Don't talk to me like that, Bev." For a minute or two I heard nothing from either man, then Clay spoke. "All right, I'll ask the courier to start the process in motion when he sees Seddon in Richmond. But the courier will carry much more important information, I'm afraid. He'll also carry news of a more sophisticated scheme than St. Albans, I assure you. It will be one that will buckle the knees of the largest cities in the North, and the death of more than one innocent victim could be the result."

I strained to hear Clay elaborate, but Tucker discouraged further discussion. "I needn't know more, Clement. I'm sure you've weighed the potential losses in Northern lives against what our sons and daughters of the South have suffered. We have many Canadian friends who abet our cause, which is comforting. Speaking of friends, did you hear that Wallace was among those arrested in Montreal along with the raiders?"

I couldn't believe my ears at this news, and evidently neither could Clay.

"Wallace? On what grounds?"

"My source isn't quite sure," Tucker said. "But he tells me Wallace is currently awaiting word of his release."

"Imagine that," Clay said. "Why would they even consider a man of his distinction could possibly be involved?"

Wallace must be covering the trial, I thought.

"It's a mystery to me, too," Tucker agreed. "I must be going. I'm due at the canal to oversee a shipment. I know I can trust that in the end you'll do right by our men."

"Yes, yes," Clay said. "I relent. Think not another moment. The men will be fine."

I heard the door to Clay's study open, and my muscles tightened as

I tried to look detached and unaffected by the conversation I had just overheard. Clay escorted Tucker to the front door.

"Thomson," Tucker greeted, nodding perfunctorily in my direction.

"Sir," I replied, rising as Tucker reached for his coat.

"Thomson," Clay said, "I'll need your help in the study. Please go inside while I see Mr. Tucker out."

"Yes, sir," I said, guiding my oil-silk bag onto my shoulder and lifting my travel satchel.

"I see you're ready to travel," said Tucker.

I found it hard to look into the man's eyes but did nevertheless. "Wherever I'm sent, sir."

Closer to the door, Tucker said to Clay under his breath, "You're still confident about this man?"

"Yes, Beverly. Don't be so suspicious. Be on your way. I'll see you for supper at the hotel." Clay held the door for Tucker and patted his shoulder as he left.

The senator's study was strewn with newspapers. From what I could gather, each was opened to various accounts of the Vermont raid. The autumn chill had crept into the house and lurked in unseen drafts by window frames and stairwells. I felt its shoulder-tightening grip. The shawled Clay entered the room, appearing slightly agitated as he shut the door behind him.

"I was unable to finish my correspondence, Thomson," he announced as he approached his desk. "The nib on my pen has split. Might you have one I can borrow?" He fumbled among his papers, trying to locate the errant pen.

"Certainly, sir," I said, reaching into my bag and handing him a nib.

"Pens are such a personal thing." Clay inserted the pen point into the slim wooden holder and gingerly dipped it into an inkwell nearby. I watched as he wiped the tip of excess ink to test the first stroke. "It's a fine point. Exactly as I prefer mine. A nib bears the inner soul of its owner, don't you think? Like a pair of shoes well worn."

Clay adjusted his chair, tilted the paper to a comfortable angle, and finished the letter he had begun earlier. I waited patiently as he wrote. His penmanship was steady with artfully formed ornate capitals and evenly angled lowercase letters. When he finished, he reached for a blotter. "I shan't sign this letter, for your safety and mine. But a seal won't hurt."

　　　　　　　　　　　　　　　　　　　　　　　　LINDA BRAMBLE

He folded the letter, placed it in an envelope, dropped some warm wax on the flap, pressed his seal, and blew until the wax hardened.

"I don't have to tell you the seriousness of this dispatch, Thomson. Deliver it directly to the secretary of war himself, none other." Clay's fingers, now translucent from the chill in the room, trembled slightly as he handed the missive to me. "Godspeed, once again, son."

To reach Richmond safely I would travel first to Montreal, then south to Plattsburgh, New York, thus avoiding the heavy U.S. Army presence at the major border crossings of Niagara Falls or Buffalo. As an added benefit, the side trip to Montreal would give me an opportunity to discover the extent of Colonel George Margrave's role in the Vermont raid. Perhaps that was why Wallace had gotten involved in the raiders' arrests.

When I arrived in Montreal, I had only a few hours before the next train to New York City via Plattsburgh, so I had to work quickly. My plan was worth a try. The oil-silk bag containing Clay's letter felt heavy as I strode down Sherbrooke Street. I pulled it closer to my chest, tapping it lightly as if to make sure its contents were still intact.

The city sprawled on the shores of the Lower St. Lawrence River and resembled a lavish Norman seaport with heavy stone warehouses, Italianate-style houses with towers and rounded arches, and stoutly built stone buildings with rooftops of iridescent green weathered copper and tin. Enough snow had fallen to cover my boots as I headed toward the financial district, which controlled most of Canada East's wealth. I'd heard that this was where the city's commercial aristocracy did business.

Nowhere else in the British North American colonies was so much power concentrated in so few hands — obviously gloved by an English-speaking minority. By the look of the store signs, the vendors were mostly Scots, with a sprinkling of Irish and English, who formed the commercial anglophone clique of dry goods, banking, hardware, boot, and clothing shops in the midst of this French-speaking province. I wasn't surprised to also find the shingles of a proliferation of lawyers and other brands of professional men who oversaw and monitored the entrepreneurial activities of the quarter. I felt rather comfortable here.

PLEASE RING BELL, THEN ENTER read the sign on the Bleury Street door. Despite some condensation on the windows, I could see a warm waiting room inside, which made escaping the early winter chill that much more inviting. Two captain's chairs nestled in a corner beside a round table, which supported a leaded glass table lamp. Hung on the centre of one wall was a solitary scene of the Scottish Highlands. But it was the other wall that distinguished this waiting room from all others. From ceiling to wainscotting was an impressive display of photographic images. It was a collective portrait of an age showing its craving for elegance, dignity, and sentimentality. There were framed portraits of what I could only guess were prominent Montrealers. It also appeared that no celebrity had journeyed to Montreal without visiting this studio — matrons in furs, little boys in sailor suits, young women in velvets and lace, all giving testament to William Notman's skill and keen eye.

I sat down to wait. The kaleidoscope of personalities before me was fascinating. As I studied their faces, I became more aware of the paradox that connected them to me. Although they presented stunning images in black and white, they were posed in front of backdrops of gardens and forests painted by competent artists who had given an illusion of reality. If the scene was indoors, it was dignified by brocaded draperies, ornate velvet chairs, potted plants, or panelled walls and rocking horses. In each portrait I found familiar backdrops mixed and matched to form different scenes in the theatre of the subject's imagination. Like mine, illusions of reality. Theirs, however, were gentle deceptions.

A jovial voice called out from just behind the door, "I'll be with ye in a flick of a wee lamb's tail." A few moments later the door opened, and the jaunty Scotsman appeared, overflowing with vitality and drying his hands on a towel. I rose as he entered.

"Mr. Notman, do you remember me?" I reached out to shake the photographer's now-dry hand.

Notman responded with a solid handshake. "A photographer, my friend, never forgets a man's visage." Notman's *r*'s cascaded gently around his words like a familiar melody. "Of course, I remember you. Mr. Thomson from the spa town by the canal." His recognition pleased both of us. "What brings you to my fair city? Nae the weather, I presume."

"I admit to being surprised at so much snow so early in the season," I said, my own words sounding dull and flat by comparison to his.

"This is a triflin'. By December's end I'll nae be able to use my back

                                                                LINDA BRAMBLE

door, for the snows will have piled high against it. Clearin' out is an hourly necessity."

"So that's what keeps you so fit? It's a pleasure seeing you so."

"And it's a pleasure to see you, but as you nae have a sweet Cavendish today, does this mean you're here on business?" Notman sat down with a sigh as if this was the first time in hours he'd a chance to do so. He motioned for me to sit beside him. "Now, laddie, what can I do for ye?"

"Perhaps you've heard the news about the Confederate soldiers being held in a local jail here in Montreal?"

"It's nae possible to escape the fact. The town's gone a wee bit wild in its jubilations at the supreme audacity of these young men darin' to test Yankee mettle, then evadin' the authorities by returnin' to our shores." Notman shook his arms in the air to illustrate the frenzy. "Did ye hear, only twenty of 'em took the entire town of St. Albans. *Achh.*" He tossed his head back in amazement, then as abruptly returned his gaze to me. "But, mind you, the needless life lost in the fray is to be pitied, but the alacrity of these Rebels gives many a Montrealer reason to rejoice." Sleeves now smoothed and cuffs buttoned, Notman sat back. "But what might these Rebel raiders have to do with ye, Mr. Thomson?"

"I trust you won't convey to another soul what I'm about to confide in you." I moved to the edge of my seat. Notman sat forward in his, as well, and placed his hand on his heart to establish the depth of his trustworthiness.

"I'm on a confidential mission to Richmond," I began, lowering my voice, wondering who I imagined would hear me. The wall's photographic images of Montreal's elite?

Notman's brows rose almost imperceptibly. He wasn't the least bit patronizing, though. *Bless him.*

"My superiors need confirmation that the men who say they're Confederate soldiers are actually so and not simply young thugs taking advantage of the times to maraud."

Notman tilted his ear and leaned in to better listen.

"If they're who they say they are," I continued, "they'll welcome the sitting. On behalf of my government, I'm here to boldly inquire as to the possibility of you shooting their photograph at the jail. I dare say their lives depend on it. Lincoln will soon demand their extradition. Richmond will fight for its own, but none other. My concern is I have to make the three o'clock train today to New York City, and you might not have the time or desire to fit me in. I'm prepared to pay you well."

Notman was on his feet. "Say no more, Mr. Thomson. Let me make arrangements with my sons to watch the shop. Have ye ever been a photographer's assistant?"

20

The "Languishing" Prisoners

William Notman's studio was an ingenious system of blinds that covered three enormous skylights cut into the ceiling. Lifeless props were stored in different corners — those same footbridges, rocks, and trees I'd seen in the photographs in Notman's waiting room, including a five-foot pyramidal mound of salt to resemble snow for winter scenes, now almost remorsefully piled without function or purpose. Posing stands stood like skeletons braced next to tripods tilted against the wall. It was like being backstage in a theatre. Every conceivable prop was available for the most elaborate theatrical productions in which Notman's subjects could enact their idealized lives for the camera.

By the time Notman was finished packing his gear, he seemed more like a field doctor than an image maker. He had assembled a movable darkroom with a tripod beside a wooden packing box in which he'd loaded small jars of chemicals, a light-tight tent, and glass plates. Pointing at the wooden box, he announced, "Your young back can carry this, lad. I'll take the tripod. I've summoned my carriage to be out in front." He surveyed his studio, tempted to incorporate a prop or two, but then thought better of the idea. "Are ye ready, Thomson?"

"Yes, sir."

"We're off to jail then!" Notman seemed to be enjoying the sport of the challenge. "Politicians and patriarchs have been before my lens," he said, lifting the tripod to his shoulder, "but I confess, I've never before had the qualified good fortune of *shooting* a prisoner." He looked back to make sure I'd gotten his pun.

"Nor have I, sir," I replied, lifting the wooden box. Both of us enjoyed a laugh as we walked to the waiting carriage.

I didn't know what to expect once we arrived at the jail. Would the jailer even permit Notman to enter? Would he release his prisoners from their cells and run the risk that their assembled strength could overpower the guards in a break? Notman didn't seem at all concerned.

The jail was an impenetrable slab structure of thick limestone set deep inside sparsely landscaped grounds entered through a stone-and-wrought-iron gate. Notman directed his driver to the jailer's home, a small cottage adjoining the jail.

"Come with me, lad. Leave the equipment in the carriage for now." Notman went straight to the cottage door and knocked. A sturdy, ruddy-faced fellow answered, dabbing his whiskers with a napkin. "McTavish, forgive the untimeliness of our visit. I see you're eating your lunch."

"Mr. Notman, come in, come in." McTavish guided us into his living room. "Trudy, set two more places. We've got more guests. It's the estimable Mr. Notman and …?"

"Thomson," said Notman. "My assistant for today, Mr. Thomson."

"Thomson, it is, Trudy. Mr. Thomson," McTavish called in the direction of the kitchen.

"You're too hospitable, McTavish, but we must forgo your kind invitation to join ye. Ye see, we're here on an assignment that compresses the time in which we have to do it. We'd hoped ye might accommodate us."

I could see past McTavish's shoulders to a dining room table groaning with food and a group of young men eating with exuberance and excited conversation.

"Anything, Notman. How may I help?"

"I understand ye have some recent arrivals who claim to be soldiers of the Confederate army," said Notman.

"Yes, I do. Don't tell me you'd like to add them to your gallery?"

"My very wish, indeed," said Notman. "Do you think that's an unreasonable request, McTavish?"

"Why don't you come in and ask them?" McTavish seemed pleased at the serendipity.

"Ask them?" questioned Notman, taken slightly off guard at the suggestion.

"Yes, of course," replied McTavish as he led us into the dining room.

"The missus and I, well —" the jailer chose his words carefully "— we felt better about having them stay with us, don't you know, here at the cottage. Since the wee ones have grown, we've plenty of room, and it's a reward to hear the laughter of such fine youth again charming these old cottage walls. These lads accomplished what we Canadians only talk about. By putting the fear of God into those arrogant American bastards, eh, Notman? I daresay they're heroes to me and the missus. I lost a brother to an American gun in that foolish war in 1812." He paused at the entrance to the dining room and said in a voice loud enough for the others to hear, "Let it not be said that the jailer McTavish doesn't take good care of his prisoners."

A loud "Hurrah" went around the table.

Mrs. McTavish had just placed two plates of sausages and potatoes on the table. "Mr. Notman, what a pleasure to have you visit our humble cottage. Won't you join our Southern friends?"

McTavish interrupted. "May I introduce the captain of this courageous band?" A young man in his early twenties rose, clean-shaven with a full head of black hair and ice-blue eyes. "Misters Notman and Thomson, meet Lieutenant Bennett Young."

The lanky Kentuckian shook hands. "Pleased to meet you, sirs," he said, slowly drawing out his vowels.

"Mr. Notman, here, is Montreal's, aye, all of British North America's most famous photographer," said McTavish, "and he's come to see if you and your men would sit for him."

"For what reason, Mr. Notman?"

Notman glanced at me.

"Merely to add to the maestro's repertoire of celebrities who have visited Montreal," I replied, hoping Notman wouldn't add anything more.

Lieutenant Young considered the idea for a moment. "I can see no harm in that if it's all right with my men." He looked at the others around the table. Their shrugs of feigned indifference didn't mask their delight. "I can only muster half my men. The rest are doing work for Mr. McTavish. Do you still want so small a group?"

Again Notman glanced at me. I nodded as if to say better than nothing.

"That would be fine," said Notman.

"So be it," said Young. "Where would you like us?"

"By all means finish this fine repast while it's hot," suggested Notman. "We'll set up our equipment. How about we take it in front of the jail? I'll need the light outdoors for a good exposure."

When they joined them, Bennett Young was the only one who came out wearing the familiar grey Confederate uniform. The other six men were in civilian clothes, seeming more like a group of young lawyers at the bar than defendants at the dock. Notman positioned their arrangement with the eye of an artist, staggering them on the steps of the jail's front door: three going up, three going down, and Young standing slightly apart in the front to the right. He shot eight exposures with a stereoscopic camera, explaining to his subjects as he shot why it was necessary to hold perfectly still for the fifteen seconds it would take to enable the light-sensitive nitrocellulose to react onto the glass plate. Notman worked silently beneath his tented darkroom with mastered discipline and steady nerves, performing the delicate wet-plate processing operation. Rather than go inside, the men assembled to wait, smoking and talking to pass the time, shifting their weight from one leg to the other to keep warm.

I took the opportunity to speak to the jailer. "Mr. McTavish, I understand a James Watson Wallace was also arrested, but I don't see him here today."

"You know Wallace?" asked McTavish.

"Yes, I do. I've been concerned for his welfare."

"No need, Mr. Thomson. I released him yesterday. Seems the authorities got him confused with another Wallace who actually was involved in the raid but escaped. Curious man, that Wallace, though."

"Why's that, Mr. McTavish?"

"The damn fool seemed more upset at being released than at being arrested. Hard to figure some people." McTavish shook his head in disbelief.

"Do you know where I might find him?" I asked.

"I believe he took rooms at the fancy St. Lawrence Hall where so many of the other Confederates stay."

If you lost an intimate contact to a major story, you'd be upset, too, I thought.

Within twenty minutes, Notman emerged and made his first appraisal of the prints he'd developed. "Under the circumstances of this overcast day, a fine print, I'd say." He motioned for the young soldiers to gather around. They nudged one another's elbows, trying to get a good view, joking and gibing, proud and awed at the outcome of such a magical art.

Packing up his gear, Notman promised to return with prints for them all. He thanked the jailer and his wife for their kindness and led the way to the carriage. "Well done, Mr. Notman," I said as we pulled away.

"Not quite yet, Mr. Thomson." Notman checked his watch. "We've just enough time, I believe, to complete our mission before your train leaves."

"Complete it?"

"Give me a half-hour or so and I'll make sure the federals at the line won't create havoc with your passing through."

The St. Lawrence Hall Hotel was within walking distance from Notman's studio. I told Notman I would go to look for an acquaintance and be back within the half-hour. Snow was starting to fall again, dusting the planked sidewalks. A hot coffee with a touch of rum at the hotel seemed fitting company while I inquired about Wallace's whereabouts. As I approached the hotel, as luck would have it, Wallace was walking in the front door. I went straight to the bar where I expected to find him.

"Wallace," I said.

He turned abruptly. "Thomson! What the devil are you doing here?"

"I could ask you the same."

"Believe it or not, I just got released from jail."

"Yes, I know."

"News travels fast."

After the barman took our orders, Wallace motioned to a table in a quieter corner of the taproom. Removing his gloves and hat, he asked, "What brings you to Montreal, Thomson?"

"I needed a border less busy with detectives. How about you? Is your friend Margrave working out of Canada East now?" I got right to the point, aware of the little time I had before the train left. Who was Wallace working for? He presented himself to me as a Southern sympathizer, an industrialist from a wealthy Baltimore family, so I went along with his ruse, or perhaps this was his truth and his journalistic pursuits were a ruse.

"Perhaps, but there are others here with the same agenda," Wallace continued. "Look around you, man. In this dining room alone, who do you see?"

I scanned the room cautiously lest my eyes meet a familiar face

                                                          LINDA BRAMBLE

from another life. Jacob Thompson was known to have a suite of rooms upstairs. I didn't want to replay the episode of the Queen's Hotel in Toronto. Impatient, Wallace directed my line of sight.

"Over there," he said, slightly tilting his head toward an arched window.

"That's George Sanders," I said warily. "I understand Clay's meeting Sanders tomorrow with funds to hire lawyers for the Raiders' defence."

"You don't say?" said Wallace, mocking the fact that it wasn't news to him. "Now look again. Who's Sanders with?"

I strained. The man with Sanders was good-looking, with dark wavy hair and a full handlebar moustache.

"Could that be the actor John Booth?"

"You tell me," said Wallace, toying with me.

"Yes, I'm certain. That's John Wilkes Booth, the actor. Is he in a play up here?"

Wallace baited me further. "A better question might be, my good man, 'What might a turncoat Northern actor be doing with a man of Sanders's ideological proclivities?'"

"How do you know Booth is a turncoat?"

"Wake up, man. Booth has made no secret of his zealous patriotism for our cause."

"But what could Booth offer Sanders?" I asked, trying to simultaneously hold two opposing views of Wallace's loyalties.

"Look at it the other way around. What if Sanders was offering something to Booth?"

"Booth doesn't need money."

"Of what can an actor never get enough?"

"Applause? Approval? But for what?"

"Think about it," said Wallace as he smoothed the fingers of his leather gloves resting beside his drink on the table. "What if our government is giving Booth the approval he needs to accomplish his ends?"

Wallace was enjoying the cat-and-mouse game he was playing with me. I was playing the innocent courier clerk becoming more and more glad that I hadn't confided in Wallace. "And his ends are the same as Margrave's?"

"Now you're on the right track."

"But where does Margrave fit in? I thought —"

Wallace stopped me in mid-sentence. "Hush, Thomson. Northern agents are in the woodwork around here. If overheard, we could both be arrested for conspiracy." He was speaking just above a whisper as he rattled off the information he had on Booth. "He's been involved in clandestine activities for years, most recently in the smuggling of drugs to the South, at great personal cost, I might add. With Booth's travels as an actor, he has opportunities to infiltrate the most sophisticated circles."

"You amaze me, Wallace. How did you discover this about the actor?"

Wallace looked away as if to consider whether he was going to reveal any more information. "Margrave …" he began as he reached his hand across the table to reinforce the gravity of what he was about to say, peering directly into my eyes. "Margrave's tried to recruit me on many occasions. Knowing my admitted weakness for celebrities, he tried to entice me into his fold with talk of a close association with the star himself. Tempting as it may be, I've resisted."

"Where's Margrave now?" I asked, not wanting to sound too eager.

"I can't tell you."

"Can't or won't?"

"He's asked me to trust no one regarding his whereabouts, Thomson. I hope you understand. My word is my bond."

"I see. But where will his next move be?"

"The less a courier knows the better." Wallace lit a cigar. "No offence, but couriers have been browbeaten for much less."

"Even a courier is curious. Perhaps I could include a message from Margrave about the progress of his campaign. I should think risking my life to get his message through the lines qualifies me for a little trust." I let Wallace think I was irked.

"He's chosen to stay quiet. I didn't mean to anger you. His grand scheme takes much concerted arranging. I wouldn't be surprised if Sanders and Booth are involved with him."

I pulled out my watch. "I have to go, Wallace, but stay in touch."

"Do give my regards to Clay."

"You'll probably see him before I do. He's expected here soon. I'd be grateful if you didn't mention our meeting." This put me in a beholding position with Wallace, which somehow didn't feel right. Something was telling me to question the extent to which I could trust this man. It took me years to listen to that voice in me and trace its message.

"Ah, yes, have no fear," Wallace said. "The border crossings at Plattsburgh and Kingston are far less crowded with army personnel, but

 LINDA BRAMBLE

he might not understand that necessity for delay. Stay out of harm's way," said Wallace. "There's much intrigue in this snowy town that could blind the eyes of an honest man's good judgment. Watch the Montreal papers, Thomson. I'll reach you there, if necessary."

I rang the Notman bell, then, as the sign directed, walked in.

"Is that ye, Thomson?" asked Notman from inside the studio.

"Yes, sir."

"Come on back."

I stamped my shoes free of snow and entered the studio. Mrs. Notman greeted me wearing a day bonnet and a shawl. "You must be Mr. Thomson," she said, eyes dancing with mischief.

"Yes, ma'am, and you must be the fine Mrs. Notman I've heard so much about."

"That I am. Well," she said modestly, "Mrs. Notman, that is. Now, lad, take off your overcoat, if you please."

"My overcoat, Mrs. Notman?" I said, starting to worry about making the train to New York City should she want to offer her hospitality.

"Aye," said Mr. Notman, entering the room. "Give it to Mum now, lad. Times a-wasting. Just like the bachelor in ye to board the train looking like a ragamuffin, buttons all akimbo. My good wife is at the ready with needle and thread poised to tidy ye up!"

"It's part of the service, Mr. Thomson," tittered Mrs. Notman.

"Ye don't mind if she replaces a few of those war supply buttons with some we've had specially made, now would ye?" Notman was grinning broadly.

"I assure you, I'm most pleased by your concern over my appearance," I admitted. "I am dishevelled, but my train, sir ..." I was flummoxed by the photographer's insistence.

"I haven't lost my wits, lad. Indeed, I may be saving your life."

Then it dawned on me what the photographer had done. "Masterful, Mr. Notman. Absolutely masterful."

"How did ye expect to get through Union lines with a photo of Rebel soldiers on your person? How had ye planned to explain that?" Notman looked stern.

"I'm not sure, but I won't have to explain anything now. May I see one, Mrs. Notman?" She handed a button to me, carefully separating the metal cap from its base. Tucked inside was a minute portrait of seven men looking stately and solemn in front of a jailhouse door.

"Now, young man," scolded Mrs. Notman, "don't lose your coat!"

"I won't even take it off."

"I assure ye," said Notman, "this weather won't allow otherwise." He rested his arm on his wife's shoulders and watched proudly as she cut the last threads and handed me my coat. "Now be off, lad, or you'll miss your connection."

"I can't thank you enough for this kindness, Mr. Notman," I said. Reaching into my bag, I pulled out a pouch of sovereigns. "This small token can't repay your generosity." The old Scot started to reach for the coins when his wife poked him. "Like I said, lad, be on your way." Then both Notmans nudged me out the door.

21

I Meet Another Union Agent

The fifteen-hour train ride to New York City from Montreal was scenic, yet I was indifferent. I should have been marvelling at the ancient formations of the Catskills and the Adirondack Mountains, yet my state of mind was unsettled. The Notmans had been kind to me. I was the man who they trusted was on a mission. Would they have behaved differently if they discovered I wasn't on a mission to further the Confederate cause? I questioned whether I would ever accept that deceit toward them and my exploitation of their services was just another casualty of war? By the time the train was speeding through the Hudson Valley on the last leg of the trip, even the hypnotic turning of its wheels gave me no rest.

At one point I dreamed of staying in New York City for a day to visit my parents, fall asleep near my brother, and wake up to the comforting smells of my mother's cooking. The thought snapped like a bone breaking when the unrelenting and unreconciled truth of my life entered my thoughts. My parents' grief after losing my brother at Bull Run and their resolute anger with me for abetting the escape of their slaves made such a visit ridiculously impossible. The line between my duty to support my father and what I thought was right seemed so clear in those days. I now doubted the valour of forsaking his interests for the freedom of others. I never thought I could make peace as an adult with the acts of my adolescence.

New York's central terminal was a discord of bodies and pandemonium, yet it came as a welcome relief. I could concentrate on more practical activities such as locating my departure track to Washington City rather than contemplating the integrity of my life. Romanesque archways supported two-and-a-half-storey ceilings giving the space a cavernous yet sanctified feeling. As impersonal as it was, and as without family as I was, it felt as if I had come home. Nonetheless, there were individuals in the city who knew me when I was articling, so I still had to be careful. In the middle of the large waiting area were long pews of oak benches where travellers sat back to back waiting for their trains to arrive and where I would sit anonymously among them, or so I thought.

After checking for the next train to Washington, I bought a few newspapers and found a seat in a row where I could see my track while I waited. Most of the news related to the coming federal election, hailing the Democratic nominee, General George McClellan, and caricaturing President Abraham Lincoln as ludicrous and ungainly. Then I found another piece in the *New York Herald* by Sanford Conover — one that shocked me with its candour. Wallace, writing as Conover, described how he'd gotten arrested on suspicion of being one of the St. Albans Raiders:

> I had no sooner entered the Tavern than, being a stranger, all sorts of questions were put to me as to who I was, whence I came, etc. Not feeling inclined to gratify their impertinent curiosity with the truth, I gave them to understand that I was a Rebel and had just arrived from Dixie. A few hours later I was arrested on suspicion of being one of the St. Albans Raiders and carried to Montreal ...

Wallace/Conover described how the Montreal Court of Justice held him in jail for two days because no one from St. Albans could identify him. He continued:

> You will probably find in your issue of Nov. 3rd a telegraphic

report of the arrest at Lacolle of James W. Wallace on suspicion of being one of the Raiders. I am the person referred to; and by that name, with the "W" in the middle, I am known here.

The piece astounded me. Why was Wallace making a public disclosure of his real identity? As Sanford Conover, he frequently had articles in the New York papers sympathetic to the Union side. Why had he chosen this time to reveal himself? Why had he sustained his charade as Wallace just a few hours ago with me in Montreal? Surely, he had already filed his story? If I hadn't known Wallace better, it might have seemed a foolish move. Wallace must be up to something more complex, I reckoned, something about which the Rebels were fully apprised, or else they would never have trusted him again.

"Have the man's machinations made you incredulous?" said a voice from the seat that backed mine.

Startled, I turned around. "Hyams, what the hell are you doing here?" The last time I'd seen this Union agent was in Toronto when his carriage was passing in the nick of time as Ben Wood was trying to recollect my real name. Hyams looked exhausted. A two-day's growth stubbled his face, and lack of sleep had drawn sunken dark circles under his eyes. "How the devil did you spot me in this crowd?"

"Providence, Montgomery," he said. "I haven't much time. If I can't get through to Washington, you must carry a message for me."

I turned back to avoid notice as Hyams spoke close to my ear amid the din of departing and arriving trains.

"There's a venal conspiracy in place to set fire to a number of New York hotels." Hyams voice sounded shallow and weak. This must have been the same operation I'd overheard Clay telling Tucker about while I was waiting to see him in the hallway of the residence he was staying at in St. Catharines.

"When?" I asked.

"I don't know, but soon. The Rebels will be placing a series of clockwork machines in several hotels plus one at Barnum's Museum to be set off simultaneously so that the fire department in each place will be unable to attend to the great number of calls. The conflagration could destroy the entire city. You must convince Assistant Secretary of War Charles Dana to take immediate steps to thwart their plans."

I was stunned but had to sit passively. He intended to get the message to General John Dix in New York City so troops could be on alert, but pleaded with me that I deliver the same message to Dana in Washington. "Perhaps someone along the line of command will take precautions."

"I'll do my best, Hyams," I said. "Go, get some sleep and food before you collapse. You're in no shape to make the trip back to Canada."

"I'm finished up there now. My life will be of questionable duration when Jacob Thompson figures out that it was I who betrayed him and Larry McDonald, the Canadian who's supplying the explosives from his munitions operation in Toronto." Hyams was grave to the point of desperation. "Those volatile supplies are currently being brought to New York in small bottles by a Toronto chemist. I'm here trying to learn the names of the men he's delivering them to. As soon as I find out, I'm on my way to Washington."

"Is there anything else I can do?"

"Finish reading your paper. The last time I saw you I warned you about Wallace. Maybe now you'll pay attention."

"I thought he was one of ours, but I'm doubting that now."

"Play the man like a fiddle, but don't ever sing his tune. There's something not quite right about him." Hyams slipped away.

Once in Washington, I walked to Dana's office but not without doubling back several times to be sure I wasn't being followed. I delivered the sealed dispatch from Clay requesting the Vermont Raiders' commissions and Clay's request for reassignment, but since it was wax-sealed with Clay's stamp, I was delayed in completing the leg to Richmond while Dana had another stamp engraved. On a previous trip, I had supplied Dana with Canadian stationery so that any new envelope could appear to be in the original wrapper. I also told him about Hyams's message regarding the Rebel plan to set fire to New York, but because I had no word of when, where, or how, Dana could take no actions on it.

I told him of my suspicions about James Watson Wallace and gave him the buttons Mrs. Notman had sewn on my coat. Dana's people would enlarge the miniatures into viewable size. I left it up to the department to determine if any of the men in the photograph was the disaffected Colonel Margrave.

When I finally arrived in Richmond, Confederate Secretary of State

Judah Benjamin, greeted me warmly, gave me lunch and a fresh horse, and sent me on my way back to Canada with an answer to Clay's request for reassignment. The documents that would expiate the Raiders would follow, but not with me. Benjamin had to confirm the necessary documentation with President Davis. Clay would have to send another courier the following week.

22

Washington Is Aroused

When I arrived at the Stephenson House Hotel in St. Catharines, Sarah Stephenson was in the lobby talking to Louis Contri, the Italian son-in-law of Sanders, the Confederate man who'd spoken of the necessity to assassinate Lincoln. As she talked, she continued arranging a massive bouquet of dried flowers in an urn she'd placed on top of the round mahogany table. They seemed to be speaking in whispers. I was getting more and more angry with the thought that this married man might be making overtures to Sarah and she was doing her best to ignore him without causing a scene.

Working intently clipping and positioning each stem, she hadn't noticed that I'd taken a seat on the other side of the foyer. When Contri finally left, she circled the table to see if her arrangement held its harmony from all views, then spotted me.

"James, you're back!" She rushed to sit beside me. "Why, you scoundrel, for just sitting there. Why didn't you say something?"

"I found it pleasing to watch you, but not that flirtatious Italian, Contri. Was he bothering you?" I'm not sure what I was thinking in those days about what the future might hold for us, but at that moment I felt protective and elated to see her.

"No, he's quite harmless. You've been gone over a week. I was beginning to be concerned about your welfare." She placed her hand on mind. "Are you all right? You look tired. Can I get you a cup of tea or a glass of —"

"Hold on, my sweet," I interrupted. "I'm fine for now sitting next to you." I leaned close and whispered, "But I confess to a deep desire to hold you close."

Just then a bellman appeared. "Excuse me, Miss Stephenson."

Sarah slipped her hand away. "Yes, Charles?"

"Your uncle's looking for you, miss. He says it's urgent."

"Everything's urgent with my uncle." She stood, straightened her dress, and touched my cheek. "I'll find you later."

I went to my room and prepared to report to Clay, and within the hour, I was in his study.

"You got through," said Clay, a remark made more as a confirmation than a query. "I understand the border was swarming with General Dix's troops."

"Yes, sir, but only as I was leaving Canada, not as much upon my return." I pulled Secretary Benjamin's reply from my bag and handed it to Clay, who read the message with concern.

"And the documents for Montreal?"

"No, sir," I admitted. "Secretary Benjamin said you must send another courier in a few days. The appropriate papers should be prepared by then."

Clay paced, blowing his breath into his hands to warm them. "Would you be ready to return in a day on a different assignment, Thomson?"

"I would."

"We must get as much done as we can before these frigid northern snows immobilize us." He pulled his shawl tighter around his neck.

"I understand, sir."

"You've heard about the results of the election?" he asked as he fed the fire in the hearth in his study.

"Not much, sir, just the early speculations."

"The behemoth Lincoln has won the election for a second term. All that gold we gave to the Copperheads out west was meant to rally voters in the Northern jurisdictions against Lincoln. Lot of good that did." When the log took hold, he stood watching it for a moment. "Empty promises and greedy men combine poorly when organization and leadership are lacking. I should have recognized them as rogues from the start." Clay was grey.

He dragged a wingback chair closer to the hearth and motioned for me to do the same. "Only victories are the stories of history." He studied the flames. "The South is dead. We're nearly bankrupt. Not only are we about to be vanquished, we and our cause will be erased as if we never existed. I can't bear it. I must return to my Ginnie and my Alabama."

From my point of view, I was elated with the election results. I knew that Dana had furloughed thousands of soldiers to make it to their polling stations in time to cast their votes for Lincoln. The strategy had worked, but I had to remain impassive in front of Clay. He paused for a moment to read the replies I'd handed him. "It seems Secretary Benjamin has kindly relieved me of my commission here in Canada. Before I leave there's one last diversionary campaign under way that I believe can save the few lives and what little property we have left."

Clay folded Benjamin's reply and tucked it in his breast pocket. "What I ask you to carry back to Benjamin is a measure of military necessity indispensable for diverting some of General Sherman's troops in his murderous scorched-earth campaign to the sea. Now listen carefully, Thomson."

Summoning his servant, Clay began pacing back and forth as he composed his thoughts. When the servant arrived, Clay turned to me to explain his scheme. "As you know, the federals have learned nearly every trick for searching couriers if they have reason to doubt you. Now with the snows of the north and the rains of Pennsylvania and Virginia, I've devised a plan to enable you to keep this next dispatch secure, hidden, and dry." Clay shifted his position, trying to get more comfortable with what he was about to say. "Forgive the indelicacy of my request, but may I have your trousers, Mr. Thomson?"

Without question I removed my trousers and handed them to Clay, who gave them to the servant standing beside him. "He'll be just a few minutes, Thomson. You'll be fine by the fire while he sews the dispatch between the double thicknesses of your twills. Here's a blanket for your legs."

The thought of turning right around and crossing the lines again didn't bother me. I still felt physically strong. There were many points of entry through the lines. They were long, and for the most part, unguarded, if a safe route to take was known. It was the mental acuity it demanded that exhausted me. Always watching for the furtive looks of strangers, picking out the detectives in the crowd, never trusting even the women who travelled the trains and coaches, for their spying activities during the war were beginning to equal that of the men. I could trust no one, but then again, neither could anyone trust me.

                                              LINDA BRAMBLE

Clay sat back in his chair, drawing the shawl around his shoulders and placing a woollen blanket around his legs. "I'm unaccustomed to the climate, you see, but I must admit I've never felt as strong as I do now. It's a good thing, too, since I don't expect a winter trip through Halifax to Bermuda will be a balmy one." Clay described his trip back home to his wife with mixed emotions. "If the port of Wilmington is blocked, and if I don't get arrested, I might have to go through Texas and across the Rio Grande, which might require many months, so I shall need all the strength I can rouse. Yet the thought of returning to Ginnie and being on Southern soil, no matter how it's been despoiled, fills my heart with joy. I must return home. We've lost so much. All we have left is each other. Do you have family back home, Thomson? Clay's glassy gaze was fixed on the fire.

"No, sir."

Clay paused, wanting to know more, but his sense of privacy guided him to a different subject. "Where's home, Thomson?"

I didn't want this friendly conversation to go on much longer. How long could it take to sew a dispatch into the lining of a pair of twills? Clay was so trusting. The day would come when I would betray him, too. It would be much easier if there was distance or disregard between us. As Clay continued to empty his heart, I mentally resolved that this would be my last crossing.

What I carried was very important, since Clay had never before taken such uncommon care to guard the safety of a dispatch. It would remain unsealed until I placed it in Dana's hand, but something told me it had everything to do with the Rebel plan to set fire to New York City. I arrived in Washington late Sunday morning and took it directly to the U.S. War Department, requesting Dana to come quickly. I informed his aide that I would need a seamstress because what I carried was in the seam of my trousers.

By the time Dana arrived, the aide had ordered a pair of government issue trousers for me to wear while Dana and I waited for the seamstress to carefully unlock the stitches and retrieve the dispatch. When he read it, he was visibly shaken and asked me to wait while he hand-delivered it to Secretary of War Stanton, who was home in bed with a cold.

23

"You Will Be Taken, Searched, and Jailed"

I ran my fingers around the inside of my collar, pulling at it until the knot of my tie loosened. I wouldn't have felt it proper to loosen it entirely, even though the clean collar I had buttoned on was stiff and uncomfortable. Dana had been gone for over an hour, delivering the dispatch. For Stanton to accept this on a Sunday meant that he, too, regarded the dispatch more seriously than other messages I'd carried.

The resolute look on Dana's face when he returned reminded me of a Spanish proverb I once heard about the two phrases for which there was no reply: "Leave my house!" and "What do you want with my wife?" I had the clear sense I was about to discover a third.

"Here's a pistol, Montgomery," Dana said. "The president wants you arrested." Dana took a seat behind his broad desk to better calculate my reaction.

I was aware of the sensation of heat burning my face from the inside out. He had just handed me a four-shot pepper-box revolver with intricate swirled markings cast onto its silver grip.

"You do know how to use it, I hope?" Dana asked.

"Yes, sir," I replied, even though I'd never had to fire a handgun in combat. Nor, for that matter, did I ever have the desire to do so.

Dana pulled an envelope from his pocket and read aloud the details of my next assignment. "You'll have the dispatch resewn into your trouser lining." His voice was clipped and commanding. "Your horse will be ready at dusk, at which time you'll take the road you normally use in passing through the lines. You'll be at Coxe's Tavern outside Alexandria at nine o'clock this evening to water your horse."

Both Dana and I pulled our watches out at the same time. It was one o'clock in the afternoon, and Alexandria was a two-hour ride by horse.

"Colonel Henry Wells," Dana continued, "won't permit you to reach the line. You'll attempt to evade his custody. He'll catch you after a brief resistance on your part. Your gun will be taken and you'll be searched, arrested, and jailed. You'll give your name as George Patterson. Any questions?" He placed the envelope of instructions inside a folder.

I felt like a top whose string had just been yanked, sending me reeling around the floor for the amusement of the War Department. Words seemed to flail away from me due to some centrifugal force. All I could think to say was: "What's going on?"

"You need only understand, Montgomery," said Dana, "that the Confederates, while sheltering themselves behind the British government in Canada, have succeeded in organizing and outfitting a military expedition against the United States and are taking the war in another direction of terror and civilian mass murder. The message that Hyams gave you is confirmed regarding their plan to burn New York City. With your dispatch, we now know which hotels are targeted and when."

I had come to know Dana as an approachable man with a brilliant intellect and an unabashed admiration for Lincoln. For his part, Lincoln had taken Dana into his innermost confidence because of Dana's uncompromising conduct. Dana had become the eyes and ears of the president, operating at the heart of the war through the Secret Service he'd organized only a few months before and of which I was an early initiate. I never saw him with a more sombre sense of urgency than I did that day.

"The stakes are high," he continued. "Even though there's much Canadian sympathy for the Southern cause, the British government is about to protest the violations of their neutrality. We would refuse to accept responsibility for Rebel actions, forcing the government into an ultimatum, and who knows, perhaps even a declaration of war with Britain, all the doing of the Confederates. It's very serious. We don't want a war with Canada, but we'll declare if we have to."

As if ridding himself of a menacing sense of helplessness, he took a deep breath, stood, and moved from behind his desk to stand closer to me. Picking up the dispatch, he pointed it toward the ocean as if directing it at an unseen parliamentarian on the other side. "You carried the names of twelve hotels slated to be burned on November 25, the day after Thanksgiving when the hotels will be filled to capacity with families and friends."

Dana closed his eyes for a moment before continuing, imagining the potential toll of innocent people. "While this affords evidence that can't be gainsaid, the mere possession of it isn't sufficient. It must be found in the possession of the Confederate dispatch bearer. That, of course, is you. And the circumstances attending its capture must be established in such a manner that the British Foreign Office won't be able to dispute the genuineness of the document. We must have this paper in order that the secretary of state can make his case to Britain."

"I understand, sir."

"The president has asked that we get you out of the scrape, if we can," Dana said, trying to assuage my apprehensions, which at this point were many.

"If you can?" I repeated, my voice bordering on insolence, which I immediately retracted. "Excuse me, sir. I meant no disrespect."

Dana moved nearer to me to bridge the impersonal space remaining between us. "You'll be fine. I'll see to it."

"That's what the husband must have said to the Lothario when he returned with the husband's wife."

"Come again, Montgomery?"

"Never mind, sir. Gallows humour."

Just before midnight, a carriage drove up to the door of the War Department with a soldier on the box and two more in the cabin. The forward seat was occupied by Colonel Wells and me, his prisoner. No one in the carriage knew I had walked quietly out of the War Department only a few hours before. Colonel Wells handed me over to General Christopher Augur, reporting that I had offered little resistance but was very violent and outrageous in my language and boasted fiercely of my devotion to the Confederacy and my hatred of the Union.

Throughout Augur's questioning, I remained scornful of my captors. Even as they examined my clothing piece by piece, I remained the dogged Rebel. To keep my mind clear and my attitude consistent, I conjured Clay's patrician face before me, reminding me of the virtues of being a loyal son of the Confederacy. My hat and boots were first searched. When they found the dispatch in my trousers, they paid less attention to me than they did to the nature and method of its capture. Augur dictated a memorandum to a young clerk who had it ready in minutes for Augur and Wells to sign. To be on the safe side, Augur signalled two other officers to also sign it for verification before he sent me off to the Old Capitol Prison.

Until the Civil War, the Old Capitol Prison had been a school and a boarding house. When the war broke out, the federal government purchased it to hold prisoners — rebels, prostitutes, and those men and women disloyal to the Union.

I lay on a cot, blunted by fatigue, hunger, and misgivings. If the plan backfired, would Dana keep his word or would he conveniently forget about me because he would be too embarrassed to claim me? Would I be regarded as just another casualty? If Dana were to keep his word, how long would it be until something happened? But what could happen? They couldn't simply free me. I studied the few filaments of light that laced through the window at the end of the passageway. I knew I wasn't alone. The cell smelled of urine and another man's sweat.

"Why ain't you in irons?" a gravelly voice from a darker corner of the cell demanded.

"Who's that?" I asked.

The voice came again, but this time it was more indignant. "I'm askin' the questions around here. I says, why ain't you in irons? You special or just too stupid to try anything?"

I sat up and strained to focus on the grimy face of a man in his thirties, his ankles and wrists manacled and chained to thick iron clamps in the wall.

"Don't worry, me-bucko. I ain't going anywhere, as you can see. Who the hell are you, anyways?"

"Who wants to know?"

"Thomas Jefferson, that's who. Shit, boy, don't mess with me. I been here too long to suffer a smartass. Now what's your fuckin' name?"

"George Patterson."

"Now that's more friendly-like, George. My daddy's name was George. I'm startin' to like you already, Mr. George Patterson."

I placed the man's accent closer to Tennessee or Virginia than the coastal regions of the deeper South.

"Mine's Seaborne," he said. "The Thirty-First Tennessee Regiment called me *Colonel* Seaborne. What's your rank, soldier?"

"I'm a civilian."

"Then why are you here?"

"I'm a courier."

"*Do-oo* tell, Mr. Fancy Britches. A courier? For who?"

"That would betray a trust. You know better than that, Colonel."

"Then where you from?"

"Canada."

"You're not a Southerner. You must be Canadian. I declare. I never met up with a real live *Canajun!*"

"I'm not Canadian." I tried changing the subject, but the man seized upon me like a hungry hound.

"If'n you're not Canajun and not a Southerner, what are ya?"

"I'm a Virginian, Colonel. Just educated in Northern schools." That seemed to satisfy the man's curiosity. Before I was assailed by another question, I decided to take the lead. "Have you ever been to Canada?"

"If'n I nary met a Canajun, how could I have been to Canada? You ain't too bright, Mr. Fancy Britches Northern-Educated, are ya? But I did know a guy, all's he talked about was those godforsaken provinces and how he was goin' to make his way north to gather up all our soldiers who escaped from Yankee hellhole prison camps around Lake Erie and then cross over the border by boat to lay low."

"He wasn't planning on mustering those poor men, was he?" I asked. "They've seen enough active duty for one war."

"Yup, that was his plan. He was aimin' to muster a regiment on Her Majesty's royal-ass soil. He was so bloomin' riled he could taste it. Seems he was a former Yank come over to our side, but I never did trust him. He was so fire-eatin' crazy humiliated by the federals that he swore he'd get back at them one way or t'other."

"What did they do to him?"

"He never did say, but they sure as hell caused a conflagration in him."

There was little else to do but listen as the Rebel rambled on. I felt like a prisoner's prisoner.

"Yes, sir, he swore to me he'd get back at those lousy, stinkin', slime-suckin' summa-na bitch Yanks. His very words." He had raised his voice for the benefit of the guards.

"You met him then?"

"Of course, I met him. Would I be tellin' you a story third-hand? He sat in that very cell over there." Seaborne pointed at a barred cubicle directly across from ours.

"What was his name? Maybe I know him."

　　　　　　　　　　　　　　　　　　LINDA BRAMBLE

"He called himself Margrave ... Colonel Margrave. But I never did learn how he earned his bars."

I sat straight up.

"I see I finally got your attenshun."

"I might have heard of him. What did he look like?"

"Well, when he come in, he looked gentleman-like. About six feet tall, slim, wore a handlebar with ends so neat they'd shame a prince. Brown hair, about ear length, last I seen him."

"What set him apart from other men?"

"A slight hook to his nose that disturbed an otherwise fine lookin', rather pious face."

"Did he say he came from Baltimore?"

"You know him then?"

"Yes, I might." The description came too close to that of James Watson Wallace. If Wallace was masquerading as Margrave, what did he have to gain? Fraud was one thing, but plotting to assassinate the president was something much more ominous. Perhaps Dana was already onto to him and that was why he'd him arrested and thrown into Old Capitol. But if that was the case, why had he been released — cut loose to foment and incite others to go along with his cunning plans?

"I wouldn't want him as an enemy," Seaborne said.

"Why's that?"

"You're not a very curious man, Mr. George Patterson. You haven't even asked why he was here at Old Capitol, now has ya?"

I could hear the rattle of iron against iron as he spoke. The man's needling was starting to rankle me, but this could be a setup, so I kept myself in check. "So why *was* he here?"

"Fraud, Mr. George Patterson — pious fraud, that is." The man jangled his irons again for emphasis and then dragged himself as close to me as his chains would stretch, exhaling fetid odours of tooth decay and hardened bowels. "It's the devil's shadow whenever there's pious fraud, don't you think? He deceives while payin' homage to virtue and we fools blush in consent."

The man turned to pee into an already full corner pail. I grimaced and looked away.

"Yes, sir. It was the easiest place I could think of at the moment —
before I lost my nerve entirely."

Dana examined the wound and called his aide to get me a supply of
needles and morphine for my trip back to Canada. "A more deliberate
and less dangerous wound it couldn't be. But it doesn't look trivial. How
do you feel?"

"I'll be okay, sir."

"Can you make it back without having it dressed?"

"That would raise suspicion. With the assistance of the supplies
your aide's collecting, I'll not only make it back, I'll probably enjoy the
journey."

"I have to warn you, Sergeant Major, an advertisement offering $2,000
for your recapture will be running in the *New York Herald*, Pittsburgh
Gazette, and *Chicago Tribune*."

"You're not going to make this any easier, are you, sir?"

"If it's ease you're looking for, why didn't you join the navy?"

On my way to buy another horse for the trip, for mine was confiscated
on the way to jail, I stole some bed linens from a clothesline to bind
my arm. The morning editions of the *Herald*, with the advertisement
for my capture, would be out by now, so I bypassed New York City and
rode north to Tarrytown before the morning editions had a chance to
arrive. Whenever my arm began to throb, I gave myself an injection.
From Tarrytown I made a connection on a coach to Schenectady, then
the sleeper to Buffalo. George Patterson wouldn't have passed customs,
but James Thomson did.

24

A Confusing Mark of Traits

I was aware that I smelled of dried blood as I entered the opulent lobby
of Stephenson House. In an ordinary season, the hotel would have been

quiet with summer guests gone home for the winter. But this year its guests remained long after the leaves had fallen. Either they had no home to go to, or getting through Union lines was too hazardous. They remained in suites at the hotel, waiting for winter in Canada West to begin or the war to end. There was no rush for me to report to Clay who was still in Montreal, a fact for which I was very grateful. From the reception desk, I could see my employer, Colonel Stephenson, in his office, but thought it wiser to check in with him after I could make a better presentation of myself.

I asked the reception clerk whether Dr. Mack, the hotel physician, was on the premises. My wound was in desperate need of dressing. The clerk reported he hadn't seen the doctor all day. I went to my own office to find Cyril Spears at our shared partners' desk. "Hello, Spears. Have you seen Dr. Mack?" I asked as if I'd been just down the hall and not gone for over a week.

"I'd say by the look of your lack of sea legs, you're the one who needs him, guv," sniffed Spears. "And a good bath. No offence, Thomson."

"Indeed, I do need a bath, but the good doctor's first on my list. Is he in his office?" I repeated with some exasperation. I hadn't survived the trip to St. Catharines to be waylaid now.

"He's seeing patients here this morning. And a good thing for you, I'd say. Tough trip back this time?"

"Trip?" I asked, in no mood to be challenged.

"Yes, trip. You *are* a courier for Clay, after all, aren't you? No need to answer, but everyone knows."

"Is that so?"

"Anyone here, with a good reason, could turn you into the federals for, dare I say *treachery*, at any time for running for the Confederates. There's good money in that. That's if they were of that certain turn of mind."

"I suppose so, Spears. Were you thinking of the potential in that?"

"Well, no, but I just got to thinking since anyone of us could turn you over, then why hasn't someone already done so? Then I thought, perhaps someone already has and you're being protected by Union agents."

I had removed my jacket and began unpeeling the blood-hardened strips of linen I'd tied around my arm. The scab that had formed was starting to open and bleed.

"Oh, my God, Thomson. That's a serious wound." Spears came over to take a closer look. "If I didn't know better ..." He bent to scrutinize it, but the smell of infection pushed him away. "My God, it's a bullet wound! We've got to get you to Dr. Mack fast."

"My very thought. About that other stuff, Spears. Don't think too much, or else I'll think you had something to do with this."

Spears was aghast. "But surely, Thomson, you don't think that I —" His shoulders rose as he opened his palms toward me in an exaggerated appeal of innocence. "I swear to you, Thomson, I've not mentioned my mental meanderings to a soul. And ... you certainly don't think that I —"

"I don't know what to believe." Spears placed his arm around my shoulder, but I shrugged him away in feigned valour. "I'm all right, Spears. Just get me a pass for an attendant and a bath."

Dr. Theophilus Mack was one of the most learned physicians in Canada West. His patients came from as far away as Toronto and Buffalo. Word had it that he had recently turned down an offer to assume a sizable practice in Boston. I could see the doctor was with someone — a woman with a yapping dog on her lap was prattling about the doctor's wife and whether or not Mrs. Mack would come for tea, or then again should she call on Mrs. Mack first, or might she, Mrs. Mack, want to bring their lovely daughter?

Dr. Mack waited patiently until she finished, then suggested that Mrs. Mack would be most happy to receive her but couldn't assume to know his wife's appointment calendar. He suggested that a call after tea would be most appropriate. But that was the end of his patience. When he spotted me sitting in the waiting room, he motioned for me to come in. "You'll excuse me, Mrs. Barrett. My next patient is here."

The woman uttered "Dear me" repeatedly on her way out the door with the pooch safely tucked under the shelf of her ample bosom. I took a seat beside the doctor's desk.

"Let me take a look at that arm, Thomson," Mack said as he closed his office door and pulled a tall stool over to sit by me. "It looks nasty." The doctor gingerly held my arm, turning it as he might rotate the fragile arm of a newborn.

A current of indebted relief went through my body as Mack inspected me.

     LINDA BRAMBLE

"This wound is two days' old, Thomson. Why?" The doctor was kind but stern. "Why have you waited so long before having it dressed?" He stood and began gathering soap, a basin of water, and some gauze.

"When you get shot by a Yank in Yankee territory, you don't press your luck by asking another Yank for a bandage!" I replied, hoping to stave off the doctor's further queries.

"Sounds serious. You've been carrying for Clay, I hear," said Mack, arranging his cleaning materials close to my arm.

"Is there anyone here who doesn't know?" I asked, protesting just enough to be convincing. "Excuse my impertinence, Doctor, but I'm starting to question my ability to get through the lines when almost anyone here could inform the Yankees in advance."

"You have a point, Thomson. This should, however, keep you behind the desk for a while." The doctor dabbed away small bits of gunpowder, dried blood, and cotton threads from around the wound's most open area. "Any longer and I might be reaching for a saw and not a bandage. You're lucky the bullet bypassed the bone. How did it happen?"

I fabricated a story of the guards firing and hitting me as I escaped. The doctor was commenting on my heroics when I noticed a section on the his bookshelves entitled "Diseases of the Mind."

"Excuse me, Dr. Mack, but I have a question perhaps you can help me address."

He tamped salve over my wound. "Go ahead."

"Have you ever heard about individuals who tell you they're one person but in actual fact are someone else?"

"Couriers do that all the time, Thomson. You ought to know about that first-hand."

"Yes, Doctor, but I mean a man of a different sort whose pretense isn't premised on an act of duty, as I interpret mine to be, but rather as a way of life, depending on the circles he travels in and the personal gain he can accrue."

"You mean an imposter?"

"Yes, yes. Is that written up in any of your books?" I pointed at the particular section on Mack's bookshelf as he finished wrapping gauze around my arm, tearing the ends and tying them snugly in place.

"There," Mack said as he finished. "See me in a couple of days and keep this arm dry and out of mischief." He stood to get a closer look at his books. "There are a few volumes that might be of interest to you. One is by Philippe Pinel. Another is by a researcher by the name of Benjamin Rush, and a third …" He searched the spines for the author's name. "Ah, here it is … James Prichard." Mack's collection was precise and in order. He handed the books to me. "Can I trust you to return them?"

"Yes, by this afternoon — promptly. Thank you."

"It's a confusing mark of traits you'll be reading about. Confusing because the assumptions of conduct that we apply to ourselves aren't applicable to an imposter."

"Why's that?"

"By our actions, we discover what we really believe, and simultaneously reveal ourselves to others. Because an imposter's manifest actions are illicit, he reveals not himself to us but what we *wish* to see in him."

With the help of an attendant, I struggled in and out of a bathtub and succeeded in keeping my dressing dry. I shaved, dressed, and reported to Colonel Stephenson, looking brand-new. As long as I was doing work for Clay, Stephenson made no complaint, nor did he request an explanation as to my whereabouts when I was away from the hotel. The colonel would usually nod to me with an insider's smile and a confidential wink. I suspected Clay was paying for the innkeeper's neutrality and silence.

Work had piled up while I was gone, but my focus was first on reading. *"Mani sans delire,"* wrote Pinel. "Insanity can exist without defects in the reasoning capacity." Pritchard, an alienist and ethnologist, wrote: "… a madness consisting of a moral perversion of natural feelings, affection, inclinations, temper, habits, moral dispositions, and natural impulses without any remarkable disorder or defect of the intellect or knowing and reasoning faculties and particularly without an insane illusion or hallucination." Rush was more to the point and confirmed my worst fears: "Lucidity of thought with socially deranged behaviours … a life-long pattern of irresponsibility without corresponding feeling of shame over the personally destructive consequences of their actions."

I was haunted by the description I read of the ruthless, selfish, callous, and depraved manipulations people with this disorder exhibited. The fact they had little remorse about the consequences of their actions made them extremely dangerous. Since they derived pleasure from bamboozling others, they could damage the lives of innocent

　　　　　　　　　　　　　　　　　　　　LINDA BRAMBLE

people. It was with a an illusion of sanity that these moral outlaws were able to trick others into accepting them without suspicion. They were masters of legerdemain.

Being taken in by Wallace and his multitude of personas made me feel like a fool. But his most dangerous guise was possibly that of Margrave. How had it happened? Wallace's articles on the necessity of assassination alone could be powerful instruments for fomenting acts of terrorism in the name of political necessity. It had to be Wallace that my prison mate was describing. If the proud Wallace's efforts to raise a regiment had been rejected by Union officials, that could have been motivation enough for him to seek retribution. If my hunch about Wallace's state of mind was correct, his journalistic deceptions could be excused as *noms de plume*. But to fan the flames of assassination, as he was depicting through his contrived depictions of his so-called Margrave and without any "corresponding feelings of guilt or shame," could be a mendacious act of moral perversion with most dire consequences. He would continue to be in my sights.

I finished the afternoon by completing some correspondence for hotel guests and memoranda the colonel requested I distribute to all hotel staff. My thoughts, however, kept darting in and out about Sarah. Earlier I had asked her whereabouts, but no one had seen her for the past day or two. Possibly, she was on a buying trip for her uncle, I thought.

Working methodically until I reached the bottom of the pile, I found a note that caught me completely off guard. It shouldn't have been there. I quickly covered it up with another sheet of paper before anyone could notice. Then, checking to see if Spears was around, or the reception clerk, or the colonel, I finally lifted the paper off the note. It was like uncovering a log to find a hand or someone's disembodied face smiling up at me.

Having the note didn't put me in jeopardy. It was the assumption that I might know how to decipher its coded message that would. I reached for my oil-silk bag. The bag was the visible evidence of my profession — the clerk, the lawyer, the man of letters. It was also my talisman of survival since my college days, through law school, and as a law clerk in New York City, then as a scout for Brigadier General McDowell in Virginia, and now as a spy. It was my companion, the thread of my past life that was safe to weave into my present.

I lifted the flap to the compartment where I kept my nibs and pens.

Beneath them I felt for another flap. Its unworn texture was brittle compared to the softness of its now-supple cover. With the smell of leather came a flash of the promise I'd to myself when I was given the bag: "I will fill it with honourable things."

Beneath the flap, my hands groped deeper into an inner pocket. Feeling my way through mental images of its invisible geography, I slipped my fingers through another chamber with a slit in the side lining. There, my fingers touched the cool metal of a small disc the size of a two-cent piece. I pulled it through the tiny maze of the bag's compartments and closed my hand tightly as I brought it out. No one was around. I placed the disc on the desk and began matching its outer ring of letters against each letter in the jumbled message of the note. Deciphered it read: "I could a tale unfold whose lightest word/Would harrow up thy soul."

I collected the correspondence I'd prepared for guests, filing some in their respective mail slots for signing, tying signed letters in a string for mailing. In the event Colonel Stephenson came looking for me, I told the desk clerk I was going to the post office to get the letters into the afternoon mail. On my way out, I passed the barbershop and left a note requesting Aaron to be at the storage tunnel at 6:00 p.m. when late autumn's dusk would turn into a protective shield.

25

Trapped

The black guard at the mouth of the tunnel recognized me and gave me a lamp while I waited for Aaron Young to arrive. The cases of summer bock and amber ale were all but gone with the exception of a few stacked by the door. I pulled out two cases to sit on, helping myself to two bottles in the process.

Aaron soon arrived, shaking his head. "What does it take to catch you?" he said, referring to our literary guessing game.

I handed him a beer. "That's not a very cordial greeting to a wounded soldier of war."

                                                        LINDA BRAMBLE

"What do you mean *wounded*? Has someone else gotten to you before I could?" Aaron unsnapped the top off the bottle as he spoke.

Feeling safe that no one was around, I related the events of the previous week, which amused him at the foolish extremes I'd gone to convince the Rebels of my loyalty. Admittedly, it wasn't the smartest act, but that day it had seemed like the only act I could play to maintain my cover. I wouldn't repeat it, however.

"I could put your brains in a gnat's butt," Aaron said. "You're lucky you didn't lose a limb."

"What's this secret that would 'harrow up my soul'? And where in hell did you get hold of that Rebel cipher? Washington cracked it and gave a decoder to me. Only a few in the Rebel government have one."

"Where I got it isn't important right now. It's about Sarah."

Just then a whistle blew, like the trill of a cardinal sending a warning to invaders in his territory.

"Somebody's coming," Aaron said.

"Who knows we're here?"

"No one — and no one must see us together or your work in Canada is over for good. Let's get out of here. They're probably here to smoke me out. Come on. I'll explain."

"Is there another way out?"

"Yes, but it's at the other end of the tunnel, and I'm not sure the entrance will be open when we get across."

"Great," I said sarcastically. "I can hardly wait to find out."

"Cut the light."

I snuffed the wick in the lamp, putting us in darkness so complete that I couldn't tell if my eyes were open or shut. We hugged the narrow passageway.

"Stay close to me," whispered Aaron. "I know this tunnel. There's a split under repair farther down. One false move and we're underwater."

"Don't worry," I whispered back. "I'm behind you."

"You always have been, Richard, and I've been grateful for that."

"What's this all about?" I asked as the narrowing passage slowed our escape.

"I've complained to the city fathers about the tyrannizing way my brothers and sisters have been treated in school. They've separated them as if they were too dumb to learn what the white folks learn. They need an education. They deserve an education. Damn whites. No offence. Some folks are riled enough to show me who's the overseer around here." Feeling the passageway narrow, he warned, "This is where we have to start to crawl. Just pray they haven't sealed the other end for the winter." A small beam of light filtered through the tunnel. "They've discovered our beer bottles. Where there's light there's bound to be fire and smoke."

"Crawl faster, man," I said, twisting to see if anyone was following us.

"With that arm, you'd never keep up with me."

I punched the sole of Aaron's shoe.

"Try me."

"Okay, let's go."

We snaked through the ever-narrowing tunnel. I used one arm to pull my weight through the rock-filled channel while holding my injured arm to one side. The stones on the tunnel floor were beginning to cut through the fabric of the elbows of my coat, tearing at the tender flesh. The smoke came like a wave gathering energy as it pushed through the passageway, moving slowly at first, then hungrily filling the passageway behind us.

"Careful," Aaron said. "This is the point we need to cross over to the other wall. I'm sure of it. The pilings were loosened by a paddlewheeler last week, but no one's been out to fix the damage."

We rolled over on our sides, trying to avoid putting weight on the damaged support.

"Can you feel the water?" Aaron questioned, asking for confirmation he really didn't want to receive.

"I can. Not a good sign."

"I can think of other places I'd rather be. We've got only a few feet to go."

My lungs were starting to burn with every breath. Only half-breaths could feed my need for oxygen. The tunnel opening had narrowed to the point where we could only squeeze our shoulders through what were now the ceiling and the floor as we inched our way in front of the advancing column of smoke.

"Are you all right, Aaron?"

"I'm fine. I'm at the trap door."

I felt Aaron start to push against the tunnel exit, but with so little room to manoeuvre, he could use only the power of his forearm to try to wedge it open. There was no way I could possibly squeeze through to help him.

"It's sealed tight as a drum," Aaron said.

"Can you pry it open?" I coughed, covering my mouth from the smoke.

"With what?"

I pulled my arm down in front of my chest, trying to reach into a trouser pocket that was so jammed along the side of the tunnel wall that I could barely wedge my fingers through.

"I've got a pocketknife in here somewhere," I said as I straightened my leg to make more room for my hand to search inside. I was able to pull it through the confined space and signalled Aaron. "It's on your left. Can you grab it?"

"Yes, I've got it."

"Hurry, Aaron …"

"Quiet … I hear someone outside. I didn't think anyone knew where the trap door was on this side of the canal. This could be it, my friend. It's been nice knowing you. If only I could have taken my entrance exams, I'd be in law school now instead of ambushed in a tunnel with you."

He was able to crank the trap door open. Its hinges squeaked out years of accumulated clogged rust. Smoke puffed out the door as we peeled ourselves away from the sides of the tunnel, gasping for fresh air as we entered the crisp night. But no one was there.

"It might be an ambush," Aaron whispered. "Be careful."

"Go slowly. I'm ready when you are."

Aaron crawled out farther and crouched beside the slanted hillside door, searching for men hiding in the surrounding brush. Still no one appeared. I spotted a large figure approaching Aaron from behind.

"Behind you!" I yelled.

Aaron swung around, shouldering the figure to the ground. I swivelled behind him, searching for others.

"Get off me right now, you little chicken choker!" demanded the voice.

Aaron jumped back like a boy shocked straight by the sight of an angry bear. "Auntie? What are you doing here?"

The old woman stood, brushing grass from her vast petticoats and skirts. "You better be damn well glad I am. You can thank that snoopy little brother of yours who's always takin' after you a-lookin' for adventure. When those men hit the watchman, he hightailed it back to me all by hisself. Then took me to this side of the canal where he know'd you'd be a comin' out."

"Never thought I'd be grateful to that runt shadow." Aaron could see his little brother peering from behind me and ruffled the eight-year-old's soft black curls, then swooped him up and wrapped his arms around the proud little boy.

"We'd best be gettin' you boys outta here," Aaron's aunt said. Pointing to me, she said, "You, young man, you bleedin' from head to toe. Both of you, get behind those vegetable crates on my wagon till I gets you safely across the bridge and away from those delirious white folk. We gots us a river to cross. We ain't home yet." The black woman and her little nephew drove their wagon down the main street, dropping me off just ahead of the lamplighter as he was making his rounds.

Aaron and I had been thrown together in clandestine work, creatures of such different worlds but bound by shared secrets and the things we both valued. That night my sense of the injustice of it all was paramount. We were running from whites, whites like me, who were ready to kill Aaron for his outspoken requests for educational reform for black people like him.

26

Wild Retribution

Because I was dishevelled, I had entered the Stephenson House through the kitchen's delivery entrance. "I've got something for you, Mr. Thomson," said a pantry girl peeking behind the cupboard door when I arrived. The other girls in the kitchen giggled at her boldness, as if she were fulfilling a dare.

"What would that be?" I said, teasing her out of the package of leftovers she held behind her back. I touched her freckled cheek. "Thank you, Emma. You're the answer to a hungry man's prayers." She blushed and ran to join the other pantry girls who gathered her into their gleeful fold. Since the day I arrived, the kitchen had been a source of calm to me.

                                              LINDA BRAMBLE

Besides the attention I received from the pantry girls, which I enjoyed immensely, the kitchen was a haven. Everything was always in its place — graduated sizes of ceramic mixing bowls, butter paddles, cake moulds, tureens, iron skillets, plus pots and pans — always spotless and polished, used, and replaced each day. The kitchen gave me a feeling of order and certainty within my disordered and uncertain life.

The next day a bellman informed me that Clay had requested I meet him at his residence at three o'clock. He had returned from Montreal by rail the previous evening and no doubt had crossed the same bridge from the depot that Aaron and I had traversed perhaps moments between our separate crossings. I was learning that the intelligence business was a game of serendipity and good timing, but how long would my luck last?

Clay was at his desk when I arrived. He was as sympathetic to the trials of my journey as I had expected he would be. The additional scratches and bruises from the night before in the tunnel lent even greater credibility to my story. My loyalty was never in doubt, assured Clay, and my narrow escape from the Union prison guards was an act of valour deserving of a Confederate Southern Cross.

"It was too bad the Union soldiers happened upon you, but at least the dispatch reached its destination and is safely in Confederate hands." Clay then informed me that he had sent a number of agents to Richmond each charged with getting the papers that the boys from St. Albans needed for their release. "Sooner or later someone's got to get through."

"That must be very costly," I commented, wondering who else he'd sent.

"I assure you, Thomson, There's always plenty of money to pay for an enterprise that's worthwhile. I'd go myself if it weren't for both Canadian and Union officials. They've been alerted at the border to arrest me for my covert activities here. So I wouldn't get very far."

I wondered if he was assessing how deeply his life had plunged since his days in the Senate, to now being a fugitive at large.

Clay pushed some papers to one side and paused, stroking his beard. "By the way, I understand you made your last trip across by way of Montreal."

"Yes, sir." I realized it must have been Wallace who had told Clay, even though I'd asked him not to. "I assumed the Buffalo crossing would've been armed with border detectives. I didn't want to take a chance."

"You saw our friend Mr. Wallace there, I gather."

"Yes, as well as Mr. Sanders, but I don't think he noticed me."

"I'd be careful of Sanders if I were you," Clay said. "I wouldn't put any trust in him. He's a good man to do our dirty work — that's all. Because of his reputation as an inveigler, he can speak to people it would be unseemly for us to contact. But don't trust him. Don't trust his son-in-law, either, for that matter — the Italian Contri. Something about him gives me serious misgivings."

As if trying to locate the reasons for his doubts, Clay gazed out the window for a moment as a carriage stopped across the street to let passengers off in front of a residence — people living seemingly normal lives in contrast to his own. "Wallace, on the other hand, is reliable," he finally added, his eyes still transfixed as the passengers disembarked.

Clay's assessment of people seemed to be built on naive oppositional elements that created the rationale on which he decided who to trust and who not to. Either a man was aggressive or co-operative, wise or foolish, responsible or irresponsible, humble or proud. There was no shade in between. Wallace belonged in the category of people who were trustworthy or untrustworthy.

"As a matter of fact," he continued, "I'm thinking of giving Wallace a commission that would bestow powers of authority on him so he could do a bit of work for me. If I don't, his assistance on our behalf might be seen as the act of a renegade, as our boys in that Montreal prison are fully experiencing."

He looked at me directly and said as an afterthought, "I do trust you, Thomson. You've grown very important to me. I know you won't let me down."

Gaining Clay's trust was part of my assignment, yet I felt irresponsible, for I somehow couldn't summon up the kind of hatred I should have felt for the enemy. That was one of the problems with this horrible war. My brother had died as a Confederate soldier. If I was conflicted, there must have been others who felt the way I did. Someday Clay would discover my dissembling and his misplaced trust in me. How would he feel then? I was doing this for my country, but it was wreaking havoc on my life and how I identified myself as an honest man. I was a lot like Clay in that regard. Either a man was honest or he wasn't. Consequently, every act I engaged in as James Thomson chipped away at who I thought I was.

"I've no one to send to New York City with some boxes that must be delivered by Friday this week," Clay said. "That's within three days. I hesitate asking you, but I don't know who else to trust. Wallace is still in Montreal, and these boxes need to get out by tomorrow."

"I'll go, sir," I replied without hesitation, simultaneously snapping out of feeling deferential to a kind superior. That was one of the most difficult parts of my assignment — the necessity to compartmentalize my feelings when they started to distort my innermost reactions. I also wondered why he hadn't afforded me the safety of a commission. Was I being used as a foil to lead the federals into a diversionary campaign? I wasn't sure what to think. It took great energy to spell out the potential consequences of mistrust and subterfuge had I read the situation incorrectly. On the other hand, Clay wasn't asking me to participate in an operation, only to communicate with his superiors in the Confederate government.

"But your wound. Are you sure you're able to? The trip will be critical to the success of this operation."

"I'm fine. I can leave tomorrow and have it delivered within the allotted time."

"There are other campaigns under way in Buffalo and Rochester that are sufficiently covered, but the New York one is extremely important."

Clay held his head in his hands, occasionally rubbing his eyes, a habit he'd developed when his asthma acted up. But that day he had no symptoms. "I should be more concerned with your well-being, but I fear I have no choice but to send you. Are you certain you're well enough for the journey?"

"Yes, sir," I insisted. "Once I'm on the train, it's fifteen hours of sitting, since the cars do the work. It would be another matter if I were going on horseback."

"Then listen carefully. There are two valises at the train depot in St. Catharines under the name of T.E. Lacey, an anagram of my name. Here are the tickets for their release. Take them to the Exchange Hotel on Greenwich Street in New York City." Clay handed me a card with the address of the hotel. "Deliver them in person to Captain Robert Kennedy. He must give you this sign." He took my right hand and pressed the first joint of my forefinger in the ancient Masonic sign of trust. "He must then say to you, 'True till death.' If he doesn't, don't release the valises to him. You'd be facing someone unknown to our operation. Should he respond appropriately, you reply, 'So be it.' Do you understand all of this?"

Masonic tenets found expression throughout the Civil War. Freemasons went to great lengths to take care of their own, and in this case, to ensure trust.

I nodded and repeated his instructions verbatim.

"If you're up to offering your services, take orders only from Kennedy."

It was evident to me that Union General Dix must have gotten tired of waiting and decided to recall his troops from New York City. Why else would the Rebels feel confident enough to resume an operation in New York? The city was undefended. An attack on New York would relieve General Lee in Virginia, giving the Confederates enough leverage to force peace negotiations on the North. More than eight hundred and fifty miles away in Georgia, U.S. General Sherman and sixty thousand men had just evacuated Atlanta, leaving it savaged in the ashes of a massive Southern defeat. The South seemed to be collapsing under the weight of its humiliation and profound fear of not knowing where Sherman's next blow would be felt. The burning of New York City was an act of desperation and wild retribution.

Thursday, November 24, was the American Thanksgiving. New York City's stores were closed for the day. Friday was different. Stores would reopen to take advantage of one of the busiest shopping days of the year. But on Thursday, families welcomed a beautiful Indian summer day by going outdoors in their holiday best, strolling in Castle Garden at the Battery and along the wide paths that led to the Mall in Central Park. After dinner they retired to their rooms and enjoyed an evening of quiet comfort after a long day.

All the hotels that Hyams said were targeted for burning were glaring symbols of Yankee opulence, each filled to capacity for the weekend. The Astor House, a popular spot for politicians, accommodated five hundred guests. The magnificent St. Nicholas, in the heart of the Theatre District, was also a favourite stopping place, holding a thousand guests. The Metropolitan had six hundred lodgers, while the Lafarge and Winter Garden could house five hundred. Other hotels in town might have been less ostentatious but no less full.

          LINDA BRAMBLE

I hired a hack to drive me the short distance from the station to the Greenwich Street hotel where Captain Robert Kennedy was waiting. A porter heaved the valises onto a dolly and led the way to Kennedy's room on the third floor. It took me several rounds of identification before Kennedy cracked open his door to offer his hand, pressing my knuckle and saying, "True till death," to which I replied "So be it." Kennedy opened the door wider, dismissed the porter, and called on two of his men to lift the valises into the hotel room.

Six men crowded around, eager to unpack them and distribute the contents. They paid little attention to me as they emptied each valise of a hundred and forty-four bottles half filled with an incendiary clear liquid and sealed with plaster of Paris. In the corner of the room, I noticed tins of turpentine to provide a speedier ignition for the bombs they were unloading. From what I could piece together, they were planning to ignite the explosives around eight o'clock the following evening. Each man was responsible for targeting four hotels, twenty-four hotels in all that were confined to the business district around Broadway and the wharves of the Hudson. They were certain that the fire department would be immobilized in its inability to respond because the simultaneous fires would spark other fires and the town would soon be under a conflagration so big that Sherman's burning of Atlanta would look like a carnival by comparison.

I helped the Rebels fill more than a dozen satchels with the bottles, cushioning each one with newspapers, old clothing, and boots. When the job was done, I left, promising to return in the morning. I then boarded a Broadway bus heading for a telegraph office on the other side of town. A furloughed uniformed Union soldier entered the rear door. Although the bus contained several empty seats toward the front, the back was almost completely filled with families returning home after Thanksgiving dinner with relatives. The soldier took the last remaining seat in the back, forcing me to sit in the front facing the driver, which was against my inclination. As a boy, I always headed straight for the back of the bus where I could better survey the comings and goings of passengers. In the front, I always felt as if I was being watched. But in New York being watched was a fact of life. Long before the war New Yorkers took as their prerogative the right to size a passenger up and down in invasive appraisal, like a dog sniffing a newcomer. I knew once their curiosity had been sated all eyes would turn away in indifference.

As much as I tried to shake it, I still felt under a kind of surveillance that differed from ordinary curiosity. I tried to read the *New-York Times* so I wouldn't lapse into mindless panic and do something I might regret. But I had to know what I might be up against. My instincts drove me. I dropped the newspaper in the aisle beside me and glanced back at the rows of seats behind me as I picked it up. That was when I caught sight of the penetrating eyes of the Union soldier. Neither of us showed any sign of recognition, but I was relieved nonetheless. I resumed reading the paper until the soldier stood to pull the cord to signal the driver he was about to get off at the St. Nicholas Hotel.

I followed him off the bus, into the hotel, and up the stairs. The soldier knew I was behind him but said nothing. When he came to his room, he unlocked the door, leaving it slightly ajar. I checked the hallway before entering the room. When I was sure the hall was clear, I entered, closed the door behind me, and stepped into the sitting room where the Union officer stood waiting.

I raised my right hand at a forty-five-degree angle until the top of my forefinger touched the lower part of my forehead, my thumb and fingers extended and joined. "Lieutenant Colonel," I said.

"At ease, Montgomery."

"Permission to speak."

"Go ahead."

"Pleased to meet up with you now, sir. I'd known the thickset Thomas Eckert when he was head of the War Department's military telegraph operations where I'd briefly carried intelligence for him. He had since been brevetted as a lieutenant colonel, working directly on high-level missions for the War Department.

"I recognized you as you boarded the bus," Eckert said. "What are you carrying?"

"Information that, if not conveyed in time, could cost the lives of thousands of innocent people. I was on my way to a safe telegraph office. It's very urgent. Would you be able to transmit it for me, sir?"

"What's it all about?" asked Eckert, accepting my sense of urgency. "The provost marshal's men have been keeping an eye on these Rebels around town for the past month, and they're getting damn tired of waiting. What's going on?"

"These Rebels are serious, sir. I assume that General Dix has

                                         LINDA BRAMBLE

withdrawn his men. The only thing we can do now is solicit the co-operation of the police."

"It's that serious?"

"Yes, sir." After briefing the lieutenant colonel on the operation, the bombs, and the names of all the hotels where I knew for sure the Rebels would be, I asked for permission to sit.

"Granted. Leave this with me. In the meantime, young man," said the officer accustomed to thinking about the welfare of his men, "you look exhausted and hungry. I'm going to send for some food. I want you to eat and then get some sleep. That's an order! I'll see that no one bothers you and that you're safe here."

"I'd appreciate that, sir. Just don't let me sleep through tomorrow. This is one of the hotels they're targeting!"

"I'll have someone stationed at your door," he assured.

When I awoke the next day, it was cold and rainy. Unless the weather improved, the Rebels' plans would have to change. By noon the sky had cleared. Within hours I knew their plan would be put into action. I had imagined the dreadful scene: each Rebel, already registered as a hotel guest, would take a heavy satchel to his room. He would throw the bedding on the floor, douse it with phosphorus, pour turpentine onto the heap, and set it all on fire, then leave, locking the door behind him. This would be repeated twenty-three more times throughout the city. A bright flash from the transom would light up the hallways, smoke would curl under the doors of other rooms, and men and women would burst into the hallways, coughing and screaming for help. One after the other new alarms would blare. Hysterical children would be carried out in the arms of panicking parents. Alarms would shriek from one end of the city to the other throughout the night. I feared the holiday weekend would start with a night of terror because the fire department, though forewarned, would be powerless to cope. I felt helpless to change the course of these inevitable events if Eckert had no luck in reaching General Dix or Washington in time.

Even if Eckert succeeded in alerting the officials, the news would likely reach them too late. If the diabolical scheme went as planned, it would be devastating. But my worst fears never materialized. The hotels had five thousand guests, and if the Rebels had triumphed, many innocent people might have died. As unbelievable as it seemed, to the benefit of thousands of innocent lives, the Rebels' Greek fire merely smouldered and never actually caught fire, although there was a reported $15 million in smoke damage.

One city newspaper reacted with shock at the "diabolical attempt at arson and murder." Another insisted it was "among the most gigantic crimes of history."

My hotel, the St. Nicholas, suffered the most damage. However, by the time the fires started, I was on a sleeper train steaming for the Canadian border. My hunch was that once their work was done the Rebel arsonists would head to Canada, so I wanted to get back before federal detectives blanketed the trains.

Clay's backing of this bloodthirsty scheme was making it easier for me to separate my sympathies. He was slowly transforming in my eyes from a naive idealist loyal to his country to a rational pragmatist who could easily justify the killing of innocent civilians. By the time I reported back to Clay, I learned that all of the arsonists escaped except Captain Kennedy, whose appearance and limp made him very recognizable. If Kennedy was found, Clay was certain the captain would be tried and sentenced to death.

The next morning a hushed antimacassar of gentle snow covered the sleepy grounds. When Clay arrived at Stephenson House where we were meeting for breakfast, I was throwing a couple of logs onto the expansive lobby fireplace. He thought the hearth would be a nice place to meet, so he requested one of the waiters to place a morning tray of coffee and breakfast rolls beside the wingbacks that flanked the hearth. I hardly would have recognized Clay as the same, wheezing man from a few months ago. He was actually pink-cheeked and robust that morning. We reviewed the events in New York City as we ate. Our conversation was strangely casual.

"The use of phosphorus — baffling," Clay said as he placed a spoonful of sugar into his steaming coffee. "It failed in Vermont and again in New York." He stirred the sugar slowly as if trying to extend the mood of the morning's welcomed silence while preparing himself to tackle the more disagreeable topic of what I thought he would have considered the fiasco in New York.

"I've not had a chance to read the latest counts," I confessed.

"According to the fire marshal's report, the boys closed the doors and windows of the rooms where they set the incendiary devices, so when the phosphorous was ignited the fire smouldered from want of oxygen." Clay tore off a piece of roll and took a bite, neatly wiping away with his napkin a tuft of cinnamon that clung to his now collar-length beard. "I suppose the smoke alerted detection before much impact could be felt."

"I suppose. No one's fault, I guess."

Clay sipped some coffee. "I might have made the same error."

"And I."

"The plot's failure isn't for naught, however." He added more cream to his cup. "By all accounts, we've produced a great panic that will take some time to subside." He sank back into the soft leather chair, savouring his strategic success. Slapping the arms of the chairs to signify the end of one project and the launch of another, he sat up. "Now it's time to focus on other things."

"Such as, sir?"

"As I mentioned last week, I'm getting ready to leave the country by way of Montreal and Halifax. I'll need a secretary for the first leg of the trip as far as Halifax. Would you accompany me?"

"Yes, sir, gladly." Montreal would give me an opportunity to confront Wallace with the Margrave story I'd learned about at the Old Capitol Prison. Wallace was either a trickster, a dangerous man of self-serving moral perversion as the French doctor Philippe Pinel had described decades ago, or he was simply an extremely clever triple agent. If Clay was about to give him a commission for clandestine activity, this could be a boost for the North, if indeed Wallace was working for the North. He could be an agent for Britain or some other foreign interest, for all I knew. On the other hand, he could truly be an agent for the South, posing as a Northern journalist, who was posing as a Southern agent. At any rate, Wallace was the man I had to track.

27

Aaron Young's Message

Before I left for Halifax I wanted to find Sarah. She still wasn't back from her trip attempting to secure the documents that would ensure the Vermont Raiders were acting in compliance with military orders and weren't just rogue villains robbing a U.S. bank and taking a life.

It was the thought of her that had sustained me during my entire trip back from New York. I felt a sense of loss that I might not see her before I left again. I imagined how she would look coming in the front doors, down the staircase, or crossing the snow-covered grounds behind the hotel. I tried to imagine her fragrance and how I would inhale an ocean's breath of her when we met. Was I concerned about the dichotomy that defined our separate allegiances? Of course, I was, yet I allowed my affections for her to prevail. I could rationalize that she also provided a convincing cover for anyone who might question my political affiliations.

Scouring Stephenson House, I searched for someone who might know where she might have disappeared, but no one had any information, asking her uncle was out of the question. Then I remembered that just before Aaron and I were smoked out of the tunnel, Aaron was about to tell me something about Sarah. I disliked feeling the way I did about her. For the sake of my autonomy and security, I couldn't allow myself any attachments that might make me vulnerable, particularly with a Southern woman. But she was so lovely and so smart. Occasionally, on my trips when I couldn't sleep, I allowed myself the fantasy of a moment alone with her where there was neither war, nor sides, nor enemies.

Such yearning wasn't good for a man who had to keep a clear mind. Definitely not good. Yet I found myself taking the steps three at a time leading to the barbershop. What could Aaron have to say? Had something happened to her? Shouldn't she have returned by now?

There were no other patrons in the chairs when I arrived. Aaron was sitting at his desk in the rear of his shop, writing, no doubt, another letter to the editor or the school board trustees. I nodded to him, as any customer would to a shopkeeper. Aaron pointed to the chair farthest away from the window and sent his assistant on an errand for clean towels.

"A shave, sir?" Aaron asked as he swept the familiar striped cape around my chest.

"Yes, Mr. Young, and a trim, if you please." I slid my head into the headrest as Aaron cranked back the chair.

"We've been here before," whispered Aaron as he wrapped a strip of muslin around my neck to protect my collar.

"Yes, Mr. Young. I never did get to test your mettle with a razor, did I?"

"Came close, though." He laughed as he laid steaming towels across my cheeks, neck, and mouth.

I pulled my arm from under the cape to lift the towel momentarily so I could speak. "Tell me what you were about to confide before we were interrupted last time."

"Yes, Richard, I've been expecting you." He began stropping a clean razor. "You been away?"

I said that I had, then wordlessly narrowed my eyes and raised my brows as if to say, "Get to the point!"

Aaron mixed a bowl of soap into a lather of suds and foam as he spoke. "One of my sisters is a chambermaid here at the hotel, you see. Now I don't want you to think she's not a trustworthy one with what I'm about to tell you. Because she is."

"Um, hmmm," I mumbled as Aaron removed the towels, my beard now sufficiently softened.

"Well, you see, she found something," he began, slowly spreading the lather onto my whiskers, around my chin, and over my lip.

"Tarnation, man," I said, quickly losing patience.

"Well, you see, she was changing the linens in a guest room when she spied a locket on the dressing table beside the bed. A *golden rose* she called it. It attracted her so that she gave in to the temptation to hold it in her hands, to touch its fineness — an act for which she could've lost her job. Nevertheless, in all her born days, she'd never seen anything as fine. So she picked it up, and in so doing, discovered that the clasp of the locket was unsnapped. Figuring she'd catch a glimpse of the lady's paramour, she peered inside. Girls like looking at a face of love. But the countenance of a loved one wasn't what she found."

I rolled my eyes in exasperation.

Aaron stretched the skin tightly across my neck. Once assured he had full control of the conversation, he continued. "Inside the tiny frame was a miniature wheel within a wheel, with letters circling each wheel in gibberish formation. Now, don't misunderstand me, but she, knowing full well the other business I'm in and suspicious of the wheel's mystery, brought it to me." Aaron was now deftly stretching the other side of my neck with one hand and wiping the blade onto a towel with the other.

"And ...?"

"Patience, my friend," Aaron said as he completed one cheek in long, smooth strokes, and then the other. "Sure enough, it was a miniature Rebel decoding machine." He checked my face for any patches he might have missed.

"What does this have to do with Sarah?"

"Well, it came as a surprise to me." He wiped away the remaining dabs of lather. "And it should be a warning to you."

I sat up and grabbed the cloth from my friend, wiping my face myself. "Don't do this, Aaron. What kind of warning?"

"It would appear that the fair Miss Stephenson isn't the colonel's niece, after all, but a well-placed Rebel spy. That news isn't as bad as the next item I must tell you as a friend."

I braced for what was coming. "Go ahead."

"I saw her travelling arm in arm with the son-in-law of George Sanders — you remember, the Italian, Louis Contri?" Aaron scanned my face for clues to what I might say or do next. "Stay cool, my friend. Don't do anything you'll regret."

28

Toronto, Canada West

Before leaving Canada for the South, Clay needed to brief Jacob Thompson, his co-commissioner, in Toronto. The Queen's Hotel, where

Thompson had a suite of rooms, was Clay's first stop on his way to Halifax. It was all I could do to contain myself when I saw Sarah in the lobby of the hotel the day Clay and I arrived. "Have you been here all month?" I asked.

"Yes," she replied, then explained how Thompson mourned the dismal onslaught of winter. He had heard of her Southern sympathies and skill at entertaining and suggested she might lighten their winter-weary hearts by organizing a salon. "Of course, I was pleased to comply," she told me, exaggerating a bow so low that her skirts puffed behind her. "*Aut delectare aut prodesse est* — I exist to please and to educate. But how unkind it was of me not to leave you a note. I do feel quite thoughtless. Why don't you join us this evening? You'll be most welcomed, I'm sure. I'll see that Mr. Thompson knows all the wonderful things about you that I know."

I know some wonderful things now about you, too, my dear, I thought, then wondered what she actually knew about me. Were we playing a cat-and-mouse game?

As usual, Sarah was a stimulating presence during that evening's conversation with the guests but lingered a bit too long with Louis Contri. What he had to offer her other than Italian lessons was beyond me. I didn't like seeing them together. Wallace also appeared in Thompson's suite that night and was captivating, punctuating his stories with startling details of information only a man of connections and breeding could relate, which enthralled his listeners, not the least of whom was Clay. Wallace also entertained everyone by drawing caricatures.

"Why, Mr. Thompson, I do declare," Sarah said, "it's a frightfully admirable likeness of you that our dear Mr. Wallace has drawn." Sarah passed the sketch around the circle of guests, each one leaning over the other to catch a glimpse.

Clay leafed through the sketchbook on Wallace's lap. "You've portrayed us all, I see. Do your talents know no bounds? First you translate Colonel Dennison's recitation from the German and now this. Acuity with both language and pen!" Clay was effusive in his praise, obviously convinced he'd picked the right man to do some undercover work for the South.

Unwilling to be upstaged by Clay, Thompson stood and raised his glass to initiate a toast. "To genius and improvisation!" He held his glass high in Wallace's direction.

The admirers cried choruses of "Bravo" and "Here, here," joining Thompson in the salute. Wallace feigned surprise, overlapping his palms on his breast in exaggerated humility. Sarah's fawning over Wallace confused me. If she was a Rebel spy, she was concealing very well her awareness of Wallace's Northern proclivities.

Clay, on the other hand, had no misgivings regarding Wallace's loyalties. "You must join me for breakfast, Wallace," he announced as he prepared to leave. "I have a proposition to offer you. The South could use a man of your talent and wit."

"To serve the South would complete my purpose as a man of honour," Wallace replied with a flourish.

"Nine o clock then," confirmed Clay.

On her way to accompany Clay to the door, Sarah passed me, blanketing me with her scent. Rebel spy or not, I still wanted to pull her back under its canopy until I could breathe again.

"Are you coming?" Clay called to me. "I've got a few reports to complete before retiring."

"Of course, sir. I'll be right there." Thompson was lighting a cigar as I approached him to bid good-night. "Kind of you to have me tonight, Mr. Thompson." I felt the knot in my stomach tighten.

"Kind of you to come, Mr. Thomson." Thompson took three or four quick drags in succession, pulling deeply, studiously checking the cigar's tip to see if it was alight. He took his time, obliging me to wait until he completed the ritual. "I see my colleague Senator Clay still holds you in high regard." Thompson held his head to one side as he spoke, as if sizing me up. He clenched the cigar in his teeth as he reached for a handkerchief to dab his swollen, runny eyes.

"I've been tireless in my efforts to prove his trust is well placed," I said, receiving my overcoat from Sarah, brushing her hand with mine.

"I'll wager you have," Thompson said, still holding the cigar firmly between his teeth, squinting as he spoke. "And I've relaxed no effort in attempting to prove him wrong, but we all know what a stubborn old goat he is." Thompson scanned his audience of nearby guests for their reaction to his quip. They complied with solicitous laughter. Sarah nonchalantly tugged at her lace gloves to conceal the fact she was becoming unnerved. I could have been wrong, but it seemed that she didn't want the conversation to escalate.

Noticing Sarah's uneasiness, I interceded. "Please allow me to prove otherwise, Mr. Thompson. I'm accompanying Senator Clay until Halifax and would be in your debt if you'd allow me to demonstrate my loyalty by serving you in your next campaign."

Thompson smiled thinly. "That remains to be seen. On the other hand, you've been shot by Yankee pursuers at the lines I hear, and you do have your supporters. Some more ardent than others." He glanced fondly at Sarah as his audience tittered politely. Sarah's face reddened. "I'll need a courier with this trial in Montreal looming shortly and your employer so conveniently taking his leave."

The jab at Clay was uncalled for. Thankfully, the senator was talking to another man in the hallway, out of earshot. Curiously, I felt protective of him. "Senator Clay is doing his best to secure their commissions," I said, but Thompson paid no attention.

"Meet me in my rooms tomorrow," Thompson said instead. "See William Cleary, my secretary, about the time." He curled his arm around a passing guest and dismissed me, turning momentarily to add, "If you fail me …" Then he finished his parting words by raising his forefinger and thumb as if it were a pistol and feigned a shot aimed directly at my heart.

The next day in Thompson's suite, watching him dismiss his callers was like trying to keep a dizzy eye on a game of battledore and shuttle-cock. Each entered flattering him, while he, in turn, returned a volley of considerable vanity. Then each guest showered further compliments until Thompson squired them to the door. After shutting the door behind each sycophant, he said something disparaging such as "Another splay-footed western Democrat Yankee," or "I don't know which is worse — to be ruled by Negroes, vile abolitionists, or money-grubbing Copperhead mercenaries. All they want from me is money."

When he was finished, he locked the door and placed Cleary, his secretary, as sentinel, refusing any new callers. Then he walked to the window to watch the phenomenon of snow falling like cottonwood tufts in spring, shedding their downy seeds to a dispersing wind.

Turning to speak to me, he appeared more composed, as if mellowed by the view. "Look, Thomson, maybe I could use you, but I won't know until after next week. Our boys from Clay's St. Albans debacle will know better whether or not the U.S. will be able to extradite them. They're good as dead if the federals win this war. Lincoln's denied my courier safe passage to Richmond. For some reason, you seem to know how to get through. As long as you get through, I don't care who you're working for. Keep in touch once you're in Montreal."

And that was that. Thompson unlatched the door, indicating it was time for me to join the others standing in the hallway — the rebuffed and those still waiting, all hoping to be permitted an interview to present their cases for business. Most were Canadians there to secure contracts — ammunition dealers from Toronto, arms and torpedo manufacturers from St. Catharines, Greek fire assemblers from Windsor. Copperheads from Indiana and Ohio, too, were frequent visitors, always looking for gold. Others were there seeking commissions — the documents that ensured they were working for the Confederate government and not simply itinerant spies or organizers. Four civilian members of the Sons of Liberty, the anti-Lincoln group from the northwest, had recently been sentenced to be hanged for spying. Military duty versus civilian activism had different consequences. When a man acted on orders from his commanding officer, he was a soldier and free from legal retribution. When a civilian did the same thing, he became a renegade traitor and an egregious spy. If the South was victorious, the latter would be my fate. Jacob Thompson would make sure of that.

The hallway smelled of stale tobacco and men's breath soured by winter's constipation, ravaged molars, and the bitter prospects of a prosperous war coming to an end. I felt nauseated. Cleary reached behind me to close the door, jealously marking his territory as the faithful secretary to Thompson, just in case I was getting any ideas.

"Is it always this busy?" I asked, scarcely clearing Cleary's officious arm.

"This is of little consequence compared to some of the visitors Mr. Thompson gets."

"That so?"

"Why, yes. Just a few days ago the actor Booth, the younger brother — John Wilkes — was here. He's truly a loyal son of the South."

"Why was Booth here?" I asked. "Surely, he's no manufacturer looking for a contract."

Cleary sniffed. "He's anxious to play a part offstage for the South he loves so dearly. His determination is most impressive."

　　　　　　　　　　　　　　　　　　　LINDA BRAMBLE

"And Thompson's response?"

"He's given Booth an official rank of colonel in the detached service." Cleary scrutinized me. "Has he given you a rank?"

The secretary knew very well that Thompson hadn't but needed to reinforce his suspicions of me. Again, I ignored the man's childish remark. "His trust in my service will be rank enough. You'll excuse me, Mr. Cleary."

At the end of the hall I'd caught sight of Clay talking to a tall man with thick coal-black hair. The senator had motioned me to join them. As I approached, Clay reached for my hand, considerately, yet keeping me at bay as he listened to the other man finish talking. They spoke in undertones so muted, even as close as I was, I couldn't hear what they were saying. Then another man pulled Clay aside.

Turning to me, the senator said, "Wait for me, Thomson. I'll return."

That left me and the tall, reticent man face to face with nothing to say. I felt annoyed. The space Clay had just occupied seemed to create a vacuum, sucking me into an awkward conversation with this sombre stranger. His eyes were deep-set, wide apart, and an eerie, translucent blue that seemed embittered and mistrusting. He was tanned and clean-shaven and stood as if anchored to the centre of the earth, held by the magnetic pull of the poles.

"Cold up here," I ventured.

"I reckon."

"Don't much like the cold, do you?"

"Nope."

"Up here long?"

"Nope."

"Name's Thomson, James Thomson." I offered my hand, assuming he would accept that a friend of Clay's would be a reasonable reference for a returned gesture of civility. But the man wasn't at all inspired by the idea of sociability.

"I'm Canadian," the man suddenly volunteered with an unmistakable Southern drawl. He shoved his hands inside the pockets of his Confederate military-issue canvas coat and turned the other way. I excused myself and waited for Clay by a window instead of forcing conversation with an unwilling stranger.

A two-horse sleigh pulled into the front of the hotel. Five early-morning tourists unpeeled a layer of buffalo robes from their laps, laughing as they stood to take the hand of the footman. Sarah was hosting the group. I ran down the stairs, pushing aside men who cluttered my way. She was standing beside the sleigh until her excursion passengers were safely inside the lobby. I stood shivering to one side.

"Miss Stephenson," I called, as if I were a guest needing information on city shopping or sightseeing. "Might I have a minute?" She untied her bonnet and smoothed her hair. Her cheeks, crimsoned from the cold, looked like a schoolgirl's — freckled and crystal, smelling from the outdoors. She approached, glancing around imperceptibly to be sure she wasn't noticed responding any differently to me than she would to any other guest.

"Yes, Mr. Thomson?" Her indifference bothered me.

I pulled her to a more private alcove. "Are you avoiding me, Sarah? I miss you. And I'm worried about you."

"You needn't be, my dear. I'm fine, but I must parcel my time with judicious care lest I betray us both. You do understand?"

"Perhaps."

"I'm leaving for Montreal tomorrow morning. The trial of our boys will resume. I'll be staying at St. Lawrence Hall. Clay's told you no doubt by now that I, too, am serving our beloved South. Will I see you in Montreal? We may have more time to be together then."

She noticed a lost-looking elderly couple and offered to escort them to the buffet of hot cocoa and cookies that was being served. I hoped she would glance back, but she didn't. *In what way is she serving her beloved South?* I thought. *Don't let affection cloud your duty.*

I returned upstairs. Clay had been searching for me. "Ah, there you are, Thomson." He motioned to a bench. "I understand you spoke with my young friend," he added, fishing for a voluntary summary of the conversation.

"You mean the tall chap?"

Clay nodded expectantly.

"Yes, we spoke. If you could call it that."

"Did he tell you who he was?" Clay seemed worried that a great secret might have been exposed.

"Only that he was Canadian. I got the impression I was to mind my own business."

Clay laughed. "Yes, he's a Canadian all right ..." There was a suggestion that I should take the tall, taciturn fellow's comments with a grain

                                                        LINDA BRAMBLE

of salt. Then he leaned over to my ear and confided, "But he's one we trust. Now let's be on our way to Montreal. I intend to give our boys in jail a piece of my mind and some money for their defence to quiet the likes of Jacob Thompson and his lackey, Cleary. Let it not be said that I abandoned our boys, as idiotic as I think their behaviour in Vermont was."

29

The Trial of the Raiders

The St. Lawrence Hall Hotel, where I was staying, was a five-minute walk to the courthouse where the trial of the St. Albans Raiders was taking place. It was the most important trial Montreal had ever witnessed. Since the trial's last session, the case had reached international proportions when U.S. Secretary of State William Seward threatened Governor General Lord Monck of the British Provinces with trade reprisals and the possibility of more severe retaliatory measures if the provinces didn't act quickly to prevent future U.S. invasions by Rebels operating in Canada.

The scales in the balance of power had tipped and were spilling a mist of hostile uncertainty over U.S. and British North American relations not felt since the War of 1812. Both sides could now say, "Once invaded, twice shy." Compared to the appalling wreckage of lives and property that General Sherman and his troops had left in Atlanta on their march to the sea, the Raiders' invasion of Vermont was paltry. However, it had greater consequences, for now four "nations" were involved rather than two: the Union and Confederacy, Canada, and Great Britain. Trivial events could have enormous consequences, so I watched this one carefully.

Sarah agreed to meet me for breakfast the next day. "Have you seen the report of the trial filed by our mutual acquaintance?" she asked, handing a newspaper across the table to me. "It just makes my blood boil to read his Union bias, yet he so ingratiates himself among us." She removed her gloves with quick, angry tugs. "I hope you didn't think

I was taken in by him in the Toronto salon. However, before I tell my superiors of my suspicions, I need more evidence."

I couldn't tell her that Clay was about to commission Wallace for some unknown clandestine operation he'd planned. If only I could confess to her who I really was, I thought, perhaps the hole of guilt that had opened up in me would go away. This was prevarication at its best: lying for the sake of one's country, for an ideal preserved, was a man's duty. But being untruthful to the woman one loved was an act of treachery.

"James, are you paying attention to me?"

"Yes, of course. The paper." I started to stretch for it but stopped. "You know I've missed you." I reached instead for her hand, which she withdrew for fear of being noticed.

"Yes, James," she whispered. "And I you, but we must postpone our own concerns and conceive a plan to disclose the insidious and perhaps diabolical Northern sympathizer Wallace. If, indeed, he works for the Southern cause, his motivations will be confirmed, so either way, for good or ill, his intentions will be transparent."

"Go ahead. You have a plan?"

She was still clutching the paper. "After you read this, I'll tell you what I have in mind." She pointed to one section in particular. "Read this part most carefully."

The Southerners here are jubilant, and boast of all kinds of bloody work that they have in progress, and the people must lose no time in rallying to the defence of their property. It is rumoured that the Raiders have gone to take part in a raid in Detroit.

"There," she said, refolding her napkin and placing it defiantly next to her plate. "You see? Very few knew about that plan. Now the Union will redouble its troops along the border. I wouldn't be at all surprised if that weak-kneed Lord Monck also follows suit, proving Jacob Thompson's point. He says the bane and curse of carrying out anything in this country is the surveillance under which we act."

Another couple took a table nearby, forcing Sarah's to find a more composed way to express herself. "I declare, James," she almost whispered, "we must expose this Wallace for the Yankee spy that he is. Right now no one would believe either you or me. We must find evidence or

                    LINDA BRAMBLE

else the facile Wallace will charge us with libel. We must get into his room again, but this time to take out the evidence of his double identity."

"That could be very dangerous, Sarah, unless you have access to the chambermaid's keys again."

Crestfallen, she said, "No, of course I don't."

I tried to give her some comfort. "My hunch is that he's convinced Thompson and Clay that he's a double agent, acting as a spy for the North, but in actual fact, he's really working for the South."

"If he's working for the South, why would he reveal our plans in Detroit?"

"Perhaps Thompson agreed that would be good propaganda. Get General Dix to send troops to Detroit, then invade another border city such as Buffalo."

"Do you trust him, James?"

"No, not at all."

"I guess all we can do is bide our time and keep an eye on him when we can."

"I agree, Sarah. One step before the other. I shall be in New York City on my return from Halifax. Senator Clay and I leave today."

"James, you must be vigilant."

"I'll interpret your concerns for my welfare as acts of affection that will carry me through the overland journey to Halifax. I must admit to a certain jealousy when I see you with Louis Contri."

"Louis? Oh, my darling. Make no never mind about Louis. I'll explain someday. For now, I, too, may be travelling."

"To where?"

"Richmond. I thought Clay might have told you."

"He mentioned he was sending a few couriers but didn't mention you. My God, Sarah, that's too dangerous."

"Please don't worry about me, love. Jacob has requested an escort for me, a Mr. Surratt, John Harrison Surratt, to accompany me for safety's sake. And the boys will need me. It's certain the governor general will issue a new warrant, and I'm afraid the whole St. Albans affair will start all over again and our boys, just released from jail, will still have no papers to confirm their military affiliation."

"I beg you not to run the risk of going through enemy lines."

"They'll never question a woman, James. Never a woman." Sarah peeked around my head, catching a glimpse of someone coming. "Put the newspaper away, James." There was urgency in her voice.

"Pardon, Sarah." I misunderstood and gave the paper back to her.

She tucked it underneath her napkin. "He's in the dining room and approaching our table. Don't look back."

"Wallace?"

"Yes."

"Good morning to you, Miss Stephenson," an ebullient Wallace greeted. "Thomson. May I join you? A long way from home, aren't we?" He flipped his coattails out from under him as he sat down.

"Do join us, Mr. Wallace," Sarah said. "Blustery morning, wouldn't you say?"

Wallace smiled. "But pleasant here by the hearth. You've finessed one of the best tables in the dining room."

"You won't mind if I'm only able to stay a short while, Wallace?" I asked. "I must get my valises ready."

"Your valises? Such impedimenta on a day like this?"

"Yes. We're taking the train."

"Would you be accompanying Senator Clay on his trip to Halifax?"

"As a matter of fact, yes, I am. He's asked me to assist him so he can use the travel days profitably."

"Do I assume he has matters to attend before leaving his post here in the provinces?"

I tried to appear noncommittal.

"If so, he'd better hop to it. If the authorities are aware of his presence in town, he might as well unpack his trunks."

"They're not about to find out, are they?" I said.

"Not if we can help it." Wallace laughed, trying to deflect my remark.

"I declare, Mr. Wallace," Sarah interjected. "Do try the marvellous Brittany crepes they make here filled with apple and cinnamon. A most pleasant taste of warmer weather against these winter winds."

Wallace wasn't about to be diverted by Sarah. "Have you heard anything about this so-called raid on Detroit by our boys? War gossip, you know. Out of the frying pan and into the fire, I say." He placed his elbow against the back of his chair, surveying the breakfast room as he spoke.

Suddenly, it occurred to me how I might discover more about the elusive Wallace. "No, I know nothing about that, Wallace, but have you heard of the latest mission under way?"

Wallace sat forward, eager for my insider's information.

"I hear Clinton State Prison's next — same as St. Albans, only there will be more of our men involved. The forces are mustering in Baltimore and New York City as we speak. What I heard was they're proceeding at various points near Ogdensburg disguised as hunters, and on the appointed day, they'll take the train, seize it, and invade Plattsburgh. Other cities across New England will be next until Dix can get his troops together to drive them out."

Sarah appeared thunderstruck, at first, as I revealed a plan to the man we were only minutes before trying to prove a traitor and a spy.

"My dear," Wallace said, "certainly this is more than your delicate ears can sustain."

"No, no, Mr. Wallace, I'm a woman of the war. We're hardened to the necessary acts in which the military must engage and in which our boys and their leaders have the fortitude and will to carry on the good fight."

"Yes, Wallace, the good fight," I added. "We all must contribute to that in our own fashion, and now I must be going to do my small part." I took Sarah's hand and brushed my lips against her fingertips. "Will you excuse me, Miss Stephenson? The next time we meet won't be soon enough." I acknowledged Wallace as I returned my chair to the table. In turn, he gave me a dismissive nod.

"Goodbye, Mr. Thomson," Sarah said. "Safe journey. On second thought, would you wait a moment for me?"

"Apple and cinnamon, you say?" Wallace murmured, apparently indifferent to me or Sarah. "*Incroyable!* Don't mind if I do."

"Mr. Wallace," Sarah said, "would you mind terribly if I left you, as well? I feel most rude, but the manager promised to meet me at this time to help me prepare an itinerary for a day of French shopping for some of his guests."

"As it pleases you, Miss Stephenson, as it pleases you. You leave me in good disposition, however, here by the fire." Wallace leaned across the table and slyly lifted Sarah's napkin in a way, I surmised, she found invasive. "I see you were reading a Yankee journal and have it opened to an account of the trial. If you're finished, in the absence of your delightful company, I should be ever so pleased to have the news, no matter how vile the rag."

"Be my guest, Mr. Wallace. But reading the Yankee press can be a disturbing introduction to the day."

"Your felicitous warning is kindly accepted. However, I'm most used to their outrageous elaborations of the truth."

"I'm sure you are," Sarah said.

30

Tracing Wallace

Clay was safely aboard the blockade runner *The Rattlesnake* on his way back to the South as I made my way to New York City with an idea of my own how to track the true identity of the inscrutable Wallace. Sarah never had a chance to tell me her proposal, but I pursued a hunch, just the same. I began my investigation of Wallace by visiting one of the papers I knew he wrote for, the *New-York Tribune*, where I had a trusted contact.

The *Tribune* was located in one of the noisiest pieces of real estate in New York, Printer's Square, across the street from the *New-York Times*, where printers and other newspaper suppliers were nearby to keep the papers running smoothly. During the spring and summer when I was a law clerk, I recalled going to the top of the *Times* building to scan the cityscape through telescopes mounted on the top floor. The telescopes were probably still there, but what was missing at street level were the air- and strength-testing machines, run by Gypsies who would coax my friends and me to test our manhood by seeing who among us could hold the most air in his lungs or decide once and for all who was the strongest.

On the steps in front of the *Tribune*, the peanut vendors, however, were still there. Fresh roasted and fragrant, for a penny a bag. I couldn't resist. The warm bag in my hands evoked happier times.

The previous managing editor of the *Tribune* was now my boss, U.S. Assistant Secretary of War Charles Dana. I was in the city to look up the old friend on the staff of the paper who had originally encouraged me to enter the intelligence service.

The editing room was busier than I'd remembered. Tables were arranged adjacent to one another in an open room. Some of the sub-copy editors were gathered around examining proofs of early stories that were already set in type. Others were turning the material put before them into balanced stories — scrutinizing the dull parts, excising the unnecessary with the ruthless scratch of a pencil. These were the detached fact-finders, the newspaper's conscience, the priceless men with an instinct for news, working in obscurity yet who were the sober backbone of the paper.

My friend, Rodney Burke, was one such sub-copy editor. When I arrived, his head was bent over his desk as he assembled a story from telegraph files submitted from field correspondents. I pulled a chair in front of the desk, crowding him.

"Hey," said my offended friend, disturbed at the invasion of his space. "What the … Richard — Richard Montgomery. How the blazes are you?"

"It's been a while, Rodney."

Burke was the man I strove to be like — careful, studious, inventive, disciplined, with a sharp memory for detail. Our friendship went back to our college years. He swept around his desk at the same time I stood to better greet him. We embraced ruggedly as friends do, patting each other's shoulders and standing back to assess each other, shaking hands and giving each other playful jabs.

"Son of a bitch," said Rodney. "How the hell have you been? Where have you been? Last time I got wind of you, you'd been shipped off to places unknown."

"Thanks to Dana, your old boss, remember that?"

"Dana couldn't have picked a better man." He sat on the edge of his desk. His hairline had thinned, his eyes had darker circles, and he appeared more serious than I recollected. I wondered how my face wore the past year.

"I was sorry to hear about your brother," he said.

"Thanks, Rod. I think of him every day."

"So what brings you here?"

"You know I can't tell you my business and I know you won't ask, but I need a favour."

"Say it, Rich. I'll do whatever I can."

"I need some information on a certain correspondent your editor uses from Canada. I can give you the articles he's written, but I know he also files under different names. Sanford Conover, for one, James Watson Wallace is another. He also uses Harvey Birch when he submits to the *Daily News*."

Rodney grimaced at the mention of the *Daily News*. "He's writing for that pennysaver of a propaganda sheet *and* the *Trib*?"

"Yes. I need to know his real name and address and where his pay is mailed. Can you get that for me, Rod?"

"Like I said, Rich, I'll do whatever I can. Where can I reach you?"

"I'll contact you by wire in a few days. I'm only here until tomorrow, then I have to return to Canada."

"Oh," said Rodney. "Canada, you say?"

When I arrived at the St. Lawrence Hotel in Montreal by train a few days later, William Cleary summoned me immediately and escorted me to Jacob Thompson's rooms. Thompson looked spent. Filaments of red webbed his watery, swollen eyes. *What was it he couldn't bear to see?*

"Sit down, Thomson!" Thompson ordered sharply, pointing to a swayback Windsor. His lack of grace equalled Senator Clay's possession of it. I set my hat and gloves on the table and loosened my coat. I wasn't expected to take it off.

"Explain this!" he bellowed, shoving a newspaper into my lap and walking behind me. The story on the front page described how several gangs of Rebel desperados were organizing along the frontier to invade the United States again, this time to capture the Clinton State Prison near Plattsburgh to destroy its machine shops, rolling mill, foundry, and barracks. Plattsburgh would be the first plundered; the New England cities of Keesville, Burlington, and Haverhill would be next.

A bit of an elaboration on Wallace's part, I thought. It hadn't taken him long to get the story into print.

Thompson spun around to face me. With one arm against the back of my chair and the other on the writing table beside it, he trapped me as he spoke. "Did you write this, Thomson?"

I stayed steady. "No, sir." I blinked away Thompson's fetid tobacco breath. "I haven't a mind to do such a thing, sir. That kind of pre-emption would hurt our boys. Besides, I can't write. Even if I could, I don't have any knowledge of the proposed campaign, anyway, sir."

                                                           LINDA BRAMBLE

"There's no campaign, you fool!" yelled Thompson, striking the table so hard he tipped over an inkwell.

My reactions were swift to right the vessel before its entire contents spilled onto the carpet.

Thompson shook his head as if to question whether his swollen eyes had betrayed him. "Someone's made the whole damn thing up, for what reason I can't fathom, other than to disturb an already boiling pot." He ran his fingers through the coarse hairs that straggled across his crown.

"I'm not sure what's to be gained by such false statements, Mr. Thompson, sir."

"There's a traitor around me, and I aim to find out who he is." He glared at me as if in warning. The man still distrusted me, but he knew I was nowhere near when he'd elaborated upon the possibility of a series of raids on New England. Thompson scowled. "My secretary of war has recalled me. Are you aware of that?"

"No, sir. It strikes me there are many men relying on your intercession right now. You've too much yet to do, I'd say." I knew that was what the proud Jacob Thompson craved to hear. He wanted it plainly stated that, compared to the cowardly Clay, *he* had responsibilities he wasn't about to shirk.

"Precisely, Thomson. They've captured the last courier I sent for the St. Albans papers."

I remained impassive, but I could feel emotion inside me trying to break out. *Not Sarah, please, not Sarah.* "Who might that be, sir?" I asked calmly.

"Lieutenant Sam Davis." Thompson seemed to regard it as a personal failure that Davis, who was no relation to Jefferson Davis, had been caught. "He was taken into custody, and within only a few days, a military court tried him and sentenced the poor, intimidated soul to death as a spy. I've written to Lincoln to see if he'll commute the sentence, but I still need those other papers. The boys have been recaptured and are held once again in a Canadian jail on other charges and are waiting for extradition or their Confederate commissions proving they were ordered to conduct that preposterous St. Albans Raid."

"Send me, sir." I thought I could track Sarah and attempt to get the papers in the process.

"If I remember correctly, Thomson, you were the first one we sent and you got yourself shot. No, I've sent a total of seven couriers already.

Clay has dispatched some, as well. One of them has got to get through. I might be able to use you elsewhere."

"Where, sir?"

"I can't say yet. I'm still not convinced I can trust you, but this much I can tell you. Some bold and daring men have proposed a plan to get rid of that baboon in Washington plus some of his mates. The proponents are the kind of men who are able to execute anything they decide to do — without regard to the cost. Now, if you're the traitor in our midst, I shall expect to see this on the *New-York Tribune* front page any day now."

"The status of the plan, sir?"

"I'm waiting for approval from Richmond. When I get it, you can prove your loyalty then. I expect to hear any day, so don't go far away. I understand the British Parliament is about to pass an Alien Bill effective here in the Canadas. They'll deport you as soon as look at you if they think you're involved, so stay low."

31

Killing Not Murder

A light snowfall had wrapped the rooftops on St. Lawrence Street in a white, windless cocoon. Mounds of shovelled snow had been piled high along the side of the cleared walkways waiting for the removal wagons to haul it to the river. Young boys were clambering to the tops of these attenuated mountains of snow and trudging along the lengths, momentary heroes of the Sahara or the Alps on their way to join the troops with word of enemy positions. Younger boys were trying to gain a foothold among the travelling horde only to be shoved to the bottom as they approached, defeated by the soldiers on top of the hill.

Was that why young men went to war — to play out the improvised fantasies of their childhoods? I thought, sidestepping a tumbling bundle of mufflers and mittens. I used to think it was shame that prompted me to join the army. The shame of being alive while my brother mouldered somewhere in an unmarked grave. But there seemed to be something much more powerful, more invisible, that drove me. It would be easier to live limbless than to exist with the humiliation of succumbing to another man's will without even resisting or exerting one's limited power in the process. I once thought that a man had two choices in life: he could either be seen to be on top of the hill or valorous in his attempt to get there. Anything less would amount to humiliation. The war reinforced that kind of thinking. *There had to another choice to such madness.* At least I had come to reckon that even though spying was a dishonourable profession, I had resolved to do it in an honourable way. Others, no doubt, would cast me differently.

William Cleary and George Sanders stood in the taproom of the St. Lawrence Hall — Cleary talking to Sanders, his red whiskers bobbing as he spoke. The thickset Sanders had just emptied a mug and slapped it onto the bar, demanding the attention of the barman for another. I had followed them in, but I couldn't get close enough to hear what they were saying and still keep an eye on the front desk. Sarah had registered but hadn't returned to the hotel yet. Wallace appeared at the door. When he spotted Sanders and Cleary, he joined them. The three emptied one mug after the other. An hour had passed when Jacob Thompson made a rare public appearance.

He walked by me, giving me a perfunctory nod. When a chair was vacated about ten feet from the group, I slid in, unnoticed behind a pillar, adjusting the chair slightly so I could still keep watch for Sarah. From this vantage point, I could overhear their now more voluble conversation.

"I suppose they're getting ready for the inauguration of Lincoln next month," slurred the thin-lipped Cleary.

"Indeed," said Sanders. "But if the boys have their way, Lincoln won't be around to bother them anymore."

"How's everything going?" asked Cleary.

"All right, I guess," replied Sanders.

Thompson frowned. "You seem doubtful."

"That actor, Booth, is bossing the job," Sanders said, then put his arm around Thompson. "Forgive me, Jake. I understand you've just given him a commission but, not to put too fine a point on it, I think the man has a tendency to be a bit melodramatic offstage as well as on.

I fear he might upstage the rest of the boys and inadvertently sabotage the whole damn plan."

"The plan?" queried Wallace.

"Yes, Wallace, the plan," interjected an indignant Thompson. As much as he tried to will away the strain of the war, it was eroding him. He pulled a handkerchief from his cuff to wipe away the gelatinous film that had collected in the corners of his eyes, which were almost swollen shut and undoubtedly sore to the touch. Thompson dabbed gently, being careful not to sink his fingers too deeply into the purplish puffs of skin that crescented his eyes. "You're a man of erudition, Wallace. Have you ever read the letter addressed from Colonel Titus to Oliver Cromwell where he describes the necessity of retaliation in time of war?"

Wallace hesitated for a moment. "Was that the letter where Titus reconciled the acceptability of assassination with the greater cause of justice?"

"The very one. You see, it's killing, not murder. There's a difference. I'm tired and old at fifty-five, but not too old to seek retribution."

I nursed a shandy until the men decided to leave for dinner, all the while knowing I had to report what I'd heard as soon as possible. Before I left the tavern, I checked again with the desk about Sarah, but she'd gone. How had she eluded me? Apparently, she'd returned long enough for a quick nap and a change of clothes and had ordered a carriage for the depot.

The Montreal winds were gusting heavily off the St. Lawrence River, testing me as I quickened my step toward the telegraph office, then back to my hotel, the less expensive Donegana.

I wired my Virginia contact a rather noncommittal message regarding the conversation I'd overheard in the taproom: FOLLOW NEXT ISSUES OF NY TRIB AND HERALD STOP BREAKING STORY STOP. Then I sent another message to Rodney at the *Trib* with a postbox address in Montreal plus an alias Rod would recognize. Finally, I composed another wire, this time in federal cipher, to Dana: WOMAN COURIER WITH J. SURRATT ARRIVED FROM RICHMOND TODAY WITH COMMISSIONS STOP PROBABLY ALSO CARRYING OK FROM DAVIS TO KILL LINCOLN STOP.

                                                LINDA BRAMBLE

Within a week, Rodney reported back to me what he'd discovered about James Watson Wallace.

32

A Spring of Dread

Reports were that it was getting harder and harder for Jacob Thompson to keep his mind on his work. The last weeks of March and early April 1865 were filled with news of the final defeat of the South. Richmond was soon evacuated, and on April 9, General Robert E. Lee surrendered to General Ulysses S. Grant in the village of Appomattox Court House. Canadian newspapers were already speaking of the Confederacy in the past tense.

Thompson inhaled deeply as if trying to evoke the memory of the sultry seduction of the honeysuckle that once edged the veranda of his plantation home now burned to the ground by Union forces. Oxford, Mississippi, would be in bloom by now, but there was nothing to go home to, nothing keeping him in Canada. He let everyone know he would leave as soon as his successor arrived. Even though he was ready to depart and needed to avoid arrest for violations of neutrality, he still felt humiliated that his secretary of state, Judah Benjamin, was sending a replacement for him. He wanted to leave on his own terms, not be replaced. Thompson toyed with the bank book he'd been asked to turn over to the new man, twirling it end to end on the desk. To be supplanted by such a minor player was an insult. No one told Thompson what to do. Despite his war losses, he was, by all measure, still a very rich man. He didn't need the Confederate gold that remained in his possession, but he would take it, anyway, when he left. Life was uncertain.

Jacob Thompson knew he would have to leave Canada soon. The dispatches he was waiting for from Richmond had arrived. All that remained was his wife's arrival.

He left Montreal for Europe, faintly disguised, on April 5. Nine days later, when the U.S. agents in Halifax spotted him, they wired Washington asking whether or not they should arrest him. Union Secretary of War

Edwin Stanton brought the request immediately to President Lincoln, Jacob Thompson's one-time friend in Congress.

Lincoln responded: "When you've got an elephant by the hind leg and he's trying to run away, it's best to let him run." So Thompson was allowed to leave. Within a few hours, on April 14, Lincoln was dead.

A profound wave of universal horror rose throughout the United States and the British North American colonies. It was as if I was living a nightmare. My worst fears had materialized. Washington knew there were threats on Lincoln's life. My dispatches warning of the Confederates' machinations were among dozens of others. It was impossible for Lincoln to take precautions against them all. I knew that, but my rage overcame reason. Knowing of the possibility and then having it become reality hollowed me out. If the Confederates were responsible, I was numbed at the thought of their depravity.

Everywhere I went or read about in Canada, streets were choked with Canadians keeping vigil at local newspaper offices waiting for news of the latest developments concerning the capture of the assassin, John Wilkes Booth. Others thronged the hotels frequented by Union sympathizers, wishing to pay homage to Lincoln. Mercantile districts, churches, and civic offices were all draped in black crepe giving visible expression to their grief. The day of President Lincoln's funeral, government offices raised their flags at half-mast and citizens swamped the mails with messages of condolences to people they knew in the United States. There were, however, exceptions.

The lobby of the St. Lawrence Hall hotel was filled with Southerners holding champagne glasses high, toasting Lincoln's final exit. I tried to view them with pity as embittered aristocratic Southern refugees finding collective solace for their vanquished souls, clinging pathetically to what remained of their pride. Beverly Tucker was there, but not among the revellers. He was in the bar talking to a group of Montrealers. I ordered some supper and a beer and waited. When Tucker was about to leave, I rose.

"Excuse me, Mr. Tucker."

Tucker's obvious weariness, and presumably his lingering suspicions about me, prompted an abrupt reply. "What do you want, Thomson?"

"It's about Mr. Clay. Have you heard anything about his whereabouts? Did he arrive safely?" I found the sincerity of my own concern surprising, but it was intelligence I was after. "He asked me to forward some goods he purchased for his wife, but I haven't heard from him yet to learn of his mailing address."

"Well, the old boy got through, but not without trials." Tucker indicated that we should move to a quieter corner, and I followed. "When Clay's blockade runner reached Charleston," he continued, "it ran aground. Then his lifeboat also ran aground. I understand he had to wade to shore carrying what baggage he could manage. If it hadn't been for an oil-silk bag someone gave him on his departure in Halifax, all his personal papers would have been lost, as well." Tucker could only shake his head at Clay's bad luck. "Yet he did get through. The good news was he was reunited with his beloved Ginnie by mid-February in Macon."

"Quite an ordeal," I said. "I hope his health held out."

"My hunch not," said Tucker. "Clay's been on the go ever since he arrived, like a nomad. He felt he had to hasten to Richmond where he could deliver his dispatches to Jeff Davis in person. I heard he and Davis, with the rest of the government, were last seen evacuating Richmond, for Danville, Virginia. Officially, I guess he was discharged. He could be in Georgia, Lagrange, I believe, living at the home of a friend. I'll see if I can get a name for you."

"And you, sir, when will you be returning to our beloved South?"

"I have eight children and a good wife — none of whom I've seen in two years. Think about that, Thomson. Two years. My home in Virginia has been burned to the ground, and my debts have mounted. I have no home anymore. All the same, home is where my family is, so until they join me, here I am a homeless man living in exile. The authorities think I'm part of this devilishness, although I think it's a pity our boys didn't have it done a long time ago. It's too bad they hadn't been allowed to act when they wanted to, but I'll disavow any knowledge of their scheme."

"A spirit of Northern retaliation is spreading," I said. "The pent-up feeling of four years of war has let loose a wild and vengeful manhunt, I'm afraid."

"Yes, I know."

"Not only the federals are looking. Governor General Monck is out to arrest any one of us at the slightest provocation."

"Yes. Friends in Niagara have offered to shelter me until my family can join me. However, I won't take any accusation sitting down. I intend to counter by publishing a letter in the Montreal and Toronto papers demonstrating my innocence."

I could have reported his whereabouts to the Canadian authorities, but I felt I would learn more regarding his involvement with the conspiracy by keeping a close eye on him. I did keep Assistant Secretary of War Charles Dana posted on Tucker's whereabouts.

John Wilkes Booth, the man who shot President Lincoln, had died shortly after his capture on April 26. The United States wasted no time in charging eight others with direct complicity in the murder. The war hadn't been declared officially over, so I awaited further instructions from Dana. There was some fear that the Confederate agents remaining in Canada might attempt a final raid from the provinces. I knew of a band of able-bodied, crazed rebels who swore to murder Vice President Johnson and Secretary of State Stanton and "finish the job Booth started." So I waited.

Toward the end of April, a courier from the U.S. provost general's office delivered a dispatch to me with my orders from Dana requesting that I prepare to be a witness for the prosecution at Lincoln's assassination trial. A second assignment was to travel to the small town of Ayr, three hours by rail southwest of Toronto, to escort to Washington another key witness — Dr. James B. Merritt.

For a doctor, Merritt was surprisingly unhealthy-looking. His head bobbed precariously on slumping shoulders, connected by a long, thin neck that gave him the appearance of a wizened rooster. He was tall and bony, with a pair of brittle arms that drooped like question marks at the sides of his lanky legs. His trousers bore the crust and scars of winter's repeated dryings; a frayed collar edged with a line of unbecoming grime cupped folds of loose skin and a distracting Adam's apple, oversized and protruding.

"How long you been in Canada West?" he asked me as we settled in the train bound for Washington.

I didn't feel like making small talk.

"I say," repeated Merritt, "you been here long?" The doctor wasn't to be denied.

"About a year," I said, addressing the flat fields of tobacco of Essex County.

"'Bout that for me, too. You know Conover?"

Merritt was using Wallace's other name. "Why do you ask?"

The doctor shrugged. "Dunno. Just curious, I guess." Merritt stared out the window at the pentimento of melting snow on fields revealing patches of grass browned during winter. "Just trying to make conversation."

"I've known him about a year, I guess." I was intrigued to learn more about Merritt's connection to Wallace and why he was bringing up the man's name.

"Um-hmm. You testifying, too?"

"I expect so."

"Practised yet?"

"No, not yet," I said. "I was hoping to use this travelling time to collect my thoughts."

"I see. Nervous?"

"Yes, very. A lot's at stake. How'd you know Conover?"

"We've known each other a long time." The doctor gazed off to the side as if preparing to retell the long story of their meeting. "I joined the Confederate Army when Lincoln issued his Proclamation of Emancipation. Freed Negroes was one thing I wasn't prepared to abide. There were many Tennesseans like myself who considered this proclamation a gross infringement of the Constitution and a flagrant outrage on the people of the South. I had little choice but to join."

"Where did you serve?"

"Well, sir, I never actually fought. I served as a surgeon general, then was taken prisoner and had the good fortune to escape a year later and come here to Canada."

"And Conover?"

"Like I said, I met him at a Copperhead meeting in Windsor. Some of those attending the meeting had become patients of mine, refugees from the South like myself and from the Copperhead states — you know, Ohio, Illinois, Michigan. Northwesterners of a sort. Democrats against the war, they were. Oh, they talked of resistance, but it was all talk. Anyway, Conover was there looking for the story, and I obliged by telling him what I knew about the Southerners attending. He paid me well. 'Spect we'll get paid as witnesses?"

"Perhaps, but who will be calling you to the stand? The prosecution or the defence?"

"Well, it's the federal government that's calling on me, so I expect I'll be testifying for the prosecution. Not that I've gone over to the other side, but I need the money, and Conover's allowed there's money to be made if I testify for the Union. So, like I was saying ..."

I realized that the less I told this man the better off I'd be, so I slid down in my seat so my head could rest more comfortably, a move that Merritt hardly noticed. As my eyes closed, my thoughts wandered to Montreal and the letter about Wallace I'd received from Rodney Burke just before I left. Rodney's research was most illuminating. Wallace's real name was Charles A. Dunham, born in 1830 in Croton, New York. His father was a tanner. He studied law with a New York City firm but didn't succeed. He went back to Croton in 1853, got into the brick business with a man by the name of Auser, whose sister Dunham married. At the outbreak of the war, Dunham started to raise a regiment for the Union in New York that ended in a fiasco, greatly to the misfortune of his creditors. Revenge seemed to be on his mind, for he went to Buffalo to recruit for the Confederates. Subsequent to that, he started filing stories to the *Herald* as Conover. According to Rodney, his stories had been accurate precursors to border raids. The editor regarded him highly.

I sat up, suddenly struck by an anomaly I had to clarify with Merritt. "When was the last time you saw our friend, Mr. Conover?" I asked the doctor, who by now had given up conversation.

"Let's see now. It must have been a couple of weeks ago. Yes, Easter Sunday, it was. I remember now. April 17, it was."

"That was three days after the assassination."

"Yes, Conover helped me write a letter to Justice of the Peace Davidson in Galt, near Ayr, telling what information we had relative to the assassination. We assumed he'd let Washington know, and sure as heck, old Davidson did!"

                                                   LINDA BRAMBLE

"You have information, you say?"

"Well, Conover and me did, yes. Let's say he helped me put the words to my testimony. I owe much to Conover for the trip."

"The trip?"

"Certainly. I've not been out of Ayr since I arrived nearly two years ago. Small towns can get a bit stifling, you know. And now I'm getting out. I wouldn't want my friends to know I'm testifying. However, should they get word, they'll find that I'm what you call a reluctant witness. But I make no mind. The money's good, and I can thank Conover for that. So here I am."

I was scheduled to testify on May 12, and Dr. Merritt would be in the witness box the next day. Wallace/Conover was to appear within the week. The mystery of Wallace's loyalties would soon be out in the open, or so I thought. Judge Advocate General Joseph Holt, who was in charge of the trial, and his commissioners had granted secrecy for all three of us for our own protection. We turned out to be the three key witnesses around which Holt and Secretary of State Stanton were building their case against the Rebel leaders, including the Confederate agents in Canada. Holt had to keep us all safe from the recriminations, threats, or retaliations of hostile Southerners seeking retribution. All the court reporters were sworn to uphold the ban Holt had placed on publication of our testimonies, but it didn't quite work out that way.

33

A Trial Within a Trial
WASHINGTON CITY
May 12, 1865

Judge Advocate General Joseph Holt was a man convinced that the hardened Confederate traitors — Clay, Thompson, Cleary, Tucker, Sanders, and President Jefferson Davis — were guilty of paying Booth to kill Lincoln as an act of military necessity. Through the duration of the trial, Holt would show that they were guilty of several diabolical deeds such as plotting and financing the smuggling of blankets infected with yellow fever and smallpox into Union cities, concocting plans to poison the drinking water of thousands of New York City residents by putting strychnine into the Croton Dam, setting fire to New York City, and invading St. Albans, Vermont. He reasoned that if they were capable of plotting such acts against innocent people, they were equally capable to conspire and finance the murder of a president.

Holt believed he could show that the assassination wasn't the act of one compulsive and overwrought thespian acting in the greatest solo performance of his life, but rather it was part of a well-planned plot organized in Richmond and perfected in Canada. As far as he was concerned, the evidence was overwhelming. Eight prisoners who were directly connected to the killing had been captured and were present in court. Clay, Thompson, Cleary, Tucker, Sanders, and President Jefferson Davis would be tried in absentia.

I was the first witness, and admittedly I was nervous before the military judges who sat fixed on me. As I raised my right hand above my shoulder to take the oath, the brass buttons on my uniform strained at my chest. The quartermaster hadn't had time to fit me properly before the trial began. The single-breasted jacket was too small. It was winter issue and its shoulder straps bore the double bars of a first lieutenant, not the tri-bars of a sergeant major. Despite these shortcomings, I was still proud to be wearing Union blues once again.

"Are you a citizen of New York State?" asked Holt, perspiration beading his forehead.

"Yes, sir."

"State whether or not you visited Canada in the summer of 1864."

"I did." My pulse plugged my throat as perspiration trickled down my arms. The morning's proceedings had only just started and the room already felt dank. Everything about the hastily improvised courtroom seemed inappropriate and cramped. The proceedings were held on the third floor of the penitentiary. In spite of the freshly whitewashed walls and new cocoa mats that had been placed over its coarse floorboards, it was still a penitentiary. The only semblances of decorum were several new tables and chairs, plus an installation of the latest series of gaslights to accommodate protracted deliberations. Four opened windows provided some ventilation on what promised to be an unspeakably humid day.

"How long did you remain in Canada?"

"I was there, going back and forth, ever since, until about a week ago."

I shifted my weight imperceptibly to better disperse the tension already building in my lower back. The nine army officers sitting in front of the witness box were unnerving — three bore the braid and medals of major generals while four were brigadier generals, each braced closely around three sides of a wide mahogany library table. The sun was now burning through the iron-grated windows above them, casting their figures into a sombre inquisitional silhouette. All of them had seen combat during the war. All had shown qualities of leadership. Only my examiner, the presiding judge advocate general of the United States, Brigadier General Joseph Holt, knew the law, as did his assistant advocate generals, Henry L. Burnett and John A. Bingham.

Although I'd had trial experience when I was articling before I enlisted in 1862, my experience had been confined to the civil courts. This was a military trial, and the similarity of procedures bore only vague resemblances. I did know that the judges couldn't be challenged, the names of witnesses wouldn't be given to the prisoners, there would be no jury of the defendants' peers, and the punishments exacted wouldn't be defined by any known or familiar rules of law or legal bases.

"Did you or did you not know, in Washington City, Jacob Thompson, formerly U.S. secretary of the interior, and Clement C. Clay, formerly of the United States Senate?" Holt had raised his voice for emphasis, which made more pronounced his Kentucky drawl.

"I did."

"Will you state whether you met those persons in Canada and when?"

I steadied myself once more, slowing my pace to settle my nerves. "I met them in Canada at Niagara Falls, at Toronto, at St. Catharines, and at Montreal a number of times, very frequently since the summer of 1864 up to this time."

Holt placed a map of the Canadas on the table so the judges could become familiar with the location of the British North American cities to which I was referring. The counsels for the defence, sitting near the prisoners only a few feet away from the tribunal's table, were indignant that Holt had put a document before the judges but had failed to show the defence. They pushed their chairs away from their table with great exaggeration, making more noise than was necessary, as if demonstrating early in the proceedings the impracticability of military justice itself, of Holt's doubtful capacity to consider both sides impartially and give an unprejudiced opinion as one of the judges ruling on the case. He was simultaneously judge and prosecutor in opposition from one moment to the next. Holt looked confused for a moment, then, in a tone of disdain for their calculated manoeuvre, requested one of his assistant advocate generals to provide a copy of the maps for the defence.

The defence lawyers' tables were positioned to the left of the witness stand. Parallel and adjacent to them were the prisoners, sitting behind a railing, each gazing at a middle distance, unfocused yet defiant. I had been present when they filed in, watching the gruesome ceremony earlier that morning as seven hooded men shuffled, their ankles manacled by short chains, wrists bound by heavy iron bracelets separated by a bar to further immobilize them. The two considered most dangerous had guards walking behind them carrying the iron balls attached to the prisoners' legs.

A guard stood behind each of the shrouded prisoners, nudging and prodding as they might do with swine into a pen until the defendants sat in their assigned seats. When Holt gave the guards instructions to remove the heavy canvas hoods, the court uttered a collective shudder at the sight of their faces — all flushed, soiled, unshaven, and sinister-looking from having to squint until their eyes adjusted to the light. The last to arrive was the only woman, Mary Surratt, who sat unfettered by herself to one side, the mother of John H. Surratt, another co-conspirator not yet captured, the same man who had accompanied Sarah to Richmond to secure the Vermont Raiders' commissions.

What I had to say would have no direct bearing on the defendants in the courtroom and their involvement in the assassination. I would be allowed to tell my story, however, without objection. The Confederates in Canada whose headquarters I had infiltrated were being tried in absentia. It promised to be a trial within a trial, trying the prisoners at the dock and those yet to be apprehended.

Only ten days had elapsed since President Johnson had issued his proclamation, offering $100,000 for the arrest of Rebel President Jefferson Davis and $25,000 each for information on Jacob Thompson and Clement C. Clay, plus three more of their minions. The Military

Commission, the War Department, and the Bureau of War had proof that Jefferson Davis and his agents in Canada were guilty of committing war crimes and misdemeanours. Much of that information I had supplied. They had every reason to believe that these hardened, rebellious traitors would receive lengthy sentences, perhaps even a state hanging, each according to the nature and severity of his treachery.

Holt returned to me. "Did you or did you not meet George N. Sanders?"

"I did."

"Can you name any other Rebel citizen of the United States in Canada of note that you met?" He had formed the word *rebel* contemptuously, almost spitting it out as he pronounced it.

"Yes, sir. I met Jacob Thompson, Beverly Tucker, William. C. Cleary — I think that was his initial — and a great many others under fictitious names."

"How many different names did Jacob Thompson assume in Canada? Do you know?"

I shrugged. "It would be impossible for me to tell you. I knew him under three or four and others knew him under other names. His principal name was Carson."

The judge advocate general continued sternly. "Do you know under what name Clement C. Clay passed?"

"Yes, sir. One of them was Hope, another, T.E. Lacey. I've forgotten the initials of his name as Hope. T.E. Lacey was the principal one. Another one was Tracey."

"Tell the court when you first met Jacob Thompson."

"Shortly after my arrival in Canada West. Clay had entrusted me to act as courier to carry dispatches to Richmond and then some gold he was forwarding to Toronto."

Holt pulled a handkerchief from his sleeve and wiped away the perspiration that was collecting along his hairline and dripping inconveniently onto his notes. "What was that gold intended to finance?" He was trying to be nonchalant about the visible display of what could be seen as a lack of confidence in his examination procedures.

"The gold was intended to finance several incursions from Canada into the states of the Northwest — Ohio, Illinois, Indiana, and Missouri — to bankroll Copperhead activities designed to overthrow the federal government. They were comprised of those farmers who were angry with Lincoln for cutting off traffic down the Mississippi, their shipping lifeline."

"What kinds of activities were they planning to accomplish their end?"

"Thompson masterminded a failed attempt to liberate prisoners of war from Johnson's Island in Lake Erie, other expeditions to rescue Confederate generals on a train, the burning of New York City —"

Holt interrupted. "The court will hear testimony regarding all of these incursions at a later time. Was it your intelligence to Washington that helped to avert these incendiary acts of war?"

"Yes, sir, I helped."

"State any conversation you may have had with Jacob Thompson in Canada, in the summer of 1864, in regard to putting the president of the United States out of the way or assassinating him."

The question came out of the blue, out of the sequence I was expecting. It caught me off guard. It seemed as though Holt had grown tired of the preliminaries of examination and needed to get to the point of my testimony.

"During a conversation in 1864, Jacob Thompson said to me that he had his friends — Confederates — all over the Northern states who were ready and willing to go to any lengths for the good of the cause of the South, and he could at any time have the tyrant Lincoln, and any other of his advisers that he chose, put out of his way. That he would have but to point out the man he considered in his way and his friends, as he termed them, would put him out of it, and not let him know anything about it, if necessary. And that they wouldn't consider it a crime when done for the cause of the Confederacy."

"Do I understand you correctly to say," Holt began slowly, "that Thompson said to you that he could at any time have Lincoln and any of his advisers put out of the way and that the assassins wouldn't consider it a crime when done for the cause of the Confederacy?"

"Yes, sir."

Holt ran his fingers through his rumpled hair, pausing to give the judges the opportunity to fully grasp the significance of what I'd just testified. He rubbed his temples, pulled his handkerchief out of his sleeve again to dab his forehead, put it back in his sleeve, straightened his notes, then continued his line of questioning.

"During your stay in Canada, were you or not in the service of the

United States government and seeking to acquire, for its use, information in regard to the plans and purposes of the Rebels who were known to be assembled there?" The judge advocate general moved closer to me as if the nearness of his body was sufficient assurance to make me feel I was in hands safe enough to confide to the court.

"I was."

"To enable you to do this, did you or not deem it proper and necessary to assume a different name from your real name, one different from the one you now have before this court?"

"Yes, sir, I did."

"What name did you assume in your intercourse with the Rebels?"

"I assumed, as my proper name …" I hesitated, since I was now about to reveal my undercover identity. I knew the question was inevitable. However, I'd been reassured that the proceedings were to be withheld from publication until I could be relocated should the Confederates want to retaliate against me. I trusted that the government would keep its word.

"James Thomson was the name I used. Then, leading them to suppose that was my right name and that I wished to conceal my actual name so as not to be identified by federal spies, I adopted other names at any hotel I stopped at. I never registered Thomson on the book. I let them assume I wished to hide my 'name,' James Thomson, which was what they knew as my 'real' identity."

"Your whole object in all this was simply to ascertain their plans against the government of the United States?"

I was spying on them, Holt, not ascertaining. "Yes, sir, that was my whole object."

34

I Recognize One of the Prisoners

As the first witness for the prosecution, I knew that my testimony needed to be corroborated and my loyalty established. One mark on my character elicited by the defence would taint my credibility. What followed would become a turning point of my life, a reckoning. I thought that at last I could tell the truth as I knew it without deception or charade, yet I would learn that no matter how in earnest I reported what I knew, it didn't mean my testimony would be believed. And, if it was believed, it wasn't assured that it would be accepted. There were larger issues at stake, which I blithely never considered.

"I said," repeated Holt, aggravated that I had missed his question the first time he asked it, "will you state what Jacob Thompson then said to you, if anything, in regard to the proposition that had been made to him to rid the world of the tyrant Lincoln?" Holt's eyes bored into mine as if to reinforce the importance of getting the next recollection correct and without equivocation. I got the message.

"He said a proposition had been made to him to rid the world of the tyrant Lincoln, Stanton, Grant, and some others," I began, thinking that my words would likely mean a jail sentence or even a hanging for Jacob Thompson, so I weighed them carefully. "That he knew the men who had made the proposition were bold, daring men and able to execute anything they undertook without regard to the cost, that he himself was in favour of the proposition but had determined to defer his answer until he'd consulted his government at Richmond, and that he was then only awaiting their approval."

Holt shoved his spectacles to the bridge of his nose and gazed momentarily at the judges. He wanted to make sure they were paying attention. Once assured, he prompted me to continue.

"Thompson said that he thought it would be a blessing to the people, both North and South, to have those men killed."

The judges shifted in their seats — some sat up, others leaned over to have repeated what I'd just said.

"That was this past January?" queried Holt, making sure to differentiate Thompson's latest scurrilous admission from his earlier October statement. Three times Holt drew my attention to the date to establish the fact that assassination, not capture, had been in the minds of the Confederate agents in Canada. "Was it about that time you saw Clement C. Clay and had a conversation with him?"

"No, sir. I spoke with Clay in the summer of 1864, immediately after Thompson had first told me what he was able to do. I repeated the conversation to Clay, and he said, 'That is so. We are all devoted to our cause and ready to go to any length to do anything under the sun.' I remember his expression clearly — 'to serve their cause.'"

Holt turned the page of his notes, signalling a new line of questions. He spread an expansive arm across the line of the shackled men seated on the raised platform behind the heavy wooden bar. "Look at these prisoners. Do you recognize any of them as having been seen by you in Canada, and under what circumstances?"

I scanned them closely for the first time, as if I was finally given permission to do so. I took my time. Then I recognized one of them — the man I'd met in Toronto while in the hallway waiting for Clay. The one who said he was "Canadian."

"I've seen that one without his coat over there, but I don't know his name."

"For the record," stated Holt, turning in the direction of the court reporters, "the witness is pointing to the prisoner Lewis Thornton Powell."

Powell looked away as vacantly as he had the first time we'd met, even though I hadn't gotten his name at that time. There he sat, maybe twenty or twenty-one, on trial for attempting to assassinate U.S. Secretary of State William H. Seward. I would later learn that on the night of the assassination, this same man had broken into Secretary Seward's bedroom and stabbed him several times in the face. A jaw splint worn by Seward from a broken jaw he'd suffered from an accident a few weeks prior saved his life by deflecting it away from his jugular vein. Powell also injured two of Seward's sons, his nurse, a soldier guarding Seward, and a messenger he pushed aside as he ran out of the home. He was captured three days later at Mary Surratt's boarding house, just as she was being arrested as a co-conspirator.

Powell had a massive, animal-like force about him, with thick black hair that framed an even-featured face. He sat unflinching as if focusing on an existence outside his coil of self-righteous and defiant hate. The defendant sat slumped and motionless, immobile as a statue with an appearance of indifference, occasionally smiling as if he had no earthly fear, just a weariness of life.

"Will you state where and under what circumstances you saw him?" Holt asked.

"I had some words with him at the Queen's Hotel in Toronto, Canada West."

"State all that occurred at that time."

"I had an interview of some time with Jacob Thompson. Several others had sought an interview while I was closeted with him, and had been refused admittance. I was through with Thompson, and in leaving the room, I saw the defendant in the passageway near Thompson's door talking to Clement C. Clay. As I approached, Clay stopped me and held my hands, as if to keep me in abeyance while he finished a conversation in an undertone with that man. Then Clay left for a moment and said, 'Wait for me. I'll return.' Clay then went out and spoke to some other gentleman who was entering Thompson's door, and he came back and bid me goodbye, asking where he could see me in half an hour. I told him where and made an appointment to meet him. While Clay was away from me, I spoke to this defendant and asked him who he was. I commenced talking about some of the topics that were usual subjects of conversation among the men there. He hesitated telling me who he was, then said, 'Oh! I'm a Canadian,' giving me to understand that I wasn't to ask anything more."

The court reporter, signalled to Holt to wait for a moment so that he and his stenographic assistant could complete the verbatim notes they were keeping of the proceedings. Even though the scribbled symbols they used in what the court reporter, Benn Pitman, called shorthand was fast and capable of keeping up with the tempo of a normal speaking voice, their hands needed a momentary stretch. When Pitman gestured to Holt that he and his assistant were ready once again, Holt resumed questioning.

"Did you not ask Thompson or Clay who this man was?"

"Yes, sir. I made some mention in regard to him to Clay in an interview I had with him about a half-hour later after I saw him standing in the passageway, and he asked me, 'What did he say?' I told him that he said he was a Canadian. Clay replied by saying, 'He's a Canadian all right,' and laughed. Then he concluded by saying, 'We can trust him.'"

"What was the idea conveyed by the term *Canadian* with his laugh?"

"That was a very common expression among friends of theirs who were in the habit of visiting the United States, and gave me to understand that I wasn't to ask any more questions, that their business was of a very confidential nature."

After that, Holt grilled me on events in Canada that occurred directly after the assassination, attempting to link to the killing all of the named conspirators in President Johnson's proclamation. I testified to Beverly Tucker's desire that Lincoln's death should have occurred long ago, "that it was a pity" and "too bad the boys hadn't been allowed to act as they wanted." Although I'd never personally seen Booth in Canada, I told the court that Cleary, Thompson's secretary, told me that "Booth was one of the parties to whom Thompson had referred would "at any time put Lincoln away."

"Did Cleary make any remarks when speaking of his regret that the whole work hadn't been done? Was any threat made to the effect that it would yet be done?"

"Yes, sir. Cleary confirmed that they 'had better look out, we aren't done yet,' and remarked that they, the Confederates, never would be conquered, never would give up."

"What statement did Cleary make to you, if any, in regard to Booth's having visited Thompson?"

I felt uneasy about Holt's leading questions but even more uncomfortable about the line of questioning he was now pursuing. He was asking for hearsay and not the result of my direct observations, but that was the advantage of a military trial, I assumed — the admission of evidence was much more liberal than in a civil court.

"Cleary said that Booth had been there in the winter, that he thought the last time was in December. He had also been there in the summer and once before December. He thought December was the last time."

The humidity in the courtroom had risen to an almost insufferable level. My skin felt clammy and wet, in no good measure caused by the wool uniform I'd been given to wear, but more likely to my increasing tension. Up until that moment, I hadn't noticed, but my shirt was soaked underneath. The mental exhaustion was more taxing than anything physical I'd ever experienced.

Holt kept pressing on. "After the assassination, did you learn from these parties that they supposed themselves to be suspected in the plot to kill the president and were they taking any steps to conceal the evidence of their guilt?"

"Yes, sir. They were destroying a great many papers. They also knew they were going to be indicted in Canada for violation of the neutrality laws a number of days before they were actually indicted."

Holt proceeded to review the campaigns for which I acted as courier: to Richmond by way of Washington City to see Dana and the War

Department, carrying news regarding the attempt to burn the City of New York, the St. Albans Raid into Vermont, the intended raids of Buffalo and Rochester. Holt kindly underscored my role as admirable in preventing more severe consequences by my forewarning, a fact the press later ignored. After questioning me about the vast amount of money the Confederates had to finance all of their schemes and then establishing that they said, "We always have plenty of money to pay for anything that was worth paying for," Holt moved on to question me about the last indicted co-conspirator who had been operating in Canada.

"What seemed to be George N. Sanders's position there, if he had a defined position?"

I shook my head as if to assemble a sensible reply, because I wasn't quite sure what Sanders's role was, yet it seemed his powers over the Confederate agents were significant. "Clay told me that I'd better not tell Sanders the things they entrusted to me, that he was a very good man to do their dirty work. That's just what Clay told me."

The irony of my statement wasn't lost on the judges, who seemed to find my statement amusing. "He was then doing their dirty work?" asked Holt, realizing his question had boxed him into an answer for which he was unsure of the outcome.

I covered Holt's procedural error and again referred to Clay's words rather than my own speculation. "Clay said Sanders associated with men who they couldn't associate with, that he was very useful to them in that way, that he was a very useful man indeed."

After I answered a few questions of clarification from the defence and the court, Holt asked me to return to Canada to secure more corroboration for my testimony. Then I was dismissed.

The next witness for the prosecution was James Merritt, the doctor I'd guarded and accompanied to Washington City from Windsor, Canada West. Following him would be James Watson Wallace, who Holt knew was testifying as "Sanford Conover" to protect his identity. The thought of these two questionable men testifying after me to corroborate my testimony made me very nervous.

35

Secret Testimony Is Leaked

WASHINGTON CITY
June 7, 1865

By the time the trial got under way Tucker, Sanders, and Cleary were still in Canada. Jacob Thompson and his wife were enjoying a Grand Tour in Europe, along with the remaining Confederate gold certificates that I was confident played no small part in financing their trip. Not so lucky were Jefferson Davis and Clement Clay, who had surrendered to U.S. authorities shortly after President Johnson's proclamation for their capture had been issued. They were arrested as "arch conspirators and traitors" and taken to old Fortress Monroe in Virginia's Lower Chesapeake Bay where an eight-foot-deep moat surrounded the six-sided garrison with a fifty-foot wall of impenetrable stone around the perimeter. Clay could have escaped as Thompson had, but he didn't.

Even though the trial had begun and Clay and Davis, along with Tucker, Cleary, Thompson, and Sanders, were non-indicted co-conspirators being tried in absentia, their lack of visibility didn't hinder Holt's profound mission to continue to gather evidence against them. Their trial would be a trial against the South. Consequently, its orchestration had to be much more carefully planned than that of the direct conspirators sitting in jail and waiting for their sentences. They had committed treason, which would earn them the death penalty. Holt believed that any hope of reuniting the severed nation would be dashed forever if Clay and Davis became martyrs for a fallen Confederacy, so the two distinguished statesmen languished in the casements at Fortress Monroe. Others in the government would eventually take that belief one step farther.

Then it happened. Contrary to Holt's request not to publish the proceedings, Benn Pitman, the head court reporter, or someone in his retinue of recorders, sent our transcribed testimonies to a newspaper in Cincinnati. Pitman was never punished for this grave violation, which always made me suspicious of how responsible he really was for the actual release. No matter how or who released my testimony, this premature public revelation was devastating. Wallace/Conover, however, would manoeuvre his way through the maelstrom with a deal like no other.

Within a day, all the major newspapers of the North and South had published our verbatim testimonies. Disappointing Clay bothered me, but it would also mark the end of any thoughts of being with Sarah. Even if my testimony had been kept secret, she probably would have discovered my identity and never would have trusted me again. It was now out in the open, and my double life was about to be over, which gave me a sense of loss and at the same time relief. Before a line drawing of my face was too broadly published, I still had to return to Canada, as Holt had requested, to secure more corroboration of my testimony. To that end, Charles Dana gave me one last assignment.

On the train back to St. Catharines by way of New York City, the only place I felt comfortable was on the platform between cars, where I stood for most of the trip. The buffeting wind seemed to clear my mind. I had to find ways to evade detection. If any Confederates still operating in Canada recognized me, my life would be shortened considerably. The harder the wind pummelled my face the better I was able to think.

When I reached New York City, I went straight to the *Tribune* to see Rodney Burke, who was exactly where I'd found him the last time, crouched over copy for a special evening edition. I pulled up a chair in front of his desk.

"Richard," Burke said, surprised to see me. "I was just thinking about you and your friend, Wallace. Have you heard the latest?"

"No, Rod. That's what I came to see you about. What gives?"

"Have a look at this." He pulled a copy of an unpublished letter to the editor from the top drawer of his desk and handed it to me.

"Where did this come from?" I asked as I read the letter.

"Wallace also known as Sanford Conover or Charles A. Dunham." Rodney took a tobacco pouch and pipe from the opened drawer. "He's a strange one."

"Are you sure it's from Wallace?"

"Unless a handwriting imposter sent it in, there's no doubt. The

                                                        LINDA BRAMBLE

handwriting's Dunham's all right. My editor won't publish it. When all of this comes out, Dunham is bound to look bad. And if Dunham looks bad, so will we."

Wallace/Conover's letter explained how the *Tribune*'s editor had published, a year ago March, plots disclosing Rebel plans to assassinate President Lincoln. Then, in a peculiar twist, he wrote:

> It is of course well known that the President was destroyed by the hand of Booth, but the mad actor was a mere instrument, a tool in the hands of more wicked, designing and able villains. Southern men, Rebel officers are, as I have said, responsible for the assassination, but I am sorry to say and strange to say that the scheme was conceived and calculated, the activities under it devised, by a Northern man, now a Colonel in the Rebel service. This man is no other than Colonel Dunham of New York. Dunham went to Canada in September and immediately set on foot a series of projects of a hostile character to be executed on the frontier. Although his schemes have not been entirely successful, they succeeded in creating alarm in drawing from important posts a large number of soldiers at a great expense to the government to defend.

"This is preposterous," I said. "The man's sick, but so lucid. But why would your boss be in trouble if he printed this?"

"Seems my editor, Horace Greeley, wrote a letter to the Military Commission vouching for Wallace or Conover, as he had signed his files with us. It's about to blow up in the clever chap's face. Wallace-Conover-Dunham testified under oath that he sent the editor a letter forewarning of the assassination plot. The editor said he received no such letter, but it's his word against Dunham's.

"There's more," Rod continued. "The man doesn't stop. According to this news release from the White House, Holt has sent Dunham as Conover back to Montreal to get other witnesses to corroborate his testimony against the Confederates, and Dunham agreed! But he agreed to go back only if Holt suppressed the fact that Wallace and Conover were the same man. He stopped by our offices on his way to Montreal. I know he has no idea there will be a welcoming party there to greet him. He's aware that his testimony has been leaked to the press, but what he doesn't know is Holt failed to act in time in response to Wallace's request to withhold the name Wallace from his testimony. Some papers left out the Wallace name, but the Associated Press didn't.

"It will be interesting to see how he gets out of this one," I said.

"By the way, have you seen Dunham's testimony yet?"

"Yes," I admitted, rolling my eyes. "The problem is much of it supports my testimony, which worries me."

"Let me show you a copy of the letter Dunham wrote to the Gazette in Montreal affirming his innocence. It's better than Edgar Allan Poe."

I stood there, staring at the tear sheets Rod held out, my hands momentarily unwilling to take the documents from my friend's hands.

"Go ahead," he urged. "You'll laugh at the lengths Wallace has gone to proclaim his loyalty to the angry Confederates waiting for him in Montreal. When they confronted him, he was indignant that someone had impersonated him. To prove his innocence, he wrote an affidavit and signed it in front of a magistrate to denounce his role in the Sanford Conover testimony. He's described it all right here in an article he wrote as Wallace." Rod rolled his chair closer to me so we could both read it together.

"Look!" Rod pointed at a paragraph toward the end of the piece. "He's even put a $500 reward for anyone capturing the scoundrel Conover who so dastardly impersonated him at the Washington trial. Then he has the nerve to suggest that if President Johnson guarantees him, Wallace, safe passage to and from Washington, he'd appear voluntarily before the Military Commission to prove he isn't Conover."

My friend sat back in his chair and lit his pipe in quick inhalations until the tobacco ignited. Once the pipe was going, he exhaled and mused, "It seems Wallace/Conover is motivated to put himself into a position of authority through the press, in control of the flow of information, then he delights in withholding or manipulating it altogether."

"That's the inexplicable thing about this character," I added. "He's charming and so plausible while he manipulates people's perceptions. I fell victim to that at one point. One wonders what propels such acts in a man. He's not as vile as a killer, but he's as devious, clever, and as wretched as one."

We sat silently for a moment, trying to unravel Dunham's motivations, yet knowing such a man couldn't be explained by the measure of normal men.

In the Montreal Herald, Wallace published an offer of reward for the capture and arrest of Sanford Conover — in other words, himself! Within a day after publication, Wallace left for Montreal and was arrested four miles from the American/Canadian border by Canadian police in response to the offer for a reward. Secretary of War Stanton immediately sent a wire to General Dix in New York to get Wallace released — "to do whatever may be fit and proper to secure the presence of Conover back at Washington." Stanton and Holt had to protect one of their key witnesses. They were aware of Wallace's escapades in journalism and his work with the Confederates. I knew, because I'd informed them. Why they trusted him to be a reliable witness, though, escaped me.

36

Undercover One Last Time

In order to fulfill my last mission, I decided to grow a beard — more like a scruff of one — and disguised myself as a farmer wearing a slouch hat and overhauls. My first stop was St. Catharines to find Aaron Young.

"Good sweet Lord, Montgomery. Is that you under those whiskers?" Aaron asked as he swept his barber's cape around me.

"Not so loud," I whispered. "Not so loud. I took a chance coming here as it is. A farmer in a fine barbershop like this will arouse suspicion, anyway."

"Shave, sir?"

"No, just a trim of my moustache and my neck. It's grown to its own mind. You might tidy up my hair, but leave it long." I had to keep as much of my disguise intact as possible.

"Just a trim it is," Aaron said with a note of resignation.

He moistened his soap cup and lathered my neck and chin, then selected the sharpest razor, stropped it against his leather, and began the treacherous process of shaving the neck of a white man. Even if he hadn't grown up with that white man playing like brothers at that man's Virginia plantation, he was still aware of the double consciousness that he lived. I knew he realized his power when that razor made its first bloodless but potentially violent swipe across a man's face at the same time he accepted the perception of being the compliant black servant to a white master. To Aaron Young, however, setting up a barbershop in this little town in Canada West was his opportunity to be an entrepreneur; a man of business, not subservient to another man's commands.

Aaron was soon splashing a tonic on my neck when I asked loud enough for other patrons to hear, "Where does a man get a cheap beer in these parts?" to signal the necessity for our meeting. "I'm engaging a mighty big thirst." To the side, away from the mirror's reflection, I silently formed the words, "Tunnel, ten tonight?"

Aaron blinked in response as he whisked away errant hairs from my collar. "Try the Mermaid Inn by Market Square, sir. That's where the men of the soil congregate before shutting down their stalls."

When I arrived at the cooling tunnel, I could see the flicker of a candle midway among the barrels of beer resting before shipment.

"I've read the papers," Aaron said. "If any of these Southerners are still hanging around town and spot you, you might just as well put a halter around your neck. It didn't take them long to figure out who James Thomson was. You're a fugitive in these parts. Now you know how it feels!"

"Well, hello to you, too," I said as I grabbed the beer Aaron held out to me and sat on a nearby pallet. "I know, it's dangerous, but Dana has sent me to connect one more missing link. It's a theory Dana and I have that he's letting me test out."

"Were you telling the truth in your testimony about Booth and Thompson's admissions?"

"Yes, damn you, Aaron, of course I was. So was Conover or Wallace or whatever you want to call him. Merritt, on the other hand, was lying. He never set foot in Montreal, yet he led the judge advocate generals to believe he had. I think Wallace as Conover paid him to falsify his testimony, even though what he said happened to be true."

"Who knew what he testified to?"

"Me, Wallace, and any one of the Confederates in charge."

"You've got a problem, my friend."

"I know. If they prove Merritt was Conover's lackey, my evidence

                                                    LINDA BRAMBLE

could be tainted along with Wallace/Conover's, and the truth of this whole rotten affair will never be known."

"Why would Wallace/Conover pay Merritt to lie?" Aaron asked. "To what end?"

"That's what I can't figure out. Someone must be paying him. I'm sure it's not a case of mistaken identity. I reported to Dana what I knew about his aliases."

"Journalists use aliases all the time," Aaron reasoned.

"Yes, but this operator stretches the margins of credulity. He exposes the fears and hypocrisies of the people who want to believe him. They, in turn, become his most loyal supporters to avoid revealing themselves as fools."

"What do you know about him?"

I explained what Rodney Burke had researched about Wallace/ Conover — that his real name was Charles A. Dunham, born in Croton, New York, and he'd trained in the law. At the outbreak of the war, he'd tried to raise a Union regiment but failed. I speculated that Wallace/ Conover/Dunham's failure to do so must have so humiliated him that he turned to creating his own mythical regiment of spies, alternately claiming loyalty to both sides. He was a genius at faking news stories and suborning others to perjure themselves before the Military Commission to support his testimony, which as far as I could tell, was fairly accurate. They didn't have to lie to support his case.

Aaron's narrowed eyes glowed in the semi-darkness.

"His stock-in-trade," I continued, "was to explore wartime paranoia, and like a chameleon, he fabricated stories through multiple person-alities with just enough truth to give them credibility. He could be perceived as an agent provocateur whose aim was to destabilize the war effort, but I think he just wanted to gain notoriety and sell articles." I pulled a notebook out of my pocket, flipping through it until I got to a dog-eared page. "I mentioned the fact that his real name is Charles A. Dunham."

"Yes, an interesting monogram."

"I know. Life's little serendipities. Or maybe his intention was to live up to it. Anyway, when he wrote for Horace Greeley's *New-York Tribune,* he used the alias Sanford Conover. Here he cast himself as a Union sympathizer reporting on the activities of the spy network that Thompson and Clay ran in Canada West. Charles Dana, our boss in the War Department, knew Conover's work when he, Dana, was the managing editor of the *Trib* until 1862. When Dunham — I'll refer to him as Dunham now — filed with the *New York Daily News*, that out-and-out Rebel rag, he wrote as Margrave, submitting a constant screed of anti-democratic smears and plots to assassinate Lincoln. The Copperhead editor, Ben Wood, thought he recognized me in Toronto a few months past, but I believe I successfully disabused him of that at the time. His mind was more on getting Confederate funds for his paper."

Aaron smiled ruefully. "For your sake, I hope you disabused him."

"The *New York Herald* has Southern leanings, so as Harvey Birch, Dunham retold stories of his persecutions by Lincoln's sycophants. He also filed stories under the name of John McGill."

"Go on. It's getting interesting."

"He invented a 'Colonel Dunham' and described him as a foul renegade, traitor, and black-hearted villain who worked for the rebels in the North and Canadas but returned to the South and was now leading the conspiracy planned earlier by Margrave, another one of his inventions, to kidnap or kill Lincoln."

"That doesn't make sense. Why would he be intent on blackening his own name?"

"It could have been a way to explore his own darkness, but I don't even believe that myself. I don't know why. I don't think he cared. He seems to have no conscience. He could smear his own name and just as easily invent another persona to take its place. He's a confidence man, true, and confidence men do it for the game of duping the unsuspecting and defrauding their prey. All I know is he's dangerous."

Aaron took a slug of beer. "Men like him get others to collude in their forgeries and schemes because they think they're getting something for nothing."

"Precisely. Nor do they want to admit they were duped by their own greed in order to get whatever Dunham promised. This is what worries me about Holt."

"Why's that?"

"Holt is so convinced of the Rebels' complicity in the president's assassination that he's being blinded by the duplicitous side of Dunham's nature."

"But you said Dunham as Conover told the truth to the tribunal."

"That's the rub. He did. But if he solicited Merritt to perjure himself to corroborate his testimony, he's just as capable of soliciting others to lie before the court. If that's true, someone's got to be bankrolling the deception. How it plays out will depend on who's paying him. Whoever it is, it's damn venal."

"Are you suggesting Holt?"

"No. Holt has too much to lose if something like that got out. It's got to be someone with enough money to pay Dunham to blacken his own reputation by getting Dr. Merritt and his own brother-in-law, Nathan Auser, to lie under oath. It just doesn't make sense. Someone else must be backing him."

"Someone more devious than himself?"

"Yes, even more devious. I'm not sure who, but I have my suspicions. That's where you come in."

Aaron grinned. "Why did I know this was coming?"

The candle in the tunnel started to flicker as Aaron stood to pull two more beers from a case nearby. We knew we wouldn't be able to stay much longer before breathing would be made difficult in those close quarters. I hadn't much time left to explain.

"Tucker, Thompson, and Sanders all spoke of Lincoln assassination plots that involved Booth. Tucker and Thompson spoke of the plot as an act of war, but Sanders spoke of the assassination as one would an act of revenge. He's the man I want to track. Dana gave me the name of a man in Montreal close to George Sanders. It turns out to be Sanders's son-in-law, Louis Contri. Do you remember him?"

"I remember him. I cut his hair — black, curly, if I remember correctly, and he wore it rather short, even though he was a stylish sort of man."

"That's the fellow. He's working undercover for us. I couldn't believe it. There's no time to spare, for I'm told he'll be leaving Montreal very soon. Once Sanders realizes Contri is going back to Italy, it won't be safe for him to stay. Testifying is out of the question. He's anxious to leave the country as soon as possible, and you know how long a trial like this could be drawn out."

"He must be in deeply."

"Yes, deeper than you think, Aaron. He was originally assigned to be near Sanders's home in Kentucky. A couple of months ago he married Sanders's daughter, Virginia."

"That's undercover in more ways than one."

"He's also no saint. I understand that while Sanders was up here in

Canada, this roué also seduced Sanders's wife, the good Mrs. Sanders, on a number of occasions."

"Desperate men in desperate times."

"How charitable of you."

" Contri's behaviour does raise issues of trust. How do we know we can trust him?" Aaron trusted few white men.

"We'll be cautious."

I was about to leave when Aaron grabbed me by the arm. "Look, my friend, one more thing. I'm sorry to have to tell you this, but your friend, Sarah, found out that you were an agent for the Union. She's made it clear around the hotel that she refuses to ever see you again. She made a decision on principle rather than love, much the same way you did a decade ago with me and my family when we left your father's place. I'm sorry, Richard. I know you love her."

"In her eyes, I betrayed her. I didn't blame my father for his disowning me, and I guess I don't blame her, either."

37

The Fateful Twenty Minutes Alone

When Aaron and I arrived in Montreal, we rented a horse and wagon from a farmer, bought his cartful of cherries, and drove to the Bonsecours Market on the other side of town away from prying Confederate eyes at St. Lawrence Hall. We also rented a stall among thirty or so other vendors doing business out of the backs of their wagons. Still dressed as a farmer, I stood alongside the wagon to serve customers. A well-dressed professional man in his late twenties approached me, looking cautiously to either side. I recognized him right away from the first night in the Salon at Stephenson House.

"Montgomery?" he rasped, nudging his spectacles up the bridge of his nose. Contri was a tall northern Italian with light green translucent eyes.

"Yes," I said, motioning to Aaron to take over the sales.

"Dana wired me," Contri said. "What information do you want? Talk quickly. I don't have much time."

"Tell me about your father-in-law. Why would he want Lincoln murdered? Did he have reasons other than political expediency?"

"Ah, yes. He thinks Lincoln caused the death of his son, Reid Sanders, a major in the Confederate Army. It happened like this. Originally, George Sanders wanted to spare his son's life from the field of battle. To make money for the Confederacy, Sanders made a deal with Great Britain to build six ironclads, and he offered to carry dispatches on the side on fast shallow-draft vessels to and from Halifax. He hired his son to run the blockade with some dispatches, but instead of choosing passage on a blockade runner, Reid, *il pazzo*, the crazy, he chose a sailing steamer." Contri twirled his finger at his temple to indicate the foolishness of the son's decision. "When a federal warship caught her, the dispatches were taken and published, embarrassing Richmond into cancelling the order. Reid was arrested as a prisoner of war, where he died a sad death from dysentery within two years. Sanders still isn't over his loss."

"So, in a sense, it was revenge and expiation for indirectly causing his son's death."

"*Sì, sì*. Sanders, the operator who gets others to do his questionable bidding, got — how you say? — hoisted on his own petard." The Italian kept his head down as he spoke, glancing sideways occasionally to check whether he was being watched.

"To your knowledge, who else might have known about Sanders's meetings with Booth?" I asked.

"I was there when he met Booth, but I won't testify. I leave for *Italia* in a few days where I start my life again. *Una grande tristezza*, a great sadness it is that I will never know the *bambino* my wife now carries. *È deplorevole*, it's regrettable the life of a soldier in our business. *D'accordo*?"

With the loss of Sarah in mind, I nodded. "I understand."

"I am done. *Finito. Basta.* Enough. That is, if Sanders doesn't have me —" Contri made a rapid slashing movement across his throat.

"Is there anyone else who could verify what you know?"

He thought for a moment. "*Sì, sì.* There was a guest at the hotel who must have heard the conversation Sanders and Cleary had regarding the plot. Find him. I was sitting behind him and could hear, so I'm sure the guest could hear, too. The braggarts had much *vino*."

"His name?"

"*Non so.* I don't know. Check the hotel register. It was around February 14 or 15. I remember. I was called to the hospital that same night. The sleighs were stuck in snow that had fallen and not been cleared. Up to here." Contri pointed at his waist.

"Anyone else?"

"Maybe, but be careful. Last week when Tucker, Sanders, and Cleary confronted James Wallace for his testimony at the trial, most everyone there knew Wallace was lying, but they accepted the — how you say? — *sciarada.*"

"Charade?" I offered.

"*Sì*, charade. Wallace was too useful to them to let go, so I think they made a plan to get other people to testify. Wallace would coach them to lie, then the Confederates could later prove the testimony was false. *Presto!* Sanders claims perjury and all testimony against them would be tainted and thrown out of court. *Astuto*, no?"

"Makes sense. Every other sortie into Union lines from the North they concocted failed. If the execution of this last plot works, it'll be their single greatest victory of the war. But what's in it for Wallace?"

Contri laughed, attracting the attention of a couple of shoppers. He lowered his voice to a quieter but mocking tone. *"Seriamente?"* His wife and four children have had no money for the past year here in Montreal. Even though Jacob Thompson took millions of Confederate gold certificates with him to Europe, the *ladro* — how you say? — bastard thief. He leaves money for his *amici* to live in exile for the next decade if they so choose. Sanders could pay Wallace well to play along. And Wallace has no *scrupoli.*"

"Scruples? What about Clay? Was he involved?"

"No, he didn't know about the plot to kill the president. If he had played his hand right, he could have been sitting by the sea rather than in a prison cell in Fortress Monroe. Right now he has a noose around his neck. Just like the others they are ready to hang."

"Do you have any proof that Wallace might have made such a deal?"

"With my ears, no. With my eyes, *sì*. I saw him and Sanders move to another room after Wallace signed an affidavit swearing that someone was impersonating him at the assassination trial. The two of them were gone for about twenty minutes. More secret deals than that have been made in less time. Ask my countryman Machiavelli."

"Who else was in the room that might have seen them leave together?" I probed quickly. I could sense that Contri was getting more anxious to leave.

"Check the register for a Finestein or something. He could also tell you that Sanders bragged about paying witnesses to go to Washington to testify. That's all I've got. You are right. This will be the Rebels' greatest victory. *Ciao*, Montgomery." Within seconds Contri had melted into the crowd.

I went over to Aaron, who was making change. "Did you hear any of that?"

"Not very well in this noise."

"Never mind. I'll fill you in. In the meantime, could you check out the register at the St. Lawrence Hotel for a mention of a guest with the last name of Finestein, or something like that, staying at the hotel on February 14 or 15? I'll return the horse and wagon. You have enough for the fare back to St. Catharines?"

"Yes."

"I have to be back in Washington, so I'll be leaving tomorrow on the 3:00 p.m. train. They put us up at the National Hotel. Wire me there."

When I arrived at the hotel in Washington two days later, there was a wire from Aaron waiting for me: FINEGAS ALREADY TESTIFIED MAY 25 STOP IN TRIBUNE STOP SAID HE OVERHEARD SANDERS SAY LINCOLN WON'T TROUBLE US MUCH LONGER. BOOTH IS BOSSING THE JOB STOP.

It seemed that Finegas had contacted Judge Advocate General Holt of his own volition. I was elated by the Finegas testimony, which would corroborate my own despite the potential perjured testimony Wallace was fabricating. There was a separate wire from Aaron saying that he would soon return to the South to help in the reconstruction efforts. He thanked me for our friendship. As I read the wire, I knew Aaron's row would be a very hard one to hoe, but I also knew change had to start somewhere, and Aaron was a leader among his people.

After a nap and shower, I strolled the nine blocks up Pennsylvania Avenue from the National Hotel to the War Department located next door to the White House. The afternoon was balmy, an insufficient trope for the turbulence of the times. When I arrived, Dana's secretary sent me directly to see him — no waiting. He was a newspaper man tapped by Stanton to assist in the war effort by heading up a secret service because of his skills as an investigative journalist to organize. A fine line existed between a spy and a journalist — they both had to find ways and means to uncover information.

Dana's blue eyes, although drawn and tired, were warmly receptive as he rose from behind his desk to greet me. "Come in, Montgomery. Good to see you again."

I stood at attention in respect for my superior. "Thank you, sir. Good to see you, too."

"At ease, soldier." Dana wasn't a soldier by training, so he didn't expect the deference to the chain of command as career soldiers did. "I asked you here today to release you from duty. You're officially discharged, and honourably so. I have your papers here."

"Thank you, sir." I was surprised but not disappointed.

"I remember you coming to my office and applying for employment as a spy with my secret service inside enemy lines. You were a law clerk at the time, if I remember correctly, before joining the army. Isn't that right?"

"That's correct, sir."

"And, as an intelligence officer, you observed at a distance enemy positions and *matériel* and reported back. But as a spy, you lived among them. There's a difference. How did you find that?"

"Difficult, sir."

"Your records show you did some undercover detective work for General Murray in New York City, then served as a clerk for Secretary Chase shortly thereafter. Was it your need for living on the edge in field duty that prompted you to volunteer your undercover services in the War Department?" Dana was thumbing through my file as he spoke. I sensed a note of sorrow in his voice.

"The record of your service is unblemished. I checked, of course, before I sent you to Canada West. You came to me well dressed with an intelligent look on your face, professing to be animated by motives purely patriotic and plus fine references. All you wanted was a horse and an order that would carry you safely through federal lines. You seemed to understand perfectly well the perilous nature of the enterprise you proposed."

"Yes, sir, I did."

"You came back a couple of weeks later with a letter from Richmond stating you had Jefferson Davis's confidence. You could be trusted because of your ardent devotion to the Confederate cause. I must admit, Montgomery, that letter was so convincing it gave me pause. Had I hired the wrong man?"

"Your undercover agent in Richmond's War Department was a friend of mine and facilitated that, sir."

"Your subsequent intercepted dispatches from Clement Clay saved thousands of innocent lives," he concluded. For some reason, it was important for Dana to review my war record. "Your dispatch regarding the invasion of St. Albans, Vermont, from Canada East helped General Dix to reinforce his troops. My regrets that a self-inflicted bullet hole in your arm was necessary to convey your loyalty to the Rebels you'd infiltrated."

"It's completely healed, sir."

"I'm glad that a man with your resourcefulness is on our side. Your style of patriotic lying is sublime. It amounts to genius. Your services have been both daring and brave and of great value to your country. And now I want to give you assurance of lasting employment as a judge advocate general in New York City, if that meets with your approval." Dana still appeared stricken, even though he was giving me very good news.

"Yes, sir, thank you, but ..."

"You hesitate?"

"As you've heard, there's been perjured testimony, and I have good reason to believe there will be more. Will the truth of my testimony be believed?"

Dana removed his spectacles, as if to eliminate the barrier to the truth he was sheltering, then looked squarely at me. "It's much easier to accept errant sons back into the fold if it's also accepted that only one among them was delinquent rather than them all."

"Are you saying there's too much at stake to allow truth to prevail?" I could feel my face flush and my eyes get glassy. "If the Confederates are absolved of all complicity, then it will be murder in the time of war and the Confederacy's greatest victory."

"Yes, reunification would be impossible otherwise. I could foresee perpetual conflict and eventual separation in the decades to come. That's how much we believe in the reunification of this noble experiment we call a nation. There are always concessions in a democracy. I hope you understand.

"Before we leave today, I'd like you to meet another agent who, like you, played a significant role in our clandestine operations in Canada. As intrepid an agent as you were, you were blinded to this agent's activities. Your lack of suspicions could have been your undoing." Dana walked toward a connecting door to the office adjacent to his. He opened the inner-office door and summoned someone to enter.

"Hello, James, or should I now call you Richard?"

The moment was one etched in my memory because of all the conflicting emotions I was experiencing. Why hadn't I discovered she was an agent for the Union? Why hadn't she told me? What would Dana think of my inability to detect her loyalties? I ended up feeling proud and humbled by my dear Sarah's superior abilities at clandestine operations. She stood there momentarily allowing me to grasp the revelation. I had been outwitted by the woman I loved, yet I was never happier to accept that fact. She spoke in a Northern accent as she gently took my hands in hers.

"Richard, I hope you now understand why I had to distance myself from you during our sojourn in Montreal. Had the Confederates grown suspicious, both of our identities could have been uncovered. My real name is Elizabeth Harris. We shall both have to learn a new way of thinking about each other but, if you'll have me, my love for you will only grow."

Epilogue

Many events unfolded over the course of the months following my reunion with Sarah Stephenson, or Elizabeth Harris, as I knew her subsequently. As I had anticipated, my testimony was thrown out of court as tainted, along with that of Wallace, Merritt, and all of the seven other men and women Wallace had trained to perjure themselves. The political commentary at the time would put me down as a traitor to the United States, a dictum that has shaded my life ever since. Yet Dana and other members of the inner circle in Washington knew of my contributions, so I had solace knowing that.

I had been a lawyer, soldier, courier, and spy, and in each of these endeavours I was always uncertain about the morality of my own actions, but never so intensely as during my days as a spy. After the trial, my uncertainties extended to grasping the limits of betrayal for the sake of a larger good. I was no one to condemn what the federal government had decided to do in the end. I just didn't like it. Over the years, I've come to reconcile the fact that there are many options to the truth when one considers a greater good.

Although this part of my story is rather bleak, that ending has given rise to the writing of this recollection — a record for the sake of presenting my side of the story. The part that isn't so bleak is the fact that Elizabeth, the love of my life, and I married and had a family of four of our own. I worked as a judge advocate general for a few years after the war until I opened a small civil law practice in New Jersey where I have been to this day.

The Confederates in Canada had crafted a masterful scheme. The truth told by liars wouldn't be believed. Sanders's plan was risky but incredibly shrewd. The charges against him as a co-conspirator were eventually dropped. Through an arrangement with Wallace/Conover/

Dunham, Sanders was able to single-handedly absolve the Confederacy of any culpability in the plot to assassinate Lincoln. George Sanders, the self-appointed Confederate secret agent, was instrumental in persuading Booth to assassinate Lincoln. It is also true that he was able to absolve the Confederacy of any culpability in the plot. On November 3, 1865, Sanders left his family to spend the next seven years in Europe. When he finally returned, he died within the year at the age of sixty-five.

Dunham/Wallace/Conover's story had more unexpected twists and turns. In the summer of 1865, Dunham launched what was later referred to as his "School for Perjury" where he trained several so-called witnesses to implicate the men in the Confederate mission in Canada in the assassination of Lincoln. He supplied Judge Advocate General Joseph Holt with witnesses for the better part of the year, twisting and suppressing evidence that, at first, Washington's leaders in Congress believed to be true, but then they turned against him when one witness became so overcome with the shame of his lies, he confessed to Holt that he was lying. I, unfortunately, was tarred with the same brush.

The unfortunate thing was that much of Dunham's testimony was true. As his trained witnesses' testimony began to fall apart, he conspired to bring down Holt, who he thought had betrayed him by publishing letters from Holt that Holt claimed were fraudulent. Dunham was arrested and served a jail sentence after a weeklong trial in 1867. After making several bids for a pardon, he attempted to bring down the president of the United States, Andrew Johnson, linking Johnson to the assassination of Lincoln. All the time he was in prison, he plotted and schemed, remaining ambiguous until the end about his true loyalties. He was finally pardoned in 1869.

His later life seemed to be spent tapping into rich estates to support his wife and four children. He curiously named their last child Margrave, born in 1865. Margrave had been Dunham's incarnation of the conspir-ator who would convince Northerners that assassination was an act of patriotism. Although I never saw Dunham again after the trial, I heard recently that he passed away in Rutherford, New Jersey, a town not too far from my own, at the age of sixty-eight. Serendipitous that he was so close to me in his later years.

I was always ambivalent about Clement Clay. He seemed a patriot of principle, yet he was capable of funding operations designed to kill thousands of innocent people. When he surrendered to Union troops in

                                              LINDA BRAMBLE

Macon, Georgia, he was placed in solitary confinement for nearly a year while the determined Holt tried to gather more evidence against him. When it became apparent that Holt's evidence was based on perjured testimony from Dunham's suborned witnesses, Clay was finally released, after several appeals, on April 17, 1866, now a broken man. He practised law for the next few years in Alabama, took no active part in the reconstruction of his state, and never entered politics again. He died in 1885 at the age of sixty-six.

Beverly Tucker, the born diplomat and former consul to Liverpool under President James Buchanan, was first sent to Canada to negotiate the sale of cotton for bacon, which the Confederacy needed to feed its troops. The United Kingdom and the Union needed cotton to sustain the textile mills of both countries. He consorted with Thompson and Clay but insisted that he hadn't taken part in their operations. Tucker never felt entirely free of suspicion despite distributing a very compelling pamphlet proclaiming his innocence. Ironically, he purchased Stephenson House in 1869, just after Colonel Stephenson died, but didn't operate it for very long. He returned to the United States when amnesty was declared, leaving upward of $23,000 in debts, according to the *Buffalo Evening Courier and Republic* newspaper. He pursued a career as a Washington lobbyist but struggled with illness and poverty and died in 1890 at age seventy.

There will always be men like Jacob Thompson — slippery, conniving and brutish — who evade the consequences of their actions. When Thompson left Canada in the spring of 1865, he and his wife toured Europe for several years. There is no record of what he did with the remaining Confederate gold certificates he took with him. His wife returned to the States without him. I understand that there were many reasons why he didn't go back to his hometown of Oxford, Mississippi, not the least of which was his attitude toward the new world he would find. "To be ruled by Negroes is bad enough," he wrote, "but to be ruled by abolitionists is intolerable." However, he finally relented and returned to Memphis, Tennessee, in 1869 to manage his extensive land and business holdings until he died in 1885 at the age if seventy-five.

Regrettably, I lost track of my friend, Aaron Young. I do know that he returned to the South, along with most of the blacks in St. Catharines, to help freed men and women, who had been kept uneducated for so many years, learn the responsibilities of independent living and to help them reconstruct their self-respect as free, sentient beings. I had no doubt that they were capable enough do it, but would others allow it to happen? It has been two generations of struggle since that time. I don't see it abating soon.

Acknowledgements

James O. Hall, one of the authors of *Come Retribution: The Confederate Secret Service and the Assassination of Lincoln* (1988), was kind enough to give me his personal papers and notebooks of primary sources that he used in the preparation of his book. The notebooks proved invaluable to me. I am forever grateful to his kindness and generosity. Thank you, Mr. Hall.

Richard Montgomery, 1864.